CROOKED GOSPELS

J.G. MARTIN

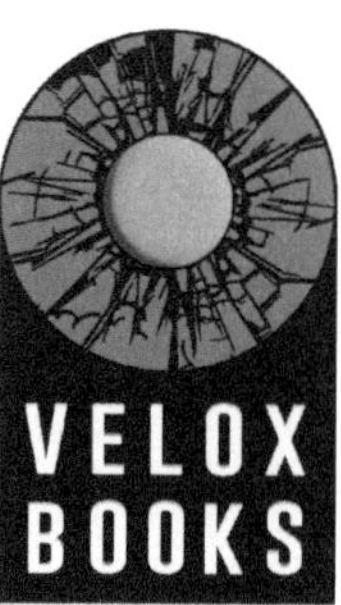

YOU'RE READING ANOTHER TERRIFYING COLLECTION FROM

**FOLLOW VELOX TO KEEP
THE NIGHTMARES COMING:**

CONTENTS

SUBJECT 21

I watch the sunset bleed.

Its outer edges drip like molten gold, and I hear the hiss of steam before I ever see the clouds rising from the arctic snow.

"Told you," Raens says. He stops short of me, slings his rifle over his shoulder and folds his arms. He surveys the sunset like it's a regular occurrence – an everyday thing. "There's a reason this place is under lockdown."

"So it's true," I say, my voice barely a whisper. "No one's left for three years."

"Not a soul."

I look back at the sun and a pit of unease grows in my stomach. The shape of it is all wrong. It's pulsing, throbbing like a living thing, like some monster born of science fiction. "What about the guy I replaced?" I ask. "They let him leave, didn't they?"

"Lentley?" Raens scratches the stubble along his jaw. "Suppose so. Flew him out last week, airlifted the kid home in a body bag."

I wait for the punchline, for Raens to crack a smile and slap me on the back, maybe chide me for being so gullible, but instead he sighs, gazes out across the white expanse. "Got a wife?" he asks me.

"Not yet."

He nods to himself, as if it were the most obvious answer in the world.

"You're cut from the same cloth as him," Raens says, words sharp as the arctic wind. "You're an extra in your own story. No loose ends. No one to raise hell if you vanish. Same as Lentley. Same as the rest of us."

"I mean, I've got family," I protest.

"Sure," he chuckles. "We all got family. The question is, do they give a damn about you?"

The question stings. It stings because I know the answer, but I can't bring myself to put it into words. It's enough to strangle our conversation before it ever gets a chance to breathe, and we spend the next hour standing silent in the fading glare of the sunset.

This is my life now, I realize. Watching over a compound at the end of the world, trading small talk with a sergeant twice my age.

"So," Raens says, clearing his throat. "How much did they tell you about the bunker?"

I swivel my gaze, squinting through the gathering dusk toward a concrete sarcophagus rising from the snow. There's a door in the center of it. Its blackened steel is covered in thick gashes painted in shades of rust.

"Not much," I admit. "Just that it was off limits, and that I'd get court-martialed if I so much as stepped within a hundred yards."

He smirks. "Figures."

"Guess I'll go ahead and ask the obvious – any idea what's down there?"

Raens scrunches his brow, lips parting as if he's about to speak but can't quite find the words. It takes him a moment. When he finally finds his voice, it's distant, hollow – somehow even emptier than the gray of his eyes. "Nightmares," he murmurs. "That's what they're hiding down there. Weapons more terrible than you can imagine."

My stomach twists as Raens' looks to the bleeding, molten sunset. The implication is clear.

"Jesus," I breathe. "Is this... Are we doing this to the sun, then?"

He shakes his head, thumbing toward the bunker. "No. Not us. That'll be Dr. Cornel Thales, Chief of Research and Engineering on this frigid rock."

I know the name. I'd heard it mentioned by the pilots when they shipped me out to this winter paradise. Thales was a genius apparently. Not your garden-variety savant, but the kind old comic books warned us about.

"I don't get it. How'd he manage to weaponize the sun?"

"That ain't the real sun," Raens explains, looking toward the darkening sky. "The real one's somewhere beyond those clouds. It's later than you think."

I tilt my head, studying the pulsating weapon on the horizon. "How's he build something like this, though? It's incredible."

"Theories float around. They always do. Some of the troops think Thales made a deal with the devil, others think he ain't properly human."

"Bit dramatic, don't you think?"

Raens slips a pack of smokes from his parka, slides one between his lips. "I don't get paid to think. You smoke?"

"Not lately."

"Smarter than you look."

He lights up, and for the first time, I'm realizing how ancient the man looks. His eyes are bloodshot, his face lined like a roadmap to exhaustion. I figure the last time he got a decent sleep was somewhere between the invention of the wheel and the fall of Rome.

"Never used to smoke," he tells me, pocketing his lighter. "Bad habit with no real upsides, but then I got posted here and it was like I needed something – anything to look forward to." He breathes out a plume, sucks it back through his nostrils. "Cigarettes became my breath of fresh air. Ain't that funny?"

My mouth dips into a frown, unsure if any of this is funny.

We stand like that for a while longer, gazing across a white glacier shimmering beneath a molten sky.

"So, this is it," I say, breath fogging the air in front of me. "You and I are just what – guarding some mad scientist until they ship us out in our own body bags, then?"

Raens' lips twist into a smile. "Nah. We ain't bodyguards. We're tripwires for what Thales has down in that bunker."

"Another weapon?"

He shakes his head, a haunted expression creeping onto his face. "Weapons are tools. You point 'em at bad guys and the bad guys disappear, but what Thales has is different. You can't aim it. Can't control it. It doesn't answer to us, and I doubt it ever will."

A shiver crawls up my neck. "You're talking about this thing like it's alive."

He shrugs. "Maybe it is. I'm not sure concepts like life or death even apply to it, though. What I can say is that it's powerful. Powerful in a way that's damn near impossible to describe."

"If it's so great, then why doesn't it just break itself out?"

"Figure it doesn't want to."

"Huh." The wind howls past us, carrying a haze of snowflakes toward the bunker. "This thing got a name?" I ask.

"Subject 21," he says simply. "Word is, it's practically catatonic. Never makes a fuss about anything. Barely even moves. Just stands in its cell and stares holes in the wall – sometimes literally, if you trust the radio chatter."

What he's describing sounds so absurd, like something out of a sci-fi novel. "Does it even breathe?" I say, half-joking. "Or is it beyond that, too?"

The sergeant ashes his cigarette with a tap of his finger. "If it feels like breathing, I suppose it could manage it. That's the thing about S21 – what makes it so terrifying. It doesn't *have* to do anything. It has no rules because it makes the rules, and all of us are just toys in its sandbox, ready to be played with whenever it pleases."

I swallow. "The hell is Thales doing with this thing?"

"Killing it," Raens tells me. "Or at least, trying to. He figures S21 is just sleeping, but he's convinced it'll wake up one day, and when that happens, we'll all be royally fucked."

Ice slithers through my veins.

"Imagine the Big Bang in reverse," Raens continues grimly. "Everything that ever was, wiped clean, with not even ashes left to mark our graves. That's what Thales believes is waiting for us on the other side of S21's catnap."

My chest tightens. The thought of this unfathomable creature being less than a mile away, locked up in a bunker beneath the ice feels surreal. Incomprehensible.

"So let me get this straight," I say, thinking aloud. "This thing is powerful beyond all measure, liable to wipe out humanity the second it wakes up, and we don't have the first idea how to stop it. What the hell is it? The damn devil?"

Raens grins. "If only. Probably be easier to deal with I'd wager."

"You're kidding. What's worse than the devil?"

Raens squints toward the horizon, a far-away glint in his eyes. "You ever wonder what happened to God?"

"God...?"

"Sure. Jesus takes one for the team, then God just ups and vanishes, doesn't he? There's no sequel to the Bible, not even after a few thousand years. Strange, ain't it?"

"Haven't given it much thought," I admit. "Always saw religion as more of a metaphor than literal history."

"Well," Raens says, his voice heavy with finality. "Now you know better."

He steps off, trudging over the hill.

It takes a second for my mind to catch up, and then I'm scrambling after him, moving as gracefully as a newborn giraffe under my six layers of winter kit. "Hold up – are you saying Subject 21 is fucking *God*?"

The old man gives a noncommittal grunt. "That's the troops' theory, but they'd tell you the moon was made of cheese if it made for decent conversation. Anything to pass the time."

"And what do you—" I catch myself, the words freezing on my tongue. "Right. You don't get paid to think."

Raens taps his temple, a wry smirk playing on his lips. "Quick study. And I might not get paid to think, but I still sneak in a little here and there – off the clock, of course." He winks, and it might be the most human he's ever looked. "There have been... incidents. Might lend some credence to the gossip around the barracks. It all started when—"

A clarion cry rings out, stealing Raens' attention. He scowls, pulling back the sleeve of his parka to check the watch on his wrist.

"Something wrong?" I ask, peering warily across the snow-drifts.

"Not yet," he says through gritted teeth.

"That's not exactly reassuring."

"Wasn't meant to be."

Raens catches the worry in my face, and he sighs. Claps a hand on my shoulder. "Listen, kid. This is your first day on the job, so I won't rush things. Not like I did with Lentley. Just try to enjoy the ignorance while it lasts."

I open my mouth to protest but he cuts me off.

"Trust me," he says, and the words fall from his lips like a judge's gavel.

We keep moving. Our boots crunch through the snow as we make our way toward the watch-turnover location: a crooked radio tower a mile out, its steel frame glinting in the glare of the false sun.

"So, these weapons," I press, still hungry for answers. "Have any of them of so much as put a dent in S21?"

"They aren't for S21."

"Then who—"

A bone-rattling screech tears through the air. Before I can wheel around, Raens is already tackling me to the snow, shoving my head to the powdery cold. "Shh!" he hisses. "They're coming ..." He scans the darkening sky as if searching for enemy aircraft. "How's your shooting?" he whispers.

"Damn good."

I reach for my rifle, but he grabs my wrist.

"Keep it on safe. Last thing I need is you punching me full of holes. Still got half a pack of smokes to finish."

"I'm a marksman, Raens. I ain't gonna panic."

He chortles. "Yeah, you and every other asshole here. Shooting a bullseye through a dick hair doesn't mean squat though, not when you're—"

His words drown in a cacophony of noise. It crashes down from above us, roaring with the fury of creation itself. I roll over, hands clamped to my ears as pressure builds in my skull like a kettle ready to shriek.

Raens staggers to his knees next to me, tears streaking his wrinkled face. He's pale. Trembling. Yet despite it all, he's grinning in a rictus of ecstasy – the sonuvabitch is *laughing*. "Heads up!" he bellows.

Light explodes through the clouds.

All at once, the world ignites, burning brighter than a solar flare. A host of winged creatures descend from above, wreathed in emerald starfire, blowing trumpets that could shatter mountains. I raise my rifle on instinct.

Too slow.

They blitz past us like avenging comets, hellbent for the bunker.

"What's our play?" I shout over the din.

Raens holds his tongue. He jerks a thumb over his shoulder, and my heart seizes. Thales' false sun has risen high, pulsing with cosmic rage. Molten rays tear away from its surface, hurtling toward the winged host like the spears of wrathful gods.

The creatures try to evade.

They dip and weave faster than lightning, but it's no use. The arrows snap through the air like guided missiles, finding their marks and engulfing them in screaming flames.

One by one, the creatures fall.

It's like watching a meteor shower, and I can't help but marvel at Thales' brutal brilliance. It only takes the weapon a handful of minutes to clear the sky; to render the invaders little more than cinders in the wind.

As the last of them dies, I'm left shaking in a snowfall of ash.

"Those things ..." I choke out, my voice strangled by awe and horror.

"Looked familiar, didn't they?" Raens answers, and somehow, it's like he's discussing the weather. "The one's with all the eyes tend to throw folks for a loop, but they're all part of the same host."

I swallow hard, tasting char and infinity. "Are you saying they were ..." The word sticks in my throat, feeling almost too blasphemous, too dizzying to speak.

"Angels," Raens confirms, joints popping like gunshots as he gets to his feet. "That's our best guess, at any rate. They've been making the rounds every couple weeks, back since Thales got his hands on Subject 21. Tricky things. Never fall for the same weapon twice." Raens says the last bit as if he's giving them some kind of begrudging respect.

"Angels ..." My voice creaks like timber. "We just slaughtered a hundred angels?"

Raens snorts. "Wouldn't bet on it."

He nods at the field before us, covered in white feathers stained black with soot. To my shock, the feathers begin to quiver, pulsing with inner light. They rise slowly as one, hanging for a heartbeat before rocketing skyward, piercing the clouds and leaving pillars of radiance in their wake.

As the last of them vanish, Thales' bleeding sun shrinks back beneath the horizon, blanketing us in the shroud of night.

Raens helps me to my feet. "You alright?"

"... I'm alive."

"Not what I asked. Lentley was alive too, right up 'til he wasn't." The old sergeant pats snow and soot from my sleeves. "Look, this job's a mindfuck, I know that – we all do, but it's still the job. You okay or not?"

My pulse is rushing so fast it hurts, goosebumps the size of dimes are peppering my skin, I'm drowning in existential dread, baptized in cosmic horror, and my ears are ringing like church bells, and ...

"I'm fine," I tell him.

He claps my shoulders, squeezing with rough compassion. "Kid, I might not be the brightest of the bunch, but I know my troops. And you? You're a long way from fine."

I take a breath, and it feels like my first in years. "This just a nightmare, right, Raens? Some Sunday School trauma clawing its way out of my system?"

He pays me a mournful smile, and it tells me everything I need to know.

"Christ," I breathe, anxiety seizing me. "We just cremated half of heaven back there ..."

"Told you already, those angels ain't dead."

"Does it matter?" I sputter. "We've probably got front row seats in hell thanks to that shitshow. I mean, you can't just torch angels, Raens. There's gotta be rules about that and ... and ..."

I trail off. Fear's got me by the throat, the weight of what we've done crushing my last coherent thought.

We're damned. All of us, irredeemably damned.

But Raens doesn't seem to care.

He pulls a fresh cigarette from his pack, lights it on fire. "Thought you didn't buy into all that religious stuff?"

"Guess I've just had a spiritual awakening."

Raens looks me over: at my mess of hair, my desperate eyes and my shaking knees. He looks at all of this and he laughs. It's the first time I've seen him do it – throw back his head, crinkle his eyes and howl with amusement. Showcase genuine joy.

Somehow, I hate it. It's like this whole thing is a joke to him, some cosmic hazing ritual for the new guy.

"What's so funny?" I demand.

"You are," he says, giving me a light punch on the arm. "Spiritual awakening? Fuck me. Lentley fed me the same line, and it killed me then, too. You two really are cut from the same cloth."

The way he's beaming at me, I wonder if this is the first time he's felt happy in ages, and it seems wrong to derail all that – to take it from him, but I need to know.

"I never asked... but how was it that Lentley died?"

The sergeant's smile fades. He turns away from me, wipes something from the edge of his eye and starts carving a path toward the radio tower. "Same as any of us do," he says with a rattling breath. "Slowly over the years, then all at once and far too soon."

"That ain't much of an answer," I say, following after him.

"Maybe not, but it's all you're getting."

Moonlight seeps through the clouds, stretching our shadows as we trudge through the snow. When we make it to the tower, Raens unslings his rifle with an exhausted sigh before sparking a fresh stick of nicotine. I slump down next to him.

"I got one more question," I tell him.

"Shoot."

"Thales. What's his angle on hating God? He some kind of militant atheist or something?"

Raens grins, amused. "That's funny. Thales might be the most God-fearing Christian you'll ever meet, now that you mention it."

"How's that work?" I say with a frown.

"What do you mean?"

"I mean what's a Christian doing trying to murder God?"

"Ah." Raens takes a moment to consider the question, his wrinkled face lit up red beneath the tower, cigarette smoldering between his calloused fingertips. "Guess he's doing it for the same reason any true believer does anything," he says, lifting the smoke to his lips. "...Cause God told him to."

The arctic wind kisses my cheeks, ruffles my hair, but all I can feel is the machine-gun rhythm of my heart pounding against my ribs.

I watch Raens tap ash onto the snow, watch him take another drag and I'm stunned by how calm he is. How relaxed. A thousand questions are pinballing around my skull, but for him this is just another Tuesday.

My eyes find my gloves, still blackened with soot, still stained with the cremains of heaven itself, and all I can think about is how much I wish I could stop thinking.

"Something on your mind, kid?"

I glance up at the sergeant, throat dry. "Yeah," I croak. "I think... I think maybe I'll take you up on that cigarette after all, Raens."

He gives me a knowing smile, weary eyes twinkling beneath the starlit sky. "Figured you would," he says, reaching into his parka with a sigh. "Folks typically do."

WE COME IN PIECES

The lockdown started the day the smiling man came by. He wore a suit that seemed two sizes too big, with a tie so tight it might've been strangling him.

"Greetings!" he sneered as I opened the door. "I have some unfortunate news for you."

I stifled a yawn, squinting in the glare of the sunrise. "Unfortunate news?"

"Indeed," he said cheerily. "I'm going to need to board up your doors and windows. With you inside, of course."

"Excuse me?" Footsteps sounded from behind me. My wife, Anne, swept onto the doorstep, her housecoat streaming behind her. "Did I hear that right – you're threatening to board us in? Is this some stupid prank?"

The man didn't move. Didn't react. He continued to smile, eyes bloodshot and unblinking.

"Hello? Did you hear me?" Anne's voice dropped to dangerous levels of impatience. "Trev," she snapped. "Call the cops. Tell them this guy's trespassing."

I brought a hand to my face, stifling another yawn and wandered inside with a shrug.

A minute later, I was back on the doorstep.

"Phone's dead," I mumbled. "Cell, too. Um... even the WiFi's outta commission."

She gaped at me. "You're kidding."

"He isn't," said the smiling man. "We cut communication utilities while the town was asleep. Less panic, you see."

I stepped forward, adopting my best impression of masculine menace. "Listen, buddy. I don't know who you think you are but—"

"Agent Cain," he said, lips trembling under the weight of his grin. He pulled out a badge that might've been real and explained he was CIA, hunting for a terrorist cell they'd tracked to our slice of suburbia. "Not to worry," he continued. "My staff will be searching every household for these vermin, and once we locate them you'll be free to go."

An engine backfired, interrupting me before I could get another word off. A semi-truck lurched to a stop on the street, its brakes screeching against the tonnage of its trailer. Soldiers spilled out the back. Their dark military fatigues blended with the dim morning light, rifles slung over their shoulders like quiet threats. They began distributing planks of wood from the truck, alongside hammers and nails.

The man's grin widened, his pale eyes shivering in his skull. "As I was saying, you'll need to step inside. For your own safety."

I tensed. We were outnumbered. Outgunned. These people held all the cards and they knew it, so with no other choice, Anne and I retreated inside.

"Ol' Ty always said this would happen," Anne muttered bitterly, pacing madly in our living room. "*Always*. And I called him crazy for it..."

"That's because he *is* crazy," I told her, watching as soldiers hammered boards haphazardly across our windows. "Nobody with that many guns is well-adjusted, Anne. They just aren't."

Anne gnawed at her fingernail, blonde hair a mess about her face. "I don't know, Trev. That Cain guy made my skin crawl. And those soldiers? I've never seen soldiers wearing black camo like that. If you ask me, *they* look more like the terrorists."

I heaved a sigh, pulling her close and kissing her hair. "Everything's going to be fine, baby. I promise."

That night we woke to the glare of lights. A truck growled down our street, hulking and armored, its spotlight cutting through cracks in our window barricade. Soldiers leapt from the vehicle, their boots hitting the pavement with ominous thuds. They marched to the house across the way and with practiced precision, painted a symbol on the door. A red sphere that gleamed wetly in the dark.

"That's Kent's house," Anne murmured, watching through the boards. "So they're vandalizing private property now? Classy."

"Maybe it's to mark that they've already cleared it," I reasoned. "You know, from those terrorists or whatever."

Anne scoffed. "Don't tell me you believe that crock, Trev."

"All I'm saying is that maybe we leave the conspiracy theories for Ol' Ty, yeah?"

"You actually think that..." Anne's voice trailed off, eyes widening. Outside, the soldiers began kneeling one by one before the sigil on the door. They leaned back, arms splayed out, fingers dancing across the ground. Started to sway. Side to side, like human pendulums.

"What the ever-loving *fuck*..."Anne breathed.

I fumbled for my glasses, swallowing hard. "Okay. I'll grant you that's a little weird."

The soldiers let their necks tilt backwards, faces toward the night sky. They went motionless, almost like they'd been shot dead on the spot, then with a sudden gasp began to speak. Chant. It resembled a sort of throat-singing, except more guttural and absent of tune.

"Crack the window," Anne hissed. "I want to hear what they're saying."

I eased the window open, letting in a rush of autumn air and that strange chorus. To me, it was gibberish. Nothing but a fever dream of consonants and vowels. But languages were Anne's life. Her career. She'd grown up speaking three, and now spoke half a dozen more better than I spoke English.

"Well?" I pressed.

She gnawed her lip, shaking her head. "I don't know, Trev. I've never heard anything like it. There aren't any familiar pronunciations, accents or... It's all just *nonsense*. I can't even place the region it's out of."

"Maybe it *is* nonsense," I suggested, grasping for some excuse to make sense of it all. "What if they're trying to freak us out on purpose? Like a practical joke or something. I've heard soldiers doing worse to pass the time."

But Anne didn't reply. Her fingers gripped the edge of the window, her eyes buzzing with anxiety as we watched. A minute passed. Two.

Then, almost as soon as the chanting started, it stopped. The soldiers lurched up to their feet. Without a word, they marched back to their truck, and with a roar of an engine, vanished into the night.

Dawn found Anne at the kitchen table, her bloodshot eyes fixed on a half-empty wine glass. She didn't look up as I shuffled in.

"So," she said, voice raw. "Any brilliant ideas?"

I blinked, still half-asleep. "About... ?"

"Last night. The ritual on our street."

"Oh. That." I poured myself a bowl of cereal and sat across from her, swishing the spoon in the milk. I'd been hoping it was just some vivid, awful nightmare.

"Well?" Anne's fingers drummed on the table, impatient. "What do you think they were doing? The chanting? That symbol? I've been through every book I own – there's nothing like it. It's practically *alien*."

I shoveled a spoonful of corn flakes into my mouth, chewing slowly. "Haven't given it much thought."

She knocked back more wine. "Well, I've got theories."

"Do you?"

"Oh yeah. I've been thinking it's a deep state program that—"

My stomach lurched. "Can we do this after breakfast?"

"What?"

I shifted in my seat, uneasy. "It's just... All this talk about conspiracies is killing my appetite."

Anne's chair scraped back. "Killing your appetite? Christ. You saw it, Trev – same as I did. This is more important than your bowl of Frosted Flakes."

"Look, we saw something weird but—"

"Unbelievable," she said, eyes narrowing. "You're sitting there in pajamas, half-asleep, stuffing your face with cereal like we didn't just witness some batshit insane military séance. You're trying to pretend it away."

I sighed. "A séance, Anne? Really?"

"Yes, *really*. Something deeply fucked up is happening and you hardly seem to care!"

"Okay," I mumbled around another mouthful.

"Okay?" she echoed, voice dripping venom. She drained her glass, fixed me with one last withering look, and stalked out. "Nothing about this is okay."

Sunset bled across the cul-de-sac. It scorched the cars and street lamps with a crimson glare, and with it came the rumble of distant thunder. A storm was coming. Anne and I sat in silence, not speaking since breakfast – her conspiracy theories still hanging between us like a toxic cloud. I knew better than to poke that bear while she was deep in her cups, so I busied myself with a novel on the sofa.

As night fell, Anne's voice broke the tense quiet. "Do you feel that?" she asked.

"Feel what?" I mumbled, turning a page.

"That shaking." She drained her wine, a red rivulet escaping down her chin, staining her white tee. "The whole house is trembling. Tell me you feel it, Trev."

I lowered my book, fixing her with what I hoped was a look of concern and not exasperation. "The house isn't shaking, Anne."

"Yes," she hissed. "It is."

I retreated behind my pages. "Maybe leave some wine for tomorrow. Your shirt will thank you."

Her lips thinned to a knife's edge. The wine glass slammed onto the coffee table as she shot to her feet. "The house *is* shaking, Trevor. See?"

It took everything I had not to roll my eyes, but I knew appeasement was my best shot at avoiding a fight so I lowered my book.

And... she was right.

Her glass *was* trembling. It was dancing like she'd set it atop a washing machine.

"Probably—" I cleared my throat. "Probably just one of those semi-trucks rolling by."

"For ten straight minutes?" Anne countered.

"An earthquake, then," I reasoned, not sure I believed my own excuse.

"What kind of earthquake lasts ten fucking minutes, Trev?"

I exhaled, frustration bubbling over. "Christ, Anne! I don't know. Maybe we're feeling the aftershocks? You got a better explanation?"

"Sure." Her eyes glinted. "How about HAARP?"

"HAARP?"

She nodded, swaying on her feet. "It's this radar array up in Alaska. Bunch of transmitters screwing with the ionosphere. Weather control. Electromagnetic fuckery. Ol' Ty says they can even trigger earthquakes when they crank it up."

I ran my hands over my face, not believing I was actually having this conversation. Oliver 'Ol' Ty' Tyler was our next-door neighbor, a Vietnam war vet with enough PTSD to make an asylum blush and a stockpile of guns to match. "So what," I started, "you think earthquakes are a government conspiracy now?"

"Not all of them," she threw back. "Just this one. Think about it. When's the last time we had an earthquake in this state? In a decade, we haven't–"

Her voice died mid-sentence. I looked up to see her frozen, staring out the sliver of visible street through our boarded window. The streetlights outside were going haywire, humming and flickering like possessed fireflies before guttering out completely.

"Oh my God... " she breathed.

"It's a power outage, Anne. Not the end of the world."

She shook her head fiercely, jabbing a finger at the glass. "No, no, no – out there, at the end of the road. Do you see that?"

"Let me guess, soldiers spray painting another house?"

Anne's finger stabbed at the window, desperation etched on her face. "Just look for fuck sakes!"

"Alright, alright," I groaned, dragging myself to the makeshift peephole. "Let's see... Parked cars, check. Our sad apple tree, check. Lawns begging for a rake, and—"

My voice shriveled up in my throat.

What. The. Fuck.

A monstrous shadow stretched across the cul-de-sac, cast by a figure that defied reason. It towered at the end of the lane, easily as tall as the streetlights. A yellow jacket hung from its frame like a tattered sail, topped by a hood that shrouded its face in empty darkness.

My jaw went slack. My brain scrambled for explanations, anything to make sense of the impossible sight before me. It was a hallucination. Had to be. Maybe that elusive "terrorist cell" had spiked the water supply and now we were all tripping balls, drowning in shared paranoia. LSD in the reservoir, maybe? Or some cutting-edge chemical weapon, Soviet leftovers, or—

The shadow moved.

The world shook.

Realization hit me like a sledgehammer. This thing, this nightmare made flesh, was the source of those tremors. But how? The creature was a beanpole, rail-thin despite its height. How could something so spindly make cars rock on their suspensions? The damn thing was rattling the photo frames on our walls, making our porchlight blink on and off.

"I don't..." I stammered. "This can't... "

Words failed me.

The creature advanced, its gait a glitchy, unsettling waltz – slow, then blindingly fast. Freeze-frame pauses punctuated by legs snapping at unnatural angles. Its torso swayed like a puppet with tangled strings, arms swinging boneless at its sides, creaking like ancient timber.

Anne and I stared in quiet horror. The thing's coat cracked like a whip in the wind, its voice reaching through the glass as it lumbered past our house. It sounded as though it were whimpering. Sobbing like a scolded child.

Suddenly, it veered left. The beast plowed through Kent's fence in a storm of shattered wood, its ponderous footfalls fading into the night.

"What... What the hell *was* that?" Anne gasped, her voice shaking.

"I don't know," I croaked.

And God help me, I wasn't sure I wanted to find out.

The next day Anne retreated to the attic. I found her hunched by the grimy window, frantically scrawling theories on scraps of cardboard. Across the way, Ol' Ty's grizzled face glowered from his own attic perch. His sign screamed ALIEN INVASION!!! in manic capitals.

Anne's cardboard proclaimed GOVERNMENT EXPERIMENTS in neater strokes.

"We call them Tall Things," she explained as I walked in, her hair a bird's nest on her head.

"Them?" My stomach knotted at the plural.

She nodded, grabbing a fresh slice of cardboard. "ARE THE SOLDIERS SATANISTS?" she scrawled. "Ol' Ty spotted more of them last night," she said, her eyes fever-bright. "Further out in town. Those ones didn't hit our street, though."

"Huh."

"Don't tell me you still think he's crazy," she chided, pressing her latest theory to the glass.

Did I? I wasn't sure.

Truth be told, I didn't know what I thought about *anything* anymore. It felt like my entire concept of reality had been unceremoniously thrown in the trash. "What's uh..." I said, gulping down my pride. "What's Ty's take on everything?"

She shot me a smirk.

"Look," I said defensively. "I'm not saying I'm buying what he's selling but..."

Anne chuckled. "It's fine. Ty thinks they're bad news – as if that wasn't already obvious."

"Bad news?"

She nodded. "He's betting it's an alien invasion, some kind of cosmic hivemind here to conquer the planet. But I'm not so sure."

"What's your guess?'

"That they're living weapons." Her eyes flashed with morbid fascination. "Think about it, Trev. Last year they opened that military base in the next town over – Newbrook – and it's so secret they won't even let the staff interact with the locals. I'm thinking it's because they were developing something. Something big."

"Or tall?" I offered.

She tapped her nose, a knowing smile on her lips. "Bingo. I'm betting the Tall Things are some kind of prototype they've been developing. Maybe cyborgs. Artificial super soldiers that managed to escape the compound, and now they're scrambling to round them back up."

"You don't think that—"

BANG. BANG.

Ol' Ty beat his fist against his window, scowling. He slapped a fresh piece of cardboard to the dusty glass.

"Soldiers not Satanists..." Anne murmured, reading the sign aloud. She frowned. Uncorked her sharpie and got back to scribbling. A moment later, her response was pressed to our own window.

"WHY'D THEY MARK KENT'S HOUSE THEN?"

Ty scratched his chin, narrowing his eyes in consideration. He bent down. Got back to writing. A moment later he shot up, his answer making my blood go cold.

MARKED FOR THE TALL THINGS, his message read.

THEY ARE HUNGRY.

WE ARE FOOD.

The night brought thunder. And with it, the Tall Thing returned. It lurched down our lane, its movements an unsettling ballet of creaking limbs. Cars groaned as it knocked them from its path. Street lights flickered and died, electricity going haywire in the monster's presence.

Anne and I watched from the living room, faces pressed to the boards.

"You think Ty's right?" I asked, horror turning inside of me. "You think we might actually be... food for those things?"

She shot me a look. "Now who's jumping to conclusions?"

"It's just—"

The Tall Thing halted outside, its teetering frame blocking out the scarce scraps of moonlight. My heart stopped. It gazed down at us, its face unknowable behind that hanging hood and I somehow knew it could see us. Feel us.

Anne's hand gripped mine. Squeezed.

Then it turned away, its yellow raincoat sweeping in a wide arc as it crossed the street. Its narrow legs looked grotesquely thin. Bandaged. Bleeding...

It crouched in front of Kent's house, its head cocking to the side with a violent crack of bone. A whimper. It almost seemed as if it were examining something.

"The symbol," Anne croaked. "Ol' Ty thinks those red symbols are how the soldiers communicate with the Tall Things. He thinks they marked Kent's house."

"But if not for food then..."

The creature lifted a long, spider-like finger to the barricade hammered in front of Kent's door. It began to pick at the boards. One by one, it plucked them away as if they were twigs from a branch.

Anne's hand squeezed tighter around mine, her teeth worrying against her bottom lip. Anxiety filled her eyes. concern. "Don't open up," she said in a low voice. "Don't you dare show yourself, Kent."

As the Tall Thing ripped the last of the boards free, it touched a finger to the door. Began to scratch. It whined, sharp and wrenching, like a dog begging to be let inside.

"Don't," Anne kept muttering. "Don't... Don't... Don't..."

The door opened.

Kent stood wheezing at the entrance, one hand trembling on his walker, the other on his oxygen rack. As usual, he was scowling. "Gotta be kidding me!" he shouted hoarsely, looking past the Tall Thing, as if he were addressing some unseen soldiers lurking nearby. "This the kinda unholy bullshit my tax dollars are going towards? Ya'll oughta be ashamed!"

Kent wrinkled his nose, smacking his gums and jabbing a finger at the towering monstrosity. "Now you listen up, you two-bit Goliath. You might be able to intimidate them dumb-fuck youngsters, but I been around long enough to know my rights. Yeah. That's it. Whine all you want, but do it somewhere else before I—"

A muffled yell. A strangled gasp.

I recoiled in horror as the Tall Thing snatched Kent from his doorstep like a child with a bug. It lifted him by his leg, dangling the old man high above his lawn. In a snapping movement, the Tall Thing tilted its head to its opposite shoulder.

"Oh fuck..." Anne said, her voice hardly a whisper.

Kent was red in the face, his frail hands swinging uselessly as he tried to catch the Tall Thing with a hook. "Get over here!" he snarled. "Get over here and let me teach you why they called me Iron Kent!"

A dull crunch.

An anguished scream.

The Tall Thing had crushed Kent's leg in its grip, and the old man was now howling, hurling curse after curse at the abomination.

"Where the fuck are the soldiers?" I demanded.

As if in response, sirens split the night. A military convoy swerved onto the cul-de-sac, their spotlights guttering as they neared the Tall Thing, megaphones crackling to life before sputtering out.

Soldiers poured out of the trucks. They started to shout. Holler.

In the chaos of it all, I assumed they were shouting at the Tall Thing – demanding it to put Kent down, to surrender but it became apparent they didn't give a damn about the monster. Or Kent. They were addressing us. Anne and myself. They were addressing the neighborhood at large, who were probably watching this unfold with the same abject terror.

"Do not look," they told us.

Do not look.

Do not look.

Do not look.

But by then it was too late. The creature started to cry, its loud weeping smothering the obscenities hurled from Kent's lips. It lifted a rake-like hand, gripped its hood and pulled it back.

I can only imagine what Kent saw then.

The old man went rigid as stone, his defiance evaporating like tears in the sun. His body went limp. Arms dangling freely beneath his head, eyes taking on a glassy, almost hypnotized sheen.

Anne shrieked, hand flying to her mouth.

Kent's face began to bubble. Blister. Steam hissed from his every pore as if he were boiling from the inside out. His skin began to stretch. Slough. It fell from his face in sheets, revealing the ashen white of his skull beneath.

Drip.

Drip.

Drip.

Drip.

Anne staggered away, dry-heaving as she scrambled for the bathroom down the hall. But I couldn't stop watching. It was like I was rooted to the spot. Paralyzed in fear. My hand shook uncontrollably at my side, left eye twitching as Kent's skin and bones – his everything poured out of his turtleneck sweater, splashing to the lawn like globs of human stew.

No, I kept thinking.

No. No. No. No. No.

This couldn't be happening. Whatever we'd seen up until now – fine. But this? It was worse than a living nightmare. It was a living Hell. A guttural drone wormed inside of my ears, and my eyes swiveled toward the soldiers, who were surrounding the monster. Except they didn't have their weapons drawn. They weren't firing on the creature.

They were worshiping it.

They sat back on their knees, swaying blissfully, voices chanting in that brutal language. Only this time, they sprinkled some English into the mix.

"Rejoice," they intoned. "Our saviors have come."

Soon after, the Tall Things outgrew the night. They stalked beneath the glare of the sun, flanked by individuals in gowns of flowing white.

"Lab coats," Anne said. "They're researchers, probably. Scientists studying the Tall Things to figure out what makes them tick. See? They've all got clipboards."

But I disagreed. To me, they seemed closer to robes – like something a priest or a nun might wear. They skulked about with bowed heads. Never looked up. Across their eyes they wore tinted visors, faces draped in hoods like the monsters they followed.

After Kent died, most of the cul-de-sac decided to make a break for it. Maybe they realized the situation was spiraling out of control, that it was only a matter of time before they became the next puddle on the pavement. Maybe they just couldn't stand the screams – the thunderous *thum thum* of footsteps in the dark. I don't know.

Whatever it was, they broke out of their homes. Usually at night. Anne and I would wake up to the crack of gunfire, and in the morning we'd find our neighbors shot dead in their yards. Nobody came for their bodies. They were left to rot, slowly decaying as a putrid example of what awaited disobedience.

Ol' Ty became our last hope.

We'd kept in contact with him through the attic window, swapping theories on those pieces of cardboard. He told us not to lose hope. He was putting together a plan, a last-ditch resistance to get us out of this mess.

MIGHT BE ABLE TO USE THE GAS LINE, he wrote.

DRAW EM IN, BLOW EM UP

BE READY

And we were.

We were ready and waiting, but eventually Ol' Ty just stopped showing up. He vanished. Anne thought he might have decided a group escape was too risky, that maybe he snuck out on his own to raise the alarm.

"He'll be back with the cavalry, Trev. T-trust me. Ol' Ty wouldn't abandon us..."

But even as she spoke the words, I could tell she didn't believe them. Her voice was empty. Hopeless. She'd even lost the blue in her eyes. They'd turned a dull, vacant gray. Stress had caused her to lose patches of her golden hair, while her paranoia kept her from sleep.

My wife was unraveling.

And so was I.

I'd rarely known death in my life, and now the sheer volume of it was numbing me. Kent. Ol' Ty. I couldn't process it. I didn't know how to feel this broken, this utterly crippled with despair. We were trapped, Anne and I. Nowhere to run. Nowhere to hide. We were prisoners slated for execution, just waiting until our names got pulled out of a hat.

And then – almost out of the blue – the military had a change of heart. They started freeing people. I watched it happen. A soldier ripped the boards from a house at the end of our lane, four whitecoats monitoring his work with clipboards in hand.

When he was finished, the door opened. A woman peeked out, trembling with anxious confusion. I think she might have said something to the soldier, but her voice was too small and too far for me to hear.

"Rejoice," he told her loudly. "You are saved."

"Rejoice," the whitecoats echoed in eerie unison.

The woman gave them a wary look, but then broke into tears of relief. She rushed inside. Returned with a baby swaddled in her arm and her young daughter close behind. The three of them darted across their lawn, jumped over their father's corpse and piled into their minivan on the street.

The entire time, the whitecoats stood only meters away, quietly observing. It didn't take long for the rumbling to begin– that telltale sound of approaching death, of one of the Tall Things coming to claim its prize. The van started up, backfiring a plume of exhaust into the air. The woman shrieked for joy, but I knew her relief would be short-lived.

See, from my vantage point at the end of the lane, I saw something that she never could: the boot locked around her tire. The van rode forward as she pressed the gas, and then clunked to a stop.

My heart broke. The look on her face, that desperation wasn't for her own life but the lives of her children in the backseat.

The rumble reached a crescendo, and in the blink of an eye a Tall Thing crashed into the van, knocking it over like a diecast toy. I couldn't make out much beyond that. Nothing but the sound of the monster tearing into the roof of the van and pulling the crying children out one by one.

My legs gave out. I slid to the carpet, hands clamped tight over my ears and screamed so I wouldn't have to listen to what came next.

"Please..." I sobbed. "No more..."

<hr>

After that, the lockdown was ostensibly over. Like hungry wolves, soldiers tore down boarded-up doors and kicked in living room windows, dragging families out onto their lawns as offerings to the Tall Things. The screams were everywhere. Omnipresent and haunting. Anne and I cranked our sound system, but it only served as background static to the symphony of suffering.

In the nights that followed we barely slept. Anne tossed and turned beside me, while I stared blankly at the ceiling fan above. There was an understanding between us: we had been abandoned. Nobody was coming to help us. Nobody was coming to destroy those monsters and save the day.

We were alone. Forgotten.

And somehow things got worse.

The darkest moment of my life occurred the morning of October 27th. I woke to sunlight peeking through our boarded-up window. Anne wasn't beside me. I looked all over the house for her before I found her note on the kitchen counter, scribbled quickly, stained with tears.

Trevor,

I wish I could have said a proper goodbye, but I know you'd try to stop me. I'm going to find help. Newbrook isn't far, and their sheriff can contact the national guard. Until then, please stay safe. We'll be together again soon.

Love always,

Annabelle

She left through the basement hatch. I know this because I spotted her corpse lying outside the kitchen window. Anne gazed back at me, a look of shock painted across her pale face, a small red dot where the bullet pierced her skull.

I couldn't even muster the courage to step out and bury her. Instead, the stray dogs took her apart piece by piece. Before long, all that remained of my wife was a scatter of bones, picked and chewed.

When they finally came for me, I wasn't there.

The man inside of me had left – all that remained was a barren husk. They kicked down my door at midnight. Found me sitting at my kitchen table, drunk with a glass of whisky in my grip. Rough hands ripped me from my chair, tossed me onto my lawn.

"Rejoice," grunted the soldier.

"Rejoice," echoed an approaching whitecoat. "You are saved, brother."

Saved? I'd beheld monsters with footsteps like thunder, watched them turn my neighbors into puddles and seen my wife rot away in front of my eyes – and I was *saved*?

I laughed.

It was so absurd, so cosmically awful that laughter seemed the only sane response.

The soldier shifted, flicking off his rifle's safety. "This one's lost it. Shall I give him the bullet, sister?"

"No," the whitecoat soothed. "He has shown courage where his fellows have fled. Our Grace will pass judgment. As it is written. So it shall be."

"As it is written," the soldier intoned. "So it shall be."

The whitecoat studied me behind her dark visor. With a smile, she cupped a frigid palm to my cheek. "You mustn't be afraid," she whispered. "When this is over, you shall know a peace beyond all concepts – an absence of suffering so complete that your emotions will reveal themselves as the messy, corruptible things they are. Rejoice."

"Rejoice," the soldier droned.

The grass began to pulse beneath my knees, bucking and trembling. Thunder rolled in the distance.

"It nears!" the soldier announced.

The whitecoat rose, joining him near my fence. "Prepare the contingency."

The soldier racked his rifle, brought it up on aim with the barrel pointing between my eyes. "How many more after this?" he asked.

"Sixteen."

"Then us, sister?"

"Yes. Then us."

"Rejoice," he said.

"Rejoice," she answered.

The rumbling deepened. Street lights flickered around the cul-de-sac. Cars danced upon whining suspensions, moving like a mechanical ballet while birds exploded from treetops. My heart slammed. It beat a rhythm of panic against my ribs, matching the frantic pace of the stampeding footfalls.

It was coming.

"Why do this?" I growled. "Why not just put a bullet in my head?"

"Because we love you, brother," said the whitecoat. "You waited patiently. Persevered. For your faith, you have earned the gift of salvation – the gift of reunion. Can't you feel it? This is the rapture."

A shadow stretched across us, stealing the breath from my lungs. A monster in a yellow raincoat stood teetering at the end of the street, only this Tall Thing wasn't like the others. It seemed larger. More imposing. Its scarecrow frame eclipsed even the moon in the sky as it sauntered toward us.

The soldier fell to his knees, swaying in the way the others did.

"What are they?" I hissed at the whitecoat. "Aliens?"

"Angels," she said with soft reverence. "Those that gifted us life in eons past."

The monster thundered forward, its feet leaving cracks in the pavement as it twisted and jerked, knocking aside cars and trees with its erratic movements. It whimpered weakly.

"Those sounds they make... It almost sounds like they're crying..."

"I believe they are," the whitecoat answered mournfully. "They take in all our pain, all of our sorrow so that we may know brief glimpses of peace. They sacrifice much for us."

The Tall Thing stumbled onto my lawn, reaching toward me with a long arm covered in bandages and scars. "Ours..." it rasped.

Matchstick fingers gripped my hair, yanking me off the ground. I cried out. Kicked, shouted as I hung in the monster's grasp, dangling above my yard like a plaything.

"Fear..." it murmured. "Anger... Sorrow..."

It was as if it were listing off my emotions – as if it were reading me, its face hidden beyond a shroud of darkness.

"Panic..."

"Shame..."

"Loneliness..."

The Tall Thing pulled in a scraping breath. "Witness..." it said. "Our Grace..."

The monster lifted a hand to its hood, pulling it down. My heart stopped. A patchwork of horror gazed back at me – a hundred visages stitched together in a tapestry of shifting eyes and gnashing teeth. It smiled. It smiled with fifteen mouths, and when it spoke, its voice was a chimera of mangled vocal chords.

With each slow syllable, the Tall Thing's many faces bled. They came apart, cutting themselves out of the monster until its head was nothing but pieces of disparate flesh floating above its brittle neck. Eyes. Ears. They spun for hardly a second before snapping back together, forming a new face. A fresh abomination.

"We... come..." it moaned, "in... *pieces...*"

I tried to speak – tried to beg for my life, but my mouth wouldn't work. I was paralyzed. A hundred mismatched eyes blinked at me. Warm piss dribbled down my legs. This was it. It was going to turn me into one of those puddles on the pavement, into nothing but a slosh of skin while it devoured the deeper parts of me.

The Tall Thing lifted a crooked finger, tapping it against my chin.

"Open... up..."

No. I clenched my jaw, shaking my head in some pathetic, final act of defiance. There was no way. No way I was going to open up for this thing, not after I'd seen what—

CRACK.

A scream tore from my throat. I howled. Writhed. My lower jaw hung limply from my face, shattered and broken. My vision became a blur of tears.

"Shhh..." the monster cooed. It slipped a finger down my throat, scraping inside of me with a serrated nail. I gagged. Choked. The monster's face began to come undone, slicing itself apart and hovering above its matchstick neck as floating pieces of mangled flesh. Then, those pieces began to spin. Expand. They swirled around us in the night, eyes blinking and mouths speaking as the Tall Thing probed deeper and deeper within.

"You..."

"Are..."

"Delicious..."

My veins caught fire. My blood began to boil, my arms and legs twitching in agony while the Tall Thing scratched at my insides, as its dozen mouths began to laugh and cry in some twisted symphony of gleeful despair and—

Gunfire.

The crack of bullets shattered the night.

The Tall Thing whirled, dropping me to the lawn as its faces snapped back together. It screeched. Roared.

The soldier stopped his chant. He scrambled to his feet, activating his radio with a static crackle. "Eden, this is Horsemen 9. We're under attack and need—"

His skull blew apart, splattering me with pieces of that thing he called a brain.

I sat, gaping on my lawn as I tried to catch up to the situation. Another shot rang out. Then another. The Tall Thing bellowed, its head snapping this way and that, trying to locate the source of the shooter as bullets tore through its raincoat, staggering it with every impact.

Bzzt.

The whitecoat's radio crackled. A slow, garbled voice spilled out of it, drowning in interference. "*Hor... semen 9,*" it said. "*Ple. .ase... confirm... prev... ious.*"

The whitecoat scrambled behind my house, pressing her back to the wall. "Yes, Eden," she wept, tears streaking her cheeks. "This is Saint Gonzalez. We are under attack. Templar Campbell is down. I say again that Templar Campbell is down."

A pause.

"*Affir...mative.... Status of the An...gel?*"

"It's taking–" Her voice cut away into a sob. "Oh, it's taking heavy fire, Eden. Our Grace's mental state appears to be deteriorating and—"

The whitecoat shrieked as a bullet carved through the edge of my house in a splinter of wood. She dropped to a knee. Clutched her shoulder. Her pale robes blossomed a deep red, blood seeping through the fabric as she forced herself back to her feet in time for the second bullet to pierce her throat.

She dropped to the grass, her visor tumbling from her face. Two white eyes gazed at me, hollow and lifeless, strangled by veins of purple.

A moment later and a rocket whistled through the air above. It slammed into the Tall Thing, exploding in a red-orange firestorm that split my ear drums. The creature roared. It lurched backward, its face splitting apart and reforming in mounting displays of fury.

And in the glow of the fire, I saw my savior.

Ol' Ty.

He stood on his roof, surrounded by an arsenal fit for a war-lord. A rocket launcher rested on his shoulder, and his mane of hair blew wildly as he let loose another RPG. The explosion sent the monster reeling. It fell backward, crashing against Kent's house in a hurricane of rubble.

Ty lowered his launcher, shouting down at me. "Christ almighty – the Hell you are waiting for, idjit? Get outta here!"

The Tall Thing shrieked. It snapped upright with a sound of crunching cartilage, beginning to sway back and forth, vibrating faster and faster until—

Oh my god.

I started running, my heart in a race against my legs. Another RPG tore through the air. Another explosion. It wouldn't matter, I knew. Not now.

Glancing over my shoulder I looked in horror at what the Tall Thing had become. Six arms had burst from the back of its raincoat, a tangle of flesh woven between them the wings of a bat. It flapped, rising into the air.

"Congrats on making yerself a bigger target, dipshit!"

Another barrage of rockets burst from Ol' Ty's roof. They connected with the Tall Thing in a series of explosions bright enough it almost turned night to day. Somewhere in the distance, sirens screamed. Rubber howled. The cultists would be closing in, the soldiers and the whitecoats – and alongside them, the low thunder of stampeding Tall Things.

I scrambled away, tears in my eyes.

Ol' Ty. I'd called him a lunatic – a nutjob, but here he was sacrificing everything for me. As I scrambled across town, ducking between bushes and moving between sheds, I heard more explosions ringing out. I'm not sure what Ty had set up but he was holding them for longer than I ever imagined he could have.

Then, a few minutes later as I crested a hill I looked back. The entire town was dark. In ruins. The one source of light was Ol' Ty's house, but I could see a small army closing in on him. A dozen Tall Things. Maybe more. Countless soldiers. All of them rushing forward and—

I blinked, blinded.

A flash erupted, and a moment later I was knocked on my ass by a shockwave. Half our cul-de-sac had gone up in flames, a massive cloud of acrid black billowing into the night sky. In the distance, I heard the anguished wails of Tall Things. The screams of soldiers and whitecoats.

"Good fucking riddance," I muttered.

Three hours later, I'd stumbled through Debby Forest and into the town of Newbrook. Tears of relief welled in my eyes. The streets were quiet and still. No soldiers. No whitecoats. No Tall Things, or the nonstop screams of their victims – just empty silence, the stuff early mornings were made for.

Squinting against the dawn, I made my way down the main road. It was odd. After so long living in a nightmare, the calm in Newbrook felt almost unnerving. Uncomfortable. It seemed impossible to me that people could just be peacefully sleeping and not dead.

When I reached the sheriff's office, I beat my fist against the door. I needed to blow the whistle on what was going on, explain that a paramilitary cult had taken over my town, that Tall Things were melting people on the street and that we needed to get our ass in gear and call in the National Guard. No—scratch that. We needed to call in fucking *NATO*.

C'mon. Open up, dammit!

But as I peered impatiently through the glass door, a reflection caught my eye. I wheeled around. And there it was – just at the edge of the curb, gleaming with the red-orange glow of sunrise.

A puddle.

Strange thing was, it hadn't rained in weeks.

JUDAS

The military base doesn't exist. Not officially. It's a rusted out corpse of abandoned hardware, a crumbling graveyard tucked away in the jungles of South America. It's lost. Forgotten. There isn't a single reason anybody should be here. Not one.

And yet I have company.

She's sitting across from me. Her eyes are squinting in the glare of the sunset, peering through the shattered window at a corroded hatch. It's an entrance. A doorway to an underground bunker that I found her lying next to an hour ago, barely breathing.

"Who are you?" I ask.

She doesn't answer. Her hands run across the purple bruises covering her forearms, and all I can think is the woman's a mess. Her blouse is torn. Her copper cheeks are flecked with red. I don't know if the blood belongs to her or somebody else, but I figure by the end of this, I'll have a pretty good idea.

"I'm not here to hurt you," I say.

She meets my eyes with a hard stare. It's quiet. Unyielding. She's not certain who I am, and judging by the look in her eyes, she's running a series of probabilities. It's the black suit that does it. Always. People see my suit, they see my briefcase, and their imagination spins into overdrive.

I try another question. "Anyone else here with you?"

A pause. Her lips part like she's thinking of speaking before pressing shut again. Then she nods. The legs of her chair squeal as she rocks back and forth, giving motion to her anxiety.

"How many?" I ask.

"Lots," she rasps, voice coarser than sandpaper. "They're close. They know exactly where—"

"I doubt that."

The woman blinks, wide-eyed like I just slapped her across the face.

"If anybody was with you," I say, "chances are they're already dead. Jobs like these? They're typically bloodbaths. They're not the sort of places you expect to find survivors – much less survivors like you."

Her lips become a thin line, defiant. "And what's that supposed to mean?"

"Only that you look more ready for a safari than a slaughterhouse." My gaze travels from her running mascara to her cargo shorts, cataloging every scratch between. "I checked you for weapons before you woke up. You've got no guns. No ammo. The closest thing you've got to a sharp edge are your car keys."

"So?"

"So you don't belong in a place like this."

She scoffs. "And you do?"

"No," I tell her. "Nobody does."

I heave a sigh, hefting my briefcase onto my lap. The clasps snap open, revealing a sea of documents and I fish out a clipboard from within. It's covered in questions. The sort of questions whose answers are typically written in blood.

"I'd like to chat, if you don't mind."

"I'll pass." She stands, swaying. The way she favors one leg tells me she's nursing a sprain, maybe worse. "I'm out of here," she tells me.

"Suit yourself."

She throws me a glare that could curdle milk, then limps for the door. I watch her go. She makes it to the threshold, even twists the knob before freezing.

"Something wrong?" I ask.

"Just figured you'd try to stop me, cuff me to a pipe or something."

"Wouldn't see the point," I say simply. "You aren't going to leave."

The corner of her mouth twitches. "Excuse me?"

"It's like this," I say, my eyes tangling with hers. "You know better than I do what's out there – so go ahead. Walk out that door if you think you're safer outside. I won't try stop you."

Her expression cracks, almost crumbles but then she finds her stubborn courage all over again. Twists the knob. The door opens with a whine. The woman looks out across a burial ground of rusted humvees smoldering in the tropical sunset. Weeds lurch up from cracks in the pavement. Every last structure is crumbling, an apocalyptic caricature of what it once was.

All of it's dead. Withering.

A grating, unnatural sound rips through the stillness, like a thousand nails dragging down a chalkboard. It echoes across the abandoned base, a twisted, electronic wail that sets my teeth on edge. Maria slams the door shut, her fingers fumbling with the lock. She turns to me, her back pressed against the weathered wood, her entire body trembling. In her eyes, I see a reflection of my own unease, a shared understanding that we're not alone out here.

"What the fuck is going on here?" she demands, her voice trembling.

"That's the million dollar question, isn't it?"

Her eyes narrow, fingernails digging into the wood.

I fish my badge out of my jacket and slide it across the floor to her. "There you go. Everything you need to know about me. I'm with The Facility, investigating a series of disappearances linked to this compound."

She studies the badge, eyes darting across the laminate. "The Facility...?"

"We're a shadow contractor," I explain. "That means the less people know about us, the easier it is to do our work."

She stalks back to her chair, eyes narrowed. "And what is that 'work'?"

"EVENTs."

"That supposed to mean something?"

"Not to you. Point is, I'm the one you call when the things that go bump in the night actually do. Think monsters. Entities. My job is to hunt these things, capture them if I can."

Laughter touches her lips. "You expect me to believe that?"

"I don't expect you to believe anything. You asked a question, and I answered it – that's typically how conversations go. All I ask is you return the favor. Now, you saw something in that bunker, and I'd like to know what it was."

Her eyes dart to the shattered window, to the corroded hatch rising from the dirt. "Who ... who says I was even inside the bunker?"

"You do," I tell her simply, pulling out a pack of smokes. "It's written on your bruises, your cuts. I see it in the way you keep stealing glances toward the entrance, with the sort of haunted look that only somebody like me could understand."

"Somebody ... like you?" she says quietly.

I nod, slipping a cigarette between my lips. "I killed my father," I tell her, pocketing my lighter and sucking back a lungful of nicotine. "Happened when I was seven years old. A shadow woke me up, some tall man with two faces and no eyes – asked me what my favorite nightmare was."

Her gaze turns stoney.

I keep talking. "Being the stupid shit of a kid I was, I screamed. Top of my lungs, I screamed. And you know who came running in without a second's hesitation?"

I feel something well up in my throat, and I press the cigarette firmer to my lips. Inhale harder. Blow out a dark plume. "My dear old dad. He came charging in, and I scrambled my ass right under that bed. Cowering. Trembling."

The woman leans forward, expression painted with sympathy.

"I watched the Tall Man lift my dad up to the ceiling," I say, trying hard to keep my voice even. "It turned to me and smiled, saying, 'I've got just the nightmare for you, kiddo.' And do you know what it did?"

She shakes her head, slowly, like she's dreading the answer.

"It tore my dad in two," I tell her. "Right down the middle, like he was made of paper fuckin' mâché."

I burn the cigarette down to the filter, then I keep going until I feel my lungs catch fire. Truth be told, I hate this story. I hate it more than anything else in the entire world and if I had it my way, I'd bury it and never think of it again – but in moments like these, it's the most valuable history I own.

Even now it's working its black magic.

I watch the woman's posture shift. Her shoulders slumping forward in horrified disbelief, her eyes welling with tears. She's doing the human thing. Empathizing. And that's exactly what I'm going to use to take what I need from her.

And there she goes again. Staring at that bunker. She's wearing the expression of a woman that's lost between a nightmare and a daydream, who wants nothing more than to wake up from both.

"My name's Carter," I tell her. "What's yours?"

She takes a breath, sharp as a knife's edge. Her eyes dissect me one final time, weighing the risk.

"Maria," she says finally. "My name's Maria."

"It's nice to meet you, Maria. I'm gonna have to insist that you to tell me what you saw in that bunker. It's important."

Her hands shift nervously in her lap. "You said that you hunted monsters ..."

"That's right."

"Well, what about demons?"

I arch an eyebrow. "What about them?"

"Are they real?"

"Depends who you ask. You saying you saw one down there?"

"I don't know," she says, voice taut as a wire. "Maybe not a demon, but... something like it." She pauses, fingernails scraping into her shorts. "I think I saw the devil down there. Satan himself."

"Satan?" I whistle low. "Now that'd be something."

"I knew it," she mutters, rising from her seat. "You think I'm a lunatic. I knew you would and—"

"Slow down," I say. "I don't think you're a lunatic. Not yet. Those disappearances I mentioned earlier? They're strange, Maria. Atypical. It's not people that are going missing, but monsters."

She settles back in her chair, eyes widening. "Monsters?"

I gesture to the fractured window, to the rotting carcass of the base beyond. "This place? It's the Bermuda Triangle for boogeymen. Entities are being drawn here, but as soon as they cross the perimeter, they vanish. Drop off every last sensor we've got. And I'm not talking about Saturday night ankle snatchers either– I'm talking about heavy hitters. Nightmare fuel. The kind of monsters that we can't destroy, much less contain."

She shrinks in her seat. "And you think all that's connected to what I saw?"

"Maybe. Maybe not. Won't know till I get the full picture."

She swallows hard. "Get me out of this hellhole, and I'll tell you whatever you want."

"Unfortunately," I say, heaving a sigh. "That's ... not possible. We've gotta do this here and now, preferably before sundown."

"Why?" she demands.

I take a moment, think hard about how much I want to traumatize the woman. A little, certainly. Some fear is always good – it's motivating, energizing, but too much of it and you get panic. And panic is messy. Panic is unpredictable. "Here's the thing," I begin, choosing my words with care. "Entities. Monsters. These things have common characteristics, Maria. One being that they're more active at nightfall. The other is that they have a habit of imprinting themselves on individuals, tracking them ... marking them."

"You're saying that I've been marked? That it's gonna come back for me?" Her voice is quivering.

"I'm saying that if it does, I need to understand what we're up against. And to do that I need your story. So talk, while daylight's still on our side."

She rakes a hand through her hair, frantic. "Let me think. It started a couple weeks back, I guess. A reader sent in a tip about this place—"

"Slow down. A reader?"

"Right. Sorry. I'm a journalist for an online paper. We chase tips, usually political dirt. But this one ... it was different."

"Your tipster have a name?"

"Arlo."

"Last name?"

She shakes her head. "Didn't give one."

Good enough. I scratch it onto the page.

"Arlo claimed he'd been hearing screams," she continues, words tumbling out. "His whole village had. Echoing from the jungle. Military convoys were sneaking through at night, their headlights off. All heading up some forgotten road. Arlo knew where it led, though. Up to an old base. One with a history of ... experiments."

I look up from my clipboard. "Experiments?"

"Human ones," she croaks. "Genetic horrors. DNA splicing. A grab-bag of the most unethical shit you can imagine."

"And how'd Arlo get read into something like that?"

"He worked there," she explains. "Years ago, during the Cold War."

My pen scratches at my clipboard, pages crinkling as I fill in a dozen different fields. "The nearest village is twelve miles out," I say. "How'd Arlo hear screams from this base?"

"That's the thing." Her voice drops, thick with unease. "The screams weren't coming from the base, but the jungle itself. Arlo said they sounded just like they did in the old days. The screams, I mean. Guttural. Inhuman. The kind of sounds only mutilated throats could make. He claimed they were test subjects set loose in the wild."

"Set loose?" The pen nearly slips from my fingers.

"Guess so. He said they'd release the guinea pigs, then send out the... more advanced models to hunt them down."

"For what purpose?"

"Food," she says, her voice as cold as a mortuary slab.

I gnaw on my pen, tasting plastic and dread. "Tell me more about Arlo. How old was he?"

"Seventy, maybe?" She wrinkles her nose. "He was fit, but ... weathered."

"Weathered how?"

"Like life had put him through the ringer. Leathery skin, half his teeth gone. His hair was a tangled mess, and I'm pretty sure I saw lice crawling in his beard." She shudders. "And his eyes... God, his eyes."

"Describe them."

"Well, they were pale – paler than the moon. And they'd pulse. Swear to God. They'd bulge out of his skull like they were trying to escape. It was freakish."

Cataracts. Not altogether uncommon for a man of Arlo's age. "And that hatch," I mutter, nodding toward the bunker's rusted maw. "I'm guessing that's how you and Arlo got inside?"

A nod.

"Walk me through it. What's down there?"

Maria's brow furrows, eyes unfocusing as she dredges up the memory. "It was ... narrow. Like this metal throat descending into darkness that seemed to stretch forever. Arlo said we'd find what we needed below. Evidence to blow the whole conspiracy wide open."

"What condition was the bunker in? Arlo made it sound operational."

"Not even close," she says, shaking her head. "It was a tomb. Looked like it'd been abandoned since the 70s. Moss crept up the walls and the ladder rattled with every step we took. The whole place was a deathtrap. Every time I put my foot down, I half-expected the rung to snap."

I keep scribbling, lost in my thoughts. One would think Arlo would clue in that the bunker wasn't fit for operation. But then, Arlo's description doesn't strike me as a man altogether *there*. Add the pale eyes, a borderline feral demeanor, and I can't help but wonder if Arlo wasn't so much an employee of the program as he was a product of it.

Maria continues, pulling me back to her story. "Fifty feet down, we hit the catwalks. Dozens of them. They sprawled out from the ladder like a metal spiderweb, each leading to a different level, a different entrance."

She pauses, a tremor running through her. When she speaks again, her words are barely audible. "The entrances were welded shut, Carter. Every last one. It's like they were desperate to keep something in. Something they couldn't risk getting out."

"Then how'd you get inside?" I ask.

"We ... we found an entrance that was different. It sat at the bottom of the ladder, half-drowned in rainwater. We waded through, the flooding up to our knees, and... "

"And?"

Her fingers curl. "It was ripped open," she breathes. "The entrance was torn apart. Like something had clawed its way out, peeled the steel back like it was tinfoil. We're talking inches of hardened metal here, enough to shrug off a nuclear blast. I mean, Christ – what could do something like that?"

For the first time, real fear slithers through my veins. It's cold. Insidious. If what she's describing is true, then there are two, maybe three entities with that capability. All of which are impossibly violent. Official protocol is to avoid contact at all costs. If contact is made, then policy dictates the elimination of all witnesses to ensure the preservation of social order.

I look at Maria, really look at her – bruised, bloodied, cradling what's likely a fractured arm. She's already been through hell. I wonder if I'll have the stomach to put her out of her misery if it comes to it.

"The door," I say, fighting to keep my voice steady. "Arlo worked there. What did he make of the damage to it?"

She gives a bitter snort. "Said it was explosives. He claimed the military blasted their way in a few months back to reboot their little science fair. But that was bullshit. The door was warped outward, not in, and there wasn't a hint of blast damage anywhere. I called him on it. Of course I did, but Arlo just changed the subject. Asked if I had *skeletons in my closet*. Asked me if I'd ever hurt people, or considered it and—"

My pen pauses on the page. "Hold on. He asked you if you'd hurt people? Why?"

"I don't know," she says. "Arlo had demons in his past, given his work at the base. I figured maybe he was looking to start a conversation, hoping we could forgive each other for our sins, sorta thing." She shakes her head. "It doesn't matter. He dropped the subject pretty quick once he realized I didn't bring anything for show and tell."

"I see," I murmur. "I'm guessing he led you through that mangled entrance then?"

Maria nods. "The passage beyond it was pitch black. We sloshed through endless corridors, our headlamps throwing twisted shadows on the walls. It felt... wrong, though. Even then. It was like we weren't alone down there, like something was watching us from the gloom."

My skin prickles. "Did it still seem abandoned at that point? Non-operational?"

"Definitely," she says. "The whole place was a time capsule. The rooms were full of ancient magazines, peeling posters, and little relics that had to be half a century old. Some floated past us in the water. Others sat on moldy tables. I fished through some filing cabinets and found old lockets, even a few wedding rings – alongside piles of classified documents." Her teeth find her lip, a distant look in her eyes. "It seemed ... strange, you know? That they'd just leave all of that stuff behind."

Yes, I think. Unless they needed to get out in a hurry. "Was the whole bunker flooded?"

"No. Before long, we climbed out of the water into a new chamber. This one was dry but ..." A violent shiver racks her frame. "Claustrophobic. Narrow. All along the concrete walls were dark streaks of paint. The air was ... musty. Rancid. And when we turned the corner—"

She stops, her face draining of color.

A beat passes. Her voice, when she finds it again, is hoarse. "Something crunched under my foot," she tells me. "*Bones*. Piles of them, a foot deep or more. It looked like they'd died clawing over each other, desperate to escape ... something. That's when I realized the streaks along the walls weren't paint. They were blood. Old and browned."

My heart pounds. Could this be evidence of Arlo's claims? "Were the bones ... mutated at all?"

Maria offers a slow nod. "Some worse than others. One skull looked ... human, maybe, but its jaw was elongated, almost like a horse. A single, twisted horn curved out of its forehead. Another was flat. Square. It looked like somebody had rolled a person's head under a *tractor*, but it had dozens of eye sockets. Multiple mouths."

Maria gags. Looks like she might be sick from the memory. And I'm feeling a little queasy myself, but for an entirely different reason. Outside, we're losing daylight. Night is fast approaching, and I'm worried it might be bringing something that I'm not yet ready to deal with. Something violent. Deadly.

"And Arlo," I croak, choking down my dread. "What did he say after showing you that evidence?"

"He ... asked me how it made me feel."

I blink. "How it made you feel?"

Maria sucks back a breath, her voice beginning to shake. "Yeah. He picked one up – another skull. But where the mouth should have been were these *mandibles*. Like a wasp. Or an ant." She pauses, twisting with discomfort. "Arlo's eyes ... they bulged. Glowed in the dark, I swear to Christ. Then he shoved that skull in my face, asked how it made me *feel*."

Her voice plummets. "He pressed me against the wall, hard. His breath smelled like rot. Decay. Then he started rubbing the skull against my cheeks, panting like an animal and I freaked out – shoved him backwards. He came back at me. So I took a swing at him. Caught him right across the jaw and he dropped, spitting out a mouthful of blood."

I narrow my eyes. "Did he get the message?"

"He got a message, just not the one I was trying to send." Maria gets up from her chair, fists pumping in and out of fists. Starts to pace. It's like she's too full of nervous energy to sit in one place, and I can relate. "Arlo started acting like a lunatic after that. Babbling. He kept alternating between crying and shrieking, shouting that I was cruel, and evil – a monster. Then he'd collapse. Curl into a ball and start crying like an infant."

"Bizarre..."

She scoffs. "Yeah, you're telling me. It was the weirdest thing. None of it felt ... real, though, you know? It felt more like an act. A performance. Like he was putting on a show and—" Realization dawns in her eyes. "Oh God ... and maybe he *was*."

"What do you mean?" I ask.

"We heard this sound after. Like *right* after. A clang. It rang through the tunnels, then it kept ringing – almost like something heavy was coming down the ladder, that long one, back at the entrance. Arlo stopped crying. He shot up, grabbed my hand and started raving, saying the military commandos were here and we needed to hide. Said he knew a place they wouldn't find us."

"And where'd he take you?"

"I'm ... I'm not sure exactly," Maria says, running a hand through her hair. "We fled down passages that twisted and turned like a labyrinth. At that point I had no idea where we were, no idea how to find my way back. He was my lifeline. My only shot. But the whole time ..." She shivers. "I heard something rumbling in the dark."

"Something?" I echo.

"It wasn't the commandos," she tells me. "It wasn't even ... alive. It sounded artificial. *Electronic*. Like feedback from a microphone, only a thousand times worse. It was just like the howl we heard earlier when ..."

"When you opened the door," I say, my jaw tensing.

I glance down at my clipboard, mind whirring. That howl. The honest truth is I've never heard anything like it, not in my entire career. It doesn't match a single entity in The Facility's database. It's a genuine anomaly, an unknown quantity and that worries me more than—

My pen cracks in my grip.

Christ. Am I actually *scared*?

"Is ... everything okay, Carter?"

Maria. I look up and she's staring at me with doe-eyed concern, her auburn hair plastered to her forehead with sweat and blood. "You kinda zoned out there for a second and—"

"I'm fine," I lie, loosening my tie with a shuddering breath. "Just having some trouble acclimating to the heat I think. It'll pass, I'm sure. Please, continue your story."

She studies me for a moment, gives me the sort of look you give a kid that just had a nightmare, then pushes on. "Arlo and I ran," she says. "He brought me to a room that made the last corridor smell like a rose garden. It was wide. Shaped like a pentagon. Machine gun barrels poked out from slots in the concrete walls, and written between them were the words ..." Her voice trails off. Maria tries to finish her thought, but it comes out as a sob. She drops her face into her hands and the tears come out like a torrent, messy and loud.

I want to give her time, but time's the one thing we don't have.

Outside, the sun is missing. It's gone. Vanished beneath the horizon. The last scraps of daylight are making crooked shadows of the tree line, spilling them across the base like decrepit fingers, reaching hungrily toward us.

My eyes find my clipboard. I scan my notes, desperate for a clue, hoping I might have missed something but my writing's a mess. It's uneven. Hardly legible. My hand's been shaking, shaking like it was the night I saw my father—

"Sector 5," Maria chokes out.

I glance up at her.

"The words on the wall in the room ..." she says, wiping tears from her eyes, recomposing herself. "They said Sector 5: Feeding Trough."

Words. Is she really getting this worked up over stupid words?

"They were food ..." she says quietly. "All the corpses in that room were food ... The bodies were everywhere. Scorched. Half-devoured. They were rotting away, with maggots pouring out of their skin. And – oh God, some of them looked *fresh*. Like I could still smell the copper in the air, could still hear the wet slap of blood with every step I took." Her eyes slide downward, gazing at the red stains painting her boots.

"What did they look like?" I ask. "Were the bodies mutated? Human?"

Maria wrinkles her nose, thinks on it for a moment. "You mentioned missing monsters earlier. Boogeymen."

My heart skips a beat. "What about them?"

"Well," she breathes. "I think I found them."

I draw back, and it's my turn to go pale with shock. Puzzle pieces begin to connect in my mind, building a picture that I'm not sure I want to see. "How can you be sure?" I demand, desperation creeping into my tone. "What if they were just more of the same – test subjects like the others?"

"No. These were different," Maria says. "Horrifying in ways the others couldn't compare to. It was like looking at a mannequin, or a doll. What's that phrase?"

"Uncanny valley," I supply, my mouth dry.

"Exactly. It was like they didn't have a soul – like they *never* had a soul. Some looked human. Nearly. Only they were too tall, or their limbs were too long, or they had too many teeth in all the wrong places ..." Her expression darkens. "But the worst part was that something had *slaughtered* those things. Ripped literal nightmares to pieces, and I knew there was a good chance it was coming to do the same to Arlo and I."

"Arlo," I mutter. "If he'd been to Section 5 before, then he must have known about that graveyard. Those bodies didn't appear overnight."

She nods, lips tight with disdain. "He knew. The bastard knew everything. He shoved me onto that pile of ... of corpses and told me as much. He started raving, calling me evil, twisted – a monster all over again. He kept pointing at me like all of this was *my* fault, like he hadn't just led both of us to our deaths."

Her voice breaks. "All while that ... *thing* howled in the darkness, its footsteps rumbling toward us. I felt terrified. Hopeless. I kept asking Arlo why me? Why go through all this trouble just to kill me?" She chokes back a sob. "But he said he didn't have a choice. He knelt next to me, put a hand on my cheek and whispered that his child needed to *feed*. Told me it was getting hungry. Desperate. He almost looked fucking remorseful if you can believe it."

Tears trickle down Maria's cheeks. "I had nowhere to run. Nowhere to hide. I didn't know how to get out of that bunker, didn't even have a working headlamp, so I just lay there, in that heap of monsters, quietly sobbing. The footsteps got closer. The nearer they came, the slower they moved. It was like that creature knew I was trapped, like it'd done this before and knew it could take its time."

"Did you see it?" I press, pen poised against the clipboard.

She cradles herself in her arms. Shivers. "Yes. It was tall, nothing but a flickering shadow. And it pulsed. Vibrated. The way it moved was jerky, haphazard, almost like it had one foot in our reality, glitching in and out of existence."

"Glitching," I mutter. The word tugs at a memory, something I can't quite grasp.

"And its eyes," Maria whispers, shrinking into herself. "It had these amber eyes. Bright and gleaming, like twin cinders smoldering in empty space. It felt like they were piercing me, like its eyes were digging through my skin and looking into my mind. My *soul*. It felt like it was taking bites out of my memories, tasting them before spitting them back out ..."

My clipboard trembles on my lap, my whole body awash with dread. "Was it painful?" I ask.

"No," she says, her eyes unfocused. "It was cold. Just cold. Like a blizzard tearing through my mind, freezing every thought to a crawl. Maybe that's why I didn't run. I just ... sat there, numb, watching as the Shadow passed through the concrete pillars like they were mist."

She grips her knees, shaking her head. "It was almost human, whatever it was. Two arms. Two legs. A head. But its body ... Jesus, its body was pure static, Carter. Like TV interference."

TV interference... The phrase shakes something loose in my mind, some half-remembered case file. I flip frantically through my clipboard, stopping at a page labeled ABERRATE EVENTS. The Facility's very own 'Most Wanted' list. My eyes scan the entries, but nothing matches. Nothing even comes close.

A thought hits me. "Your cuts and bruises, were they the work of this Shadow?"

Maria glances at her arms, at the gashes crusting with dried blood and the swollen bruising. "No," she tells me. "I picked these up running through the bunker."

And there it is. The first clue I've landed on all night. Of course the Shadow wouldn't bother with Maria – not while it already had another, far richer meal available.

"It walked past me," she continues. "It walked through that mulch of corpses and headed straight for *Arlo*. And it started … speaking."

"Speaking?"

"Remember that howl I mentioned earlier?"

"Sure."

"Well, this time it was *hissing*– like a livewire, or static electricity. Whatever it was saying, Arlo wasn't a fan. He started weeping. Pleading with it. He kept swearing that he'd done his best, that there was nothing else out there so the Shadow would have to make due with me." Her voice catches. "But the Shadow didn't care. It grabbed Arlo by his hair, lifted him to the ceiling. And its eyes … those cinderlight eyes … they blazed an *angry* orange."

My heart pounds like a war drum. "And what did it do to him?"

"What do you think?" she says darkly. "Arlo thrashed in its grip. Screamed. He begged me to help, said I'd be next if I didn't. 'She's a monster!' he kept shouting. Over and over. But then his voice collapsed in his throat, turned into this choking gurgle as the Shadow's eyes flashed red. And Arlo—Christ almighty, Arlo started to gurgle. Moan. His face started to wrinkle, melting into his skull and—"

Maria takes a deep, shuddering breath. Starts to pace. Her cheeks are blotchy with tears, her fingers anxiously picking at the hem of her blouse like she's trying to walk off the memory. Finally, she stops at the window. Look out across the darkened base, out toward that rusty hatch in the dirt.

Is she feeling it, I wonder?

That rumbling beneath our feet? That slow funeral march of an approaching nightmare? It almost feels like the ticking of a clock, and I can't help but think it's a fitting metaphor for our bleak situation. "Maria," I press, "it's critical I get these details."

"The Shadow held Arlo there," she rasps. "His legs were twitching, his face dripping onto his shirt and then …" Maria brings hand to her mouth, starts chewing her nails to the bit. "It tore his head clean off. Like a bottlecap. It lifted Arlo's head to its amber eyes, opened its mouth and screamed *fire* at him. The heat, it was like standing at the gates of Hell."

My pen flies across the page, sweat dripping down my brow. It's hard to miss now, the rumbling. *Thum. Thum.* Like a giant walking beneath earth, quaking the ground with its every footfall.

"Do you feel that?" Maria whispers, face contorting in horror. "I feel—"

"Footsteps," I hiss. "Yes, of course I do. Whatever you saw down there is coming, Maria, and unless you stop veering off I'm not going to be able to save us. Finish. Your. Story."

She nods, frantic. "Right. Right. Um … These tendrils burst from the Shadow – like limbs, and they cracked Arlo's skull like an egg. The Shadow reached inside, pulled out his brain and then brought it *into* itself. His fucking brain, Carter. Like it was assimilating him or … or …"

"Devouring him," I offer.

Her fingers clutch the edge of the window, monitoring the bunker with growing dread. "Now do you get it?" she asks. "Now do you see why I called it the devil? I mean, what else could do something like that?"

A good question. A terrifying one.

If what Maria's describing is accurate, then I can think of a single entity that fits the bill. Just one, though. If I'm right, then we'll probably live to see daybreak – but if I'm wrong?

Well, some nightmares are better left unspoken.

My fingers brush the warm steel of the glock on my hip, and I wonder if I'll have the courage to do what's necessary if the time comes. "After it killed Arlo, what did it do to *you*?" I ask.

"It glared at me," she whispers. "Another blizzard washed over my mind. It turned my thoughts into ice cubes, made me go rigid with shock and then ... then I blacked out."

"Wait," I say, lowering my pen. "If you blacked out down there and didn't know the way out, then how'd you escape?"

She leans her shoulder against the wall, heaves a sigh. "That's just it. I couldn't tell you. One second I'm in that chamber of corpses, and the next I'm outside with you dumping water on my face. That's it. Everything I remember."

I grip a fistful of my hair, staring down at the mess of words on my clipboard. Frustration boils inside of me. I was close. *This* bloody close to finishing the puzzle, to saving our lives, only to be stonewalled by her amnesia and—

Hang on.

A smile crosses my face. Memories thread together in my mind, and all at once I'm getting the full picture. The blackout. The blizzard in her skull. All of it's starting to add up and I finally know beyond a shadow of doubt what we're dealing with here. Yes. It's so obvious, has been since the start if only I—

"... police!"

I blink, Maria's standing in front of me, her expression urgent.

"I've gotta tell the cops about Arlo," she says. "Tell them about the bunker – there could still be others down there. Victims. Maybe some still alive. We need to form search parties and—"

"We're not talking to the police," I tell her flatly. "And I wouldn't worry about the victims either."

She gapes at me, stunned. "I don't understand."

"It's simple," I say, rising from my seat. "The cops won't have any record of Arlo. Sure, you can tell them what you saw down there, but they'll likely put a bullet in your head for your trouble."

I fish out my lighter, flick the wheel. A flame dances to life. "Arlo doesn't exist, Maria. Neither does this base. Neither do you."

I touch the flame to my clipboard, and the paper catches, curling with smoldering hunger.

"The hell are you doing?" Maria exclaims.

"Saving your life." I drop the clipboard with a clatter. It pops and cracks as the flames eat her story, one word at a time.

"But you said you believed me!"

"And I do," I tell her. "That's the whole problem. An hour ago, I was still in the dark on this whole thing but the more you talked, the clearer it became. You and Arlo stumbled onto something real here, Maria. A genuine conspiracy. A real cover-up."

"Then the people need to know!"

"They do," I confess. "And they will – eventually. But not from you, and not from my report either."

She shakes her head. "Then how?"

I stalk past her to the window, resting my palms against the sill. The air's thick, humid with jungle heat. "I'll find a way. I always do."

Maria studies me, glaring hard enough I can feel it on the back of my neck. Then she asks the obvious question.

"It's your employer, isn't it? The Facility's behind all this. The coverup, the experiments the—"

"Yes," I tell her. "I suspect it is."

She joins me at the window. We stare out into the darkness, at the steel hatch rising from the earth, where a devil made flesh is inching ever closer.

"I thought your job was hunting monsters," she says coldly, "not making them."

"My job is a lot of things. More than anything else, it's complicated. The Facility is ... Well, it's not what I'd call a *good* organization, Maria. Or even a moral one."

"Then what is it?"

I weigh my words carefully. "A pragmatic answer to an otherwise ugly question. How does one save our species from a force so twisted it defies all language?"

"I'm not sure I understand where this is going."

"Something is coming for this world, Maria. Something vast and twisted. A nightmare born from the coldest corners of the furthest reaches of space. It's cruel. Unfathomable ... Hungry."

"My job – the Facility's job – is hunting monsters, capturing those we can not to study them, or rehabilitate them, but to use them. To wield them." I heave a sigh, tasting guilt on my tongue. "We're drafting these creatures into an army, Maria. Using them to fight back against that cosmic force, that great evil coming our way."

"What is it exactly?"

"We don't know. Theories range from an elder god to a kind of misaligned consciousness from a higher dimension. Whatever it is, we call it The Entity."

"Okay ... I'm still not sure what any of that has to do with this base, though."

"This base was the result of that Entity. A response to it. In those days, The Facility couldn't be certain how much time we had – only that the Entity was coming. And that it was hungry. Fear made them desperate. They greenlit anything that might save us. Or so the rumors go."

"Rumors?"

I nod grimly. "Few records exist of The Facility's activities during the Cold War. Most documents were destroyed. Those that remain are buried under redactions. I wasn't around then, obviously, but I picked up bits and pieces from old timers I worked with. They'd talk about black projects in passing. Hidden programs. One project was infamous, so much so that even now, half a century later, The Facility hasn't entirely snuffed out its legend."

She stares at me, her expression unreadable in the gloom. "What project?"

"Judas," I say, the word heavy on my tongue. "Project Judas was helmed by a biochemist, a brilliant man named Arlojan Screech. The project's aim was to create a weapon. A lifeform that could assimilate targets into its being, absorbing their capabilities. Such a function would provide it with a near limitless potential. The problem was–"

Steel rattles. It's coming from out there – at the bunker. There's a groan of warping metal, like the rungs of a ladder slumping beneath the weight of something titanic, and I know that the devil is climbing out of Hell.

"It's here ..." Maria whimpers, gripping my arm. She pulls at me, but I'm rooted in place. My eyes are focused, locked on the bunker hatch bathed in moonlight. There's a whine of hinges. A snap of bolts. The hatch swings open with a dull clang, and Maria stumbles backward in stammering horror.

I watch, full of morbid wonder as a dark shape lurches out from below. It buzzes. Crackles like living static. Cinders glow in its face, twin eyes in a void of nothing. The Shadow twists as if scanning the base, emitting a low, digital hum.

"Oh my God ..." Maria cries. "This can't be ... Not again ..."

The creature sees us. It sees *me*. It takes a shambling step, kicking up dust and its eyes flare, blazing with the threat of annihilation. Maria keeps pleading, keeps begging me to run but I hardly notice she's there. This monster, this is why I've come here tonight. I know it is.

The Shadow takes another step. Its eyes burn brighter, hotter as crimson lashes from their edges like tears of lava. And all at once I feel what Maria described. I feel it pouring into my mind like ice water. I feel it rifling through my thoughts, chewing up my memories and spitting them back out. But I don't resist it. Instead I breathe deep and invite it deeper within.

Go ahead, I think. *Have your fill.*

And like a passing breeze, the cold soon begins to fade. The Shadow holds my gaze, its eyes dimming to embers once more.

Satisfied, it looks skyward. Its body begins to flicker, glowing with cathode radiance, and then—

Six wings burst from its back in a shower of obsidian static.

"How are you gonna kill that thing?" Maria hisses.

"I'm not," I tell her.

The Shadow belts one final, distorted cry before launching into the air like a streak of midnight. Three wingbeats, and it vanishes beyond the clouds.

"No," she mutters, staring at the empty sky. "You let it escape ... Are you insane? It's gonna cause a massacre out there!"

"Yes," I say. "I certainly hope so."

She rounds on me, fury and confusion warring in her eyes. "But you said you hunted these things! What gives? Are you just lousy at your job or what?"

"Project Judas had a directive," I say calmly, "a specific one. Its task was to assimilate hostile entities, to annihilate monsters and boogeymen, and ensure the survival of humanity. Simply put, it was never made to hurt people like you and me. And after everything you've told me, I'm not convinced it even can."

She gapes at me. "Were you even listening? I found a fucking *graveyard* down there, Carter! It burned Arlo's skull to a *crisp*, cracked it open and ate his *brains*! I don't care what it was designed for. I watched it kill a person right in front of me."

"Did you?" I pick up my briefcase, giving my ashen clipboard a final, farewell glance. "From everything you described, I question whether Arlo was a man at all by the time you crossed paths. If he really was Arlojan Screech – and I think he was – then it's said he conducted more than a few experiments on himself. The glowing eyes? I've never met a human with a set of those, have you?"

"Maybe not, but—"

"Arlo never brought you here for an expose, Maria. He brought you here to kill you. That was always the plan."

She blinks, stunned. "No, that can't—"

"It's like this," I tell her. "All those missing monsters I was looking for – the strange disappearances and absentee urban legends? They were being lured by Arlo. He was feeding his child a steady supply of anomalies and aberrations, just enough to keep it from entering hibernation– but then he ran out. That's why he pulled you in. Hungry. Ambitious. Willing to do anything for a career-defining story. Thought you'd be an easy mark, and he was right."

Maria's shaking her head, but I can see in her eyes she doesn't believe her own skepticism.

I press forward. "Arlo figured he could do a little … creative twisting of the narrative down there, coax you into attacking him maybe, and then use that violence to convince Judas you were food. You said he kept calling you evil. Vile. Monstrous. Almost like it was a performance – well, I don't think that was a coincidence."

I turn away from her, looking up toward the shifting clouds high above. "Unfortunately for Arlo, he misunderstood his own creation. Project Judas wasn't designed to harm humans, Maria. Never. It went against its core directive. So in that moment, when Arlo offered you as a sacrifice, a flip switched in Judas that made it realize Arlo had crossed the threshold and become a monster himself."

She's quiet.

It's a lot to throw at somebody, so I let her have some time with her thoughts as we make our way to the door. I twist the knob. It opens with a rusty whine, and this time Maria doesn't go rigid with fear, doesn't start to tremor with anxiety.

"You really think Arlo was that Screech guy?" she murmurs.

I shrug. "Hard to say. It's not as if he's got any dental records left to check … but based on what you've told me tonight, I'm inclined to think so. Seems like Screech couldn't let his project go."

We carve a path toward my SUV, gleaming black against the backdrop of ancient humvees.

"I don't get it," Maria says, circling around to the passenger door. "If Judas is as good as you say, then why'd the Facility lock it up down there?"

"Because," I say. "There was a whole lot more than Judas in that bunker, wasn't there? You mentioned legions of bones. Mutated creatures." I heave a sigh, cracking the door and clambering into the driver seat. "Chances are the Facility of yesteryear figured it'd be easier to throw the baby out with the bath water, and just sealed the whole bunker as a matter of convenience. Then they purged every last record of that base. Wiped their hands of it."

Maria gets inside, closes the door with a dull thump and takes a deep breath. "By the way," she says. "Thanks for not killing me back there."

"Don't mention it."

I twist the keys in the ignition and the vehicle rumbles to life.

"So what do we do now?" she asks. "About Judas ... or whatever?"

"Nothing," I say, pulling away from the ruins. "As far as I'm concerned, that creature isn't a monster. And that means it's not my problem."

The SUV rattles as we turn onto the uneven jungle road. Maria twists in her seat. She looks back through the rear window as her worst memory falls further and further behind us.

"If it's not a monster," she asks, "what is it?"

Words drift around my head. Definitions. I'm trying to figure out how to explain what it is that she and I witnessed, what it is that more people will see in the coming weeks. I'm trying to think of a way to tell Maria that whatever that thing was, she doesn't need to be afraid of it.

None of us do.

I open my mouth to reply, but I'm interrupted by a discordant howl. Something distant. Shrill. I squint up through a canopy of passing vines, and there—

Soaring through the sky above us. It's a dark speck against the moon-washed clouds, but I know if it were closer I'd see a shadow with six wings, cinderlight eyes, and a body of black static.

I'd see a guardian angel – one with plenty of work to do.

A VOICE FOR AUTUMN

The key was rusty, splotched red and gray. It almost blended in with the copper-gold of the dead autumn leaves, but it didn't. It stood out to the boy.

And so the boy bent down and picked it up.

"Lucky find," he said, gazing at the key with childhood reverence. Images of great adventure played in his mind, chased by phantoms of guilt and worry. He wasn't supposed to be wandering. Not here. Not today. What was it his mother had said?

Something about the stars in the sky. The angle of the sun.

"There are omens in the air," she'd cautioned, her voice tight with concern. "You get us some water from the river and you come right back, hear? Today ain't no time for play. And keep away from that old well."

"Of course," the boy had said. He'd promised that under no circumstance would he dilly nor dawdle, nor wander to that old well. She gave him a pat on the head, a kiss on his cheek, told him to give a holler if he saw anything odd, and then sent him on his way.

But this key, strange as it was, wasn't *odd*. It was just a key. The world had plenty of keys. The boy had seen several of them, and never once had any of those keys caused trouble, so why should this one?

The only question was, who did it belong to?

And what did it open?

He scanned the grassy clearing. There wasn't much around save a clutch of trees to the north, the river to the east, and that old well up on the ridge. No doors to unlock. No gates to open. Nowhere to put this rusty key save his moth-eaten pocket, and so that's just where it went.

I'll keep an eye out, he thought, trudging off toward the river.

He imagined the key might have fallen from one of his neighbors' pockets, but it looked so old. So worn. It didn't seem the sort of key one walked around with. It seemed the sort that had a purpose, the sort that unlocked things much grander than houses or sheds.

At the riverbank he lowered his bucket, filling it with babbling swirls of white-green current. The water looked peculiar today, he decided. Odd. The boy leaned forward and gave the bucket a sniff, and it smelled rancid. Dead. It smelled like touching that water on your lips might kill you worse than any plague.

"Thirsty?" a voice called.

The boy wheeled about. He looked from the grassy clearing, to the tangled trees, to the old well on the ridge with its crumbling bricks. Not a soul in sight. He narrowed his eyes, peering out toward his house on the hill, thinking that perhaps he had heard his mother call to him, but the front door was closed.

"Over here," said the voice.

The boy turned toward the well. "Over there?"

"That's what I said. Over here. Be a dear and come a little closer. I'm rather old and I'm afraid my hearing isn't what it used to be."

A clammy chill swept over the boy. The voice didn't sound so bad but it felt awful. It felt like somebody had taken a sweet person's voice and slathered it in tar and hornets, then stuffed it full of broken glass.

"Sorry," the boy said quickly. "I told my mum I'd be back in just a few, so I should really be gettin' on." He turned to leave, feeling somewhat guilty but he couldn't place why. After all, he had told the truth. He'd sworn to his mother that he'd steer clear of that old well, promising that he'd neither dilly nor dawdle.

"A moment, please," the voice croaked, feeble and morose. "You wouldn't happen to have found a key around here, would you? I seem to have misplaced mine."

The boy paused. "A key?"

"Indeed," said the voice. "An old one. Probably rusty and not much to look at, but it means a great deal to me. I should be quite thankful to have it returned."

The boy felt the weight of the key in his pocket. His heart thrummed. Threads of fantasy tugged at his mind, spinning tales of all the wonderful things such a key might open. "If I found this key," he ventured, "would you show me what it unlocks?"

The voice seemed to smile. "Why, I should think so."

The boy bit his lip. His mother would soon be wondering where he had gotten to, but surely a short jaunt to the well couldn't hurt, could it? Besides, it would only take a moment. "I think I found your key," the boy announced, clambering up the ridge.

"A fortunate twist of fate!" exclaimed the voice. "I was so distraught, worried the sun might set before I could lay my hands on it. You have saved me much woe, child."

The boy smiled, though it felt wrong to. As he neared the top of the ridge he began to look for the voice, but he saw nothing and no one, only a whisper of fog and a canvas of darkening sky.

"Down here."

The boy blinked. "You're down the well?"

"Have to be, don't I? How else am I going to use the key?"

It seemed an odd answer, but the boy knew little and less about how strange keys functioned in strange wells, so he stepped forward all the same. Yet the closer he got, the more uneasy he felt. It was his arms. They had grown all prickly with goosebumps and nervousness, as though his skin knew something that he did not.

"Almost there," soothed the voice. "Come right up to the bricks, would you? I should like to see the face of my helper."

And so the boy got right up to the stones, standing in front of that frayed rope that long ago must have held a bucket like the one he carried. He lowered his own bucket to the grass. "I don't see you," he said, peering into the well.

The voice hummed. "Don't you? How odd, for I see you just fine."

"You do?"

"Oh yes. You have such beautiful eyes, child. So blue and vast, like miniature oceans nestled inside of your skull. I could almost drink them up."

"Thank you," said the boy, though he did not feel complimented. "What are you doing down there anyway?"

There was a spell of silence, then a dreary sigh rose from the well. "I'm afraid that I was pushed."

"Pushed?"

"Indeed," said the voice. "During a twilight like this, when I was not much older than you. I had been drawing some water when an old woman crept up from behind me, all cackles and frowns. She lifted my ankles and tipped me right in."

The boy's hand flew to his mouth, horrified. He cast a wary glance over his shoulder, but saw no crones lurking in the reaching shadows, which was a relief. "Who was she?" whispered the boy.

"I do not know. I expect she must have been a witch, for only witches do such terrible things."

The boy nodded sagely. "Did you grow up nearby? Or were you out exploring?"

"I was exploring the place I grew up," replied the voice. "Many years ago I lived in a slumping house upon a hillside all speckled with lavender. If you look to the north, you might see it now."

The boy's eyes blossomed. "But that's my house!"

"Is it now? What a marvelous coincidence! If that's not fate, then I don't know what is."

The boy grinned. It was nice to know he and this voice had something in common.

"Say," said the voice. "Would you mind terribly if I asked you to toss me down that key? I suspect it's the one I've lost, and I'd like to try it on this lock."

"Not at all," said the boy. He reached into his pocket and took out the key, but just as he meant to drop it a terrible sensation swept over him. It felt like a funeral, or a deep sorrow. It felt like the kind of loneliness that turns people to stone and fills their eyes with ghosts and regrets.

It felt *odd*.

And so the boy pulled back. "I think I should ask my mum first."

"Ask your mum?"

"It might belong to her," the boy lied. "She's always misplacing things, and if I go chucking her stuff in the well then she's bound to be cross. I'll be stuck in my room all autumn." It was the best excuse the boy could come up with. "I'm very sorry," he added. "Really, I am."

He paused, uncertain if the voice deserved more apologies.

Then he decided it did not.

The boy had realized a surprising and sudden truth: he did not much like talking to the voice. It made him feel awash in strange things. Lonely things. He turned and began walking down the ridge, all the hairs on his neck standing upright.

"Wait!" cried the voice.

But the boy did not wait.

"Please!" the voice pleaded. "I'm begging you! I didn't want to tell you this but ..."

The boy turned back, squinting through the gathering gloom. The sun had all but vanished, leaving the well a dark smudge amid dancing fireflies. "What is it?" he asked. "You sound hurt."

"Oh, I am," whimpered the voice. "I didn't want to worry you but I'm hurt quite badly, and I need that key of yours to get out of this well. I need it to get help."

The boy swallowed hard. His mother had always taught him that it was a good, godly thing to help those in need. "Well, what's wrong? My mum's good at patching up scrapes. Maybe I could fetch her and–"

"No!" the voice hissed. "I'm ... I'm afraid there's simply no time for that. You see, there are snakes down here."

The boy gasped. "Snakes?"

"Oh yes," shuddered the voice. "So many. And all quite venomous, too. They're sleeping now, but they start to stir when the sun sets and the moon shines full, so they'll be waking up shortly. I see one now. Its tail is rattling – you've heard of rattlesnakes, haven't you?"

The boy had most certainly heard of rattlesnakes. They were one of his foremost fears, outdone only by quicksand and the aching sound his house made late in the evening.

His conscience twisted. It forced him back up the ridge, though each step brought a tickle of nausea with it. "Okay," he said, ignoring his misgivings. "Here's your key."

The boy opened his palm, and the rusty key fell into the opaque blackness where it never made a splash.

"Did you catch it?" asked the boy.

The voice did not answer.

"Hullo? Are you okay down there?"

But no reply came, only the faint echo of the boy's words, bouncing off the gray cobblestones below. Perhaps he hadn't been fast enough, he thought. Perhaps the rattlesnakes, angry and vicious, had sunk their fangs into the voice before it could free itself, and all of this because he had hesitated.

What would his mother think?

Tears nudged out from his eyes, and he lowered his head in shame and remorse. He was a sinner, the boy. This was his lot now. Soon everybody would know how rotten he was, and maybe they'd even throw him into jail for it.

A scream.

It broke in the distance, shattering the boy's melancholy. He whirled around. Far up on the hill, the front door of his house swung freely in the autumn breeze. Light spilled out from within. It illuminated a billowing shape sprinting down the lavender slope, cloaked in moonlight and despair.

"Stop!" his mother cried. "Get away from there!"

And the boy tried, but the ground began to shift, lurching and rolling like squall-tossed waves. He lost his footing, tumbling to the grass. The well shuddered violently, its ancient bricks crumbling inward like the last breath of a dying star.

"Don't look!" his mother shrieked. "You mustn't look, baby!"

But curiosity is the great vice of all children, and this boy was no exception.

He leaned forward, peering into a fantastic, terrible darkness that had no place in the dirt. It was the sort of darkness that belonged beneath haunted stairwells, or deep in forests made of myths and dreams.

And as the boy beheld this darkness, it beheld him in turn.

Eyes swam to the surface. They pulsed and swirled, exploding like the tainted starscape of a long-dead galaxy. The sight of them filled the boy with winter. He felt suddenly ill. Dizzy. His hair began to fall away, floating from his scalp in great swathes of gold, and he tried to pick up the strands but found his fingers had turned brittle and stiff.

"Darling ..."

His mother. She called to him, yet her voice sounded so far away, as though she were a distant memory of a thing that never truly was.

"Leave my darling ..."

The boy's thoughts began to unravel, unspooling like threads upon a loom. *Help,* he thought. He needed help, yet as he cried out it was not his words that fell from his lips, but his teeth. He spat them onto the grass. They were blackened things, all wretched with decay.

"Sweetheart ..."

"Don't you dare ..."

"Not my sweetheart ..."

Somebody kept calling, a woman whose name he no longer knew. His memories wilted. They withered into nothing and less, and the boy's eyes faded until they were emptier than glass. His mind dimmed. It guttered, flickering like a candle in a storm and he wondered briefly who he even was, how he had ever come to be here.

"Have mercy ..."

"He doesn't belong to you ..."

"Not anymore ..."

The void atop the ridge widened. It crawled toward the boy, jaws agape in primordial hunger, devouring the grass and the dirt and everything else until there was nothing left beneath the boy, not even the ground.

And so he fell.

The boy sank and sank, and the deeper he went the more certain he became that the whole world was sinking beside him. All its laughter. All its love. The darkness was eating up all the beautiful things that had ever been, and as it swallowed the last light that would ever shine, the boy heard something familiar.

A voice.

It spoke with the grace of a genocide, its words slower and more aching than a man bleeding upon a cross. "Thank you," it whispered. "For I have been so very lonely ... for so very long ..."

HEADLIGHTS

They built the research lab on Brayford Hill – something called the Ryvel Institute for Emerging Technologies. Whatever that means.

Our mayor sold us on the idea. She promised the lab would stimulate the economy, help Brayford's lagging industries. The idea was that all those scientists would come through town and spend and spend, and maybe some of their fancy STEM cash would trickle down into our blue-collar pockets.

But it never did.

Only thing Ryvel managed to do was cast a shadow.

I never spoke with any of the personnel that worked there. Not sure any of us did. They mostly kept to themselves. Didn't come through town for supplies, lunch, or even a lousy beer after their shift. They avoided us like we were crawling with disease; like we were ghosts, invisible and make-believe.

Maybe they'd been ordered to, or maybe they just didn't care. Not sure it matters. What does matter is that Ryvel ruined my town. It brought something evil to Brayford, and all of it started with the alarms.

They sounded a week ago, just past 10 p.m. Must've woken up half the town. Then the other half woke up when half of Ryvel went up in flames. An explosion blew apart its southern compound, sending concrete raining down on us like meteors and turning the night sky a blazing red.

Our mayor claimed it was a gas leak. *Nothing to worry about,* she assured us. *Just sit tight in your homes while emergency crews isolate the leak and Brayford will be back up and running in no time.*

Sure. No problem.

But then that gas leak became a chemical spill, and then that chemical spill turned into radioactive snowfall that'd turn our skin to mush, and next thing you know, I'm waking up to Sheriff Milton dropping off a box of 'rations'.

"Lockdown's been extended," he said. "Don't open the door, boy – ain't safe."

My neighbor, Benny West, stuck his bald head out his trailer window. "Extended? For how long? Been a week already, and I ain't got much booze left."

Milton folded his arms and wrinkled his snub nose. "Can't say I give a fuck, Benjamin. Figure It'll go on as long as it takes. Now close your damn window afore you get yourself sick. Christ almighty ..."

"But you ain't sick!" Benny called as Milton clambered into his truck.

"That's cause they got me takin' special pills, ain't it?" Milton shouted back, arm draped out the driver-side window. "I'll be by with another supply drop in a week, but until then stay the hell put. Both of you."

"Bullshit!" Benny spat. "You'll be back tonight like you were last night and the night before. I seen your fuckin' headlights glarin' through my window, Milton! You're a goddamn creep, you are!"

Milton craned his head out of his truck, incredulous. "The hell you talking about? You don't think I got better shit to do than watch you twiddle your shrimp dick all night? Ain't my headlights you're seeing." He jerked a thumb toward my trailer. "Maybe it was Danny's. Reckon he'd get off on that shit."

The Sheriff chuckled to himself, his heavy hand slapping the outside of his truck as he pulled out of our driveway.

"Wasn't me," I called to Benny through my screen door. "Ain't stepped outside since the explosion. Swear it."

Benny West regarded me for a moment, his lip curling and revealing what was left of his teeth. Guy had more chemical vices than just alcohol. Everybody in town knew that. "I know it weren't you, Danny," he told me with a sigh. "Them headlights made my skin crawl in a way you never could. Truth be told, ain't convinced it was Milton neither."

I shook my head. "Then who? Dawson?"

Benny snorted. "Doubt it. Dawson may be dimmer than a busted light bulb, but he ain't rotten. Not like Milton." Benny met my gaze from across our driveway, his bloodshot eyes darkening. "Listen, kid. I been around a while, and I know when things ain't right – and right now, things ain't right. Something strange is afoot in Brayford, and if you ask me ... I reckon Ryvel's behind it."

My stomach knotted. Ryvel gave me the creeps for reasons I couldn't put to words.

"You take care now, Danny. Give a holler if you need anything."

I gave him a smile as he slid his window shut, vanishing behind his cardboard curtain. And that was it.

The last time I ever saw Benny alive.

The shot rang out the next day, just past sunrise. Nearly leapt out of my bed. I rushed to my window, worrying there might've been another explosion up at Ryvel, but the concrete tower was untouched.

The snow outside, on the other hand...

It was glistening red.

Benny West lay motionless in nothing but his underwear, a smoking handgun beside what remained of his skull.

I didn't think. Just moved.

I dashed outside, dropped to my knees. Started scooping Benny's brains back in his skull, as if it'd fix him. Stupid. I found his suicide note scrunched in his fist. Rigor mortis, they call it. Didn't matter much cause the damn page was soggy, so messy with blood it couldn't be read.

Then again, it didn't need to be.

Benny's last will and testament was written across his face. Struggle was etched into his every wrinkle, poverty mottling his jaundiced skin. The smell of whisky still hung in the air. A ghost of his last breath.

Benny West hadn't killed himself. This was a murder.

He'd been done in by his own demons, cornered by them in that snow-capped trailer, and with nowhere to run and nowhere to hide, they'd taken their pound of flesh.

I called it in, my voice rattling with grief. I'd never seen a dead body before. Not like that.

Twenty minutes later, a white Chevy growled up the driveway and Sheriff Milton hopped out, beady eyes leaking fury. He started marching my direction. I sat there, trembling in Benny's blood and I thought we might share a moment of sorrow, that he might wrap an arm around me and say something like '*sorry you had to see that, Danny,*' but instead his boot caught me in the chest. Knocked me onto my back.

"The hell's wrong with you, boy?" he spat, gripping me by my collar and heaving me back up off the ground.

He shoved me forward. Walked me down until I was scrambling back into my trailer, his hulking frame eclipsing the doorway. "Didn't you hear what I said? The snow's made of poison. Radioactive. It'll kill you worse than any bullet, and it'll take its time doing it, too."

But the Sheriff's hair was flecked with snow. His boots were covered in it. There was a melting pile of snow on my WELCOME carpet too, courtesy of him.

"All due respect," I began, choosing my words with care, "but the snow didn't kill Benny, Sheriff – it was his demons. They ate him up. Spat him back out."

Milton fixed me with a glare. "You think you're a detective now? Here's a bright idea for that spacious skull of yours: how about you leave the policing to me, and I'll leave the drinking to you. Sound fair?"

He reached forward, ruffled my hair like I was some punk. It set me on edge. I opened my big mouth, and started talking about things I probably shouldn't have. "Snow ain't killed the deer yet, Sheriff! Seen 'em passing by all week. Smaller game, too. Rabbits. Squirrels. They ain't immune to radiation so far as I know, and I doubt you're sneakin' 'em those fancy pills of yours. So how do you explain that?"

The Sheriff met my gaze, his mustache quivering dangerously. Milton was a big man – twice my age maybe, but also twice my size. He got right up to my face and took off his gloves, curled his hands into fists that made his knuckles crack and sent my balls up into my stomach.

"Alright," he said in a quiet, uneven voice. "Let me put it to you in simple terms. This ain't your town, Danny. Sure, you might've been born here, maybe your ma and pa even helped make it the shit heap it is today – I don't know. Don't care either. What I do know is your place, and do you know where that place is, Danny?"

I didn't answer. Wasn't sure I knew the right answer.

Milton's fist connected with my stomach. I dropped to my knees, wheezing. He lifted his arm, brought it down across my jaw and I collapsed onto the floor of my trailer. He rested his boot against the side of my head.

"It's right here," he whispered, and I could almost hear the smile in his voice. "It's here under this fine boot of mine. You see it?"

I struggled, but Milton pressed down harder, and pain lanced across my temples. "Asked you a question!" he snapped. "Do. You. See. It?"

"Y-Yes, Sheriff," I stammered. "I see it."

He lifted his boot, but not before wiping the dirty snow from the bottom into my hair. "Good," he said. "Now, I'm gonna give you a piece of advice. Stay indoors tonight. Don't step so much as an arm outside, and keep your eyes away from your windows. Better yet – did I fucking say you could get up?"

I paused, half-risen on my hands and knees.

A smirk played at the edge of Milton's lips. "Good, boy. You sit there like the mutt you are until I'm finished. Now, where was I? Right. Stay the fuck inside or I'll break your damn legs to keep you here." He sucked back a mouthful of saliva, then spat in my face. "Anywho, nice chatting with you, Danny. Take care now."

Milton left, slamming my door behind him. From the window, I watched as he hefted Benny's corpse into the back of his truck, whistling like he was out fishing on the lake.

"Betty," he said into his radio. "It's Milton. Just headin' back to Ryvel now. Mind sending word up that Benjamin West was a suicide – didn't see no black bile or nothing. Ain't their problem, I guess."

A woman's voice crackled over the radio. *"Understood. Will do, Sheriff."*

Milton clambered into his cab, and the truck roared to life, tearing off down the driveway and veering right onto the valley road.

"Fuckin' psychopath ..." I muttered.

Still smarting and bruised, I stomped over to my liquor cupboard and cracked a bottle of whisky. Started to sip. I set up shop at my window, looking out at Benny's trailer and the swaying pine trees towering behind it – and the bloodstained snow sitting out front.

I scowled.

Black bile. That was what Milton had said to Betty; there wasn't any black bile, so this wasn't a Ryvel problem. The bottle hit my lips again. Seemed to me Benny had it right. This whole thing looped back to Ryvel, and the radioactive snow was nothing but a means of keeping us outta their business.

But what was that business?

Another drink. Then a few more. Before long, I'd polished half the bottle and the sun was creeping low on the horizon, making gnarled shadows of the trees. My thoughts turned. They became tangled things, all outta control and veering into territory I swore to never again set foot.

Territory like her.

Vanny Williams. The love of my life and the one that got away.

The thought of her made me smile, only not in a happy way but more a glum, wistful sort of way. I'd driven Vanny out of my life. Ironically, for just this reason: my damn drinking.

My demons had ruined the one good thing I ever had.

Grimacing, I threw open my trailer door and hurled what was left of my bottle into the trees. I hiccupped. Warmth flooded my veins, that fiery impulsiveness born of late-night benders and a lifetime of regrets.

"Vanny ..." I mumbled, staggering out of my trailer. "I'm sorry I ..."

The more I stood out there mumbling to myself, the more my thoughts got moving. Before long, I was wondering how she was. If she had enough supplies to weather this lockdown, if she was going stir crazy being cooped up on her own – if she wasn't just a bloody smear on the snow like Benny ...

I zipped my jacket up. Fired on a pair of gloves and a beanie.

That's the thing about being shit-faced drunk, you don't think things through. You just act. Whatever seems right in the moment, you go along with it. Hard to help. And at that moment, it seemed like I needed to see Vanny come hell or high water.

My boots crunched as I trudged down my driveway, swaying slightly. That night, there wasn't much of a moon. Just clouds and dark. I stuffed my hands into my jacket, shivering with misty breath and marveling at the temperature. It was frigid. Damn near the coldest I'd ever felt.

I kept near the edge of the road, walking beneath the pines creaking their timber song. Through their branches, I could make out the dark monolith of Ryvel. I glared at it. It sat perched up there like some kinda concrete gargoyle, its black tower reaching skyward, peppered with a dozen antennas. It seemed to look down on Brayford, almost like it owned us.

And maybe it did.

A diesel roar split the night. I wheeled about, squinting as a pair of headlights flickered through the treeline, barreling in my direction.

Sheriff Milton?

I couldn't be sure, but I wasn't curious enough to steal a look either. Scrambling over the shoulder of the road, I pressed my back against a wall of snow. Lights painted the treeline in front of me. Their glow magnified as the truck rumbled closer, casting rioting silhouettes of the reaching branches.

It wasn't that I was afraid of being thrown in jail, it was more that I figured Milton might actually have been serious about breaking my legs. The Sheriff carried a lot of power in Brayford. It was an open secret that he had a short fuse and a penchant for violence, and more than a few folks had earned a lifelong limp after getting on his bad side.

The truck closed in. Its bright gaze struck deeper into the woods, pouring past layers of frosty pines. I tensed. A weight settled on my chest, as if an invisible hand was slowly pressing the air out of me. The engine growled closer. The earth rumbled against my back as it rolled around the bend, its heavy tread thundering on down the road.

My breath, held captive, finally escaped. A smile found my face. Lucky sumbitch I was, dodging Milton like that. If he'd been that bold in my own trailer, I couldn't imagine what he would've done out here in the woods had he—

Brakes screeched.

There was a thunk of shifting gears, and then the Chevy began to reverse. It wheeled to a stop right above me. My muscles coiled tight, ready to spring but stuck tight with anxiety. A door opened. Heavy boots thumped down onto newfallen snow, and a radio transmitter whined.

"Dispatch, this is Milton."

A crackle of static. Then, a woman's voice.

"—you loud and clear, Sheriff. What can I do for you?"

"Evening, Betty," Milton said, chewing on his words like they were made of gravel. "Be advised I've got some fresh footsteps in the snow here, just off Grant Passage, about halfway between... oh, Rickson and Creatsfield. Appears they're heading down into the valley. Might have another runner on our hands."

"One of Ryvel's?"

"Doesn't look it. Can't see none of that black bile, but could be they ain't ripe yet. Go ahead and have Dawson start heading my way, and I'll have myself a lookie-loo in the meantime."

"Will do, Sheriff," Betty replied, her voice tight with concern. *"By the way, Ryvel reckoned you oughta avoid the trees tonight, they—"*

"I know what they think, Betty, but I don't take orders from Ryvel. They pay well, but this is my town. Always has been. Always will be. I'll be just fine. Now go ahead and give Dawson a ring while I handle things here. Am I clear?"

"Yes."

"Yes what?" Milton growled.

Betty's voice returned with an anxious tremor. *"Yes, Sheriff."*

"There. That's better, darling. Now, you get to your work and I'll get to mine. Milton out."

His radio beeped, and I heard him clear his throat on the road above. "Alright," he said loudly. "Don't know who you are, but I'll make this nice and easy. You got two options. Option one is you come out, and maybe if I like the story you give me I'll let you off with a handful of broken fingers and teeth for my trouble."

Snow crunched under Milton's boots as he stepped into the glare of his headlights, his monstrous shadow engulfing the trees before me. His silhouette raised a shotgun. Racked it. "Your second option," he thundered. "Is that I drag your corpse out of those trees. You got three seconds."

Gunfire split the night. I flinched violently, biting down on my knuckles as a storm of splinters fell over me.

"One..."

Another rack of the shotgun.

My lungs burned, starved for a breath I couldn't risk taking.

"Two..."

Another blast. More bark exploded, this time so close the shrapnel cut into my face. My muscles locked, every fiber of my being trembling uncontrollably. Tears stung my eyes as reality sank in—he was gonna kill me.

"Final warning—"

The Sheriff's radio beeped loudly. *"Sheriff? Sheriff Milton, do you read me?"*

Milton heaved a sigh, grinding his teeth. "Christ alive, Betty – the fuck is it now? Didn't I just tell you I was in the middle of—"

"It's Dawson," Betty cut in, frantic. *"You asked me to send him your way, but I'm not getting any response."*

"God help me ..." Milton muttered, lowering his shotgun and stalking back to his truck. "Alright. Give me Dawson's last location and I'll swing by and have a look."

"You don't think that one of Ryvel's might've—"

"It ain't one of Ryvel's," Milton spat. "Dawson's probably passed out in his cruiser again, snoring through his bloody shift.

Don't worry. I'll be sure to teach the boy a lesson he won't soon forget."

"But what about Ryvel's escaped—"

The truck door slammed shut. The engine roared as Milton slammed the gas, and a moment later he was peeling down the valley road in a powdery whirlwind.

My heart pounded as I watched Milton's headlights vanish around the hill. It took a while for my adrenaline to wear off, for my muscles to start working again, but once they did, I lurched up from the snowdrift. Dusted myself off.

Betty had said somebody escaped from Ryvel just then. And the way her voice had been shaking, it didn't sound like she thought Dawson had fallen asleep on duty. Not even a little bit.

A shiver ran through me.

My eyes found the specter of the Institute, looming high on Brayford Hill. My stomach churned. Were they capturing people? Imprisoning them? Whatever this was, it seemed to go far beyond some nonsense about radioactive snow – something sinister was going on in this town. The only question was, what?

Thoughts for later. If things were half as bad as Betty made them sound, then I knew without a doubt I needed to get to Vanny's. My hands curled into fists. If anything had happened to her ...

No.

I wouldn't let myself think like that. I started moving again, scrambling back up the ridge and marching double-time, boots pounding over the road. I hardly made it a few feet when I stopped in my tracks. There, glinting up near Ryvel were a pair of headlights.

"Probably just some night shift employee ..." I mumbled, stalking off bitterly. "Hope they're paying 'em as well as they're paying Milton."

Time stretched on. Minutes passed. Ten. No, twenty of them.

The cold was getting mean now, biting at my cheeks like it had a grudge. I picked up the pace, hugging the curve of the valley road tight as a lover. Ryvel disappeared behind the treeline, and with it, a weight lifted off my shoulders.

Suddenly I was grinning like a loon.

Christ, when was the last time I'd felt this ... alive? This human? Here I was, sticking it to the man. I'd danced through Milton's fingers, given Ryvel's lockdown the middle finger, and even stumbled ass-backwards into some grade-A conspiracy dirt. And the cherry on top? I was on my way to see Vanny.

For a moment, I felt like that punk-ass kid again—eighteen, dumb as a box of rocks, and sneaking into the valley for some cheap thrills and cheaper booze. Only this time, I was on a different kind of bender. A secret trek into the heart of something bigger and darker than I could've imagined, armed with knowledge that felt like it could get me killed.

A chuckle bubbled up in my throat, but it died faster than a snowball in hell.

There, halfway up Brayford Hill, nestled in a thicket of pines so dense they nearly choked out the glow, were a pair of headlights.

I blinked hard, convinced my eyes were playing tricks. But those suckers were real as sin, staring down at me like twin moons hanging in a pine sky. Was Milton really tearing through the woods in his pickup like some backwoods Rambo? Or was it ...

"Got my ... eye ... on you ..."

My muscles seized up. It was Milton. His voice echoed down from that hilltop, but it sounded all distorted, warped like it was being played through a faulty megaphone. The headlights blinked. On. Off. On. Off.

"Can't run ... from me ..." he droned.

A chill ran up my spine. Surely Milton couldn't actually recognize me from all the way up there, could he? I'd be just a speck to him. Faceless as a mannequin. And that meant I could still get out of this with my legs intact, just so long as I made myself scarce before he got down from those trees.

I sucked in a sharp breath. Bolted. I dove toward the wood, launching myself over the shoulder of the road. My stomach hit the valley slope and started sliding, the icy ground as slick as a luge track. My chest went numb. Branches lashed out, snapping across my face as I careened faster and faster downhill until—

Poof.

I hit bottom in an eruption of powder, coughing and sputtering. It was dark down there beneath the canopy. Almost pitch. Fishing out my phone, I turned on the flashlight. An army of trees materialized before me. Birch. Pine. Fir. They all swayed, creaking like decrepit phantoms in the cold breath of winter.

Betty's words echoed in my mind: *Ryvel reckoned you oughta avoid the trees tonight.*

"To Hell with Ryvel," I muttered, swallowing my unease.

With no path back, I pressed onward. Wandered aimless. I'd walked this valley countless times, but never amid the midnight shadows, and that made it disorienting. Familiar landmarks seemed alien beneath a blanket of gloomcast snow. Twigs snapped underfoot. They were joined by the brittle crunch of leaves shaken loose from withered branches.

Time passed. Can't recall how much. Before long I started worrying I was lost, though, that I'd got myself stranded when—

A boulder. Up ahead. A monolith I couldn't forget if I tried. It was shaped like a giant pineapple, and steeped in the best kind of memories. It was our rock. Belonging to Vanny and me. We whiled away countless summer days nestled in its shade, making music with our bodies which meant ...

There. Just as it should be—the crooked tree. A ragged pine split by lightning's fury, its trunk cleaved in two and hollowed by flame. I was orienting myself at last, gathering my bearings in the lightless wood.

My breath fogged before me as I jogged ahead, buoyed by success. Each stride felt lighter, my heart too. With luck, I'd reach Vanny's before her head hit the pillow. I could already picture her face, stone-gray with confusion at my doorstep arrival, then melting into belly laughter as I recounted this madness.

"Danny," she'd say, giving that trademark toss of her hair, that mischievous magpie smile. "You're some kinda fool, you know that?"

And she'd be right. I was some kind of fool, the kind who—

Snap.

I spun toward the sound, my light scouring, but only a maze of trees stared back.

A bear, maybe?

No ... they'd be hibernating now.

"Dawson?" I whispered. Milton was a giant of a man, but also overweight and past his prime – doubtful he had the stamina to chase me down here on foot. But maybe he'd sent his deputy. "Dawson, that you?"

No reply. The forest was deathly still. Not a scurry of squirrels or flap of wings stirred the cold air.

CRACK

I stumbled backward, the sound ringing out like a gunshot. A low groan followed. Branches began to snap, falling away as a whistle sang overhead.

Whip-like tendrils lashed my back, smashing me to the frozen earth. The forest erupted with a cataclysmic roar as something gigantic crashed beside me, the ground quaking beneath its weight. I wheezed and spat slush, scrambling frantic through the snow. Long, groping fingers slid from my spine. I lurched to my feet, sweeping my light over the hulking form, a primal scream clawing up my throat as—

"You gotta be kidding ... " I said, collapsing with an exhausted sigh.

Just a tree—a stupid hunk of wood, frozen solid and toppled over. I shook my head. Laughed. I'd actually panicked over getting jumped by Bigfoot – what would Vanny say to that? Probably tell me to lay off those horror novels. Then she'd ... My laughter died. Then she'd tell me to lay off the booze because it was making me skittish and paranoid.

And she'd be right.

I heaved a sigh. Maybe I'd just keep this story to myself.

Brushing snow from my jacket, I continued on. Had to be close now. Down below was a frozen stream, one that Tommy Welt and I used to catch crayfish in as kids. Six months ago, Vanny and I had sat beside it discussing marriage and kids.

My stomach sank.

"You really are some kinda fool," I whispered. "You had everything, Danny, and you ..."

Something swept past. A feeling—it jolted through me like electricity, prickling the hairs on my neck. It felt familiar somehow. And *awful*. Like that punishing glare up on the valley road.

I squinted, casting light between the trees. Nothing. No one. Just shadows dancing ominously.

The feeling lingered though, raising gooseflesh on my arms, so I quickened my pace. Don't panic, I told myself, the beam of my phone trembling. It's just your mind playing tricks. Nothing but trees and ...

A shape darted behind a trunk. Swift. Silent.

"Sheriff?" I called out. "That you, Sheriff Milton?"

No response. Probably a deer.

I shivered and kept walking, spotting a twinkle of lights visible atop a distant ridge through the shifting pines. Vanny's cabin. I'd made it. My fear seemed to evaporate then, replaced by a spreading warmth. It reminded me of better days, happier times.

It felt a little like hope.

BOOOOOOYYYY!

A distorted holler pierced the night. Milton. My heart leapt into my throat, my feet dancing a pirouette as I raked the darkness surrounding me. It sounded like he'd screamed into a megaphone.

"Sheriff," I said, desperately trying to control the tremor in my voice. "Listen now, I wasn't meaning to cause trouble by stepping out it's just—"

A blaring scream. Warped, artificial – like a siren played backwards. But there wasn't any sign of Milton's red-blue flashers, only endless towers of timber and the darkness that lay between them.

"To hell with this," I spat.

I took off at a waddling sprint, my boots sinking into shin-deep snow. My breath came in great white clouds. If Milton was lurking in these trees, then he'd well and truly lost his mind and I wasn't going to stick around for the show.

Another digital holler, Milton's voice scratching and skipping through the megaphone.

GO-GONNA TAKE A PIECE OUTTA YOU, I RE-RECKON!

I came up against the slope of the valley, Vanny's cabin visible through the pines. "Vanny!" I shouted. "Get your damn gun! Milton's gone and lost his mind!"

My gloves pawed at the slope, desperate for purchase as my chest hammered. I could hear Milton closing in. Heavy footfalls. They crunched across a carpet of snow, uneven and unsettling.

I punched another handhold, kicked in a foothold. Grunting, I hauled myself up another foot, breath pluming. Don't panic, Danny. Slow and steady. I can do this.

Almost there ...

"Vann-!"

My voice died as my foot slipped, my handhold crumbling away in a flurry of snowflakes. I slid, tumbling down the steep slope in a dizzying blur of branches and brush and—

Crack!

My jaw hit stone, the taste of blood flooding my mouth. My vision swam. I kept rolling, out of control. My body bounced, nothing but a spinning mess of limbs and strangled shouts until my spine slammed into a tree.

Pain.

My whole body throbbed with pain. I sat there, delirious and dizzy, a trickle of blood running from my forehead down my cheeks. "Vanny ..." I coughed, spitting a tooth into my lap.

I looked around in a blurry daze. Darkness. It was all darkness. I'd lost my phone in the fall and now – footsteps. Out there, roaming in the night. He was circling me, Milton. I could hear his lumbering strides, and maybe it was the fear pounding through my veins but he sounded so much more terrifying than he ought have. He sounded bigger than a grizzly. Bigger than a moose.

AIN'T I T-TOLD YOU TO STAY PUT B-BOY?

Milton's megaphone. Maybe it'd be loud enough to get Vanny's attention. Maybe she could get out here and put a bullet between his eyes before he finished putting one between mine.

Milton drew nearer. His breathing was shallow, sharp – almost like the sound an old television might make flipping between channels.

IT AIN'T AS BAD AS IT SEEMS, DANNY

I blinked, not sure I'd heard right. That voice. It sounded like Benny West.

THE HARD PART IS LETTING GO

"B-Benny?" I stammered, unable to see a thing in the dark.

I'LL BE HERE WITH YOU, KID

"You're dead," I said. "I saw your body ... your brains all over the drive ..."

AND PART OF YOU ENVIED ME, DIDN'T YOU?

My throat went dry. This was some kind of nightmare – some horrible hallucination brought on by booze. It couldn't be real. There was no patching up somebody that looked like Benny West. There just wasn't.

YOU DREAMED OF DEATH, DANNY
I SAW IT IN YOUR FACE
ONLY THING WE EVER HAD IN COMMON
WE HATED OURSELVES, YOU AND I
HATED OUR MISTAKES
OUR ADDICTIONS

The more Benny spoke, the more his voice seemed to churn, hissing with static. It felt garbled. Broken. The sound of it made me want to curl up into a ball, to press a gun to my head and—

"You're wrong ..." I whimpered. "I don't ..."

I AIN'T WRONG, KID
YOU DIDN'T COME OUT HERE FOR VANNY
YOU CAME OUT HERE TO ESCAPE
TO RUN AWAY FROM THE VOICE IN YOUR—

Light exploded before me. Vicious, vibrant. My hands flew to my eyes. After endless dark, the sudden brightness felt blinding, disorienting.

TIME TO GO, BOY

Milton's voice rang out. I slowly lowered my hands, squinting ahead and saw a pair of headlights glaring back at me. But how? There weren't any roads that lead through the valley floor, and it didn't seem possible Milton drove his Chevy down that slope.

More footsteps, heavy, uneven.

The headlights drew closer, swaying, blinking on and off and ...

No. This wasn't right. I stumbled away, shaking my head and struggling to find my voice. Headlights didn't sway. They didn't blink. And wheels certainly didn't crunch like footsteps.

"What are you?" I demanded.

A voice answered in a low, digital moan.

HUNGRY ...

An arm snapped forward like a spring-loaded trap, snatching me in its grip. Long fingers coiled around my torso. I struggled, pulling at them but the harder I fought, the tighter they squeezed. They were like wires, humming with electricity.

"Let me go you ..."

My voice vanished as a wave of hopelessness washed over me.

My jaw went slack. My eyes, hazy. It was like those fingers, those wires were tuned to the frequency of sorrow. Suddenly I felt empty. Hollowed out. Like there was nothing left inside but all the bad I'd ever done ...

Images poured through my mind. Memories. It was like a mental reel of every last mistake I'd ever made – everything from getting belted by my father for staying up past bedtime, to having my stepmom use my hand as an ashtray for giving her lip. I saw the disappointment in my teacher's every time I handed in a failed report. Heard the laughter in the throats of my classmates when I'd screw up a presentation.

And then there was Vanny.

Vanny Williams, the one good thing I ever had – and I ruined it by passing out drunk four nights a week. She'd left me. Word was she Charlie Keen were a thing now, and I could only imagine how much happier she was with a man that wasn't an absolute fuck-up like me.

Benny was right.

I did want to die.

I wanted it badly, but I kept running from that truth because I was afraid of it. Only I'd spent my whole life afraid. It was time I manned up. It was time I did what was best for me, and the people in my life.

The fingers coiled tighter, cracking my ribs and laughter escaped my lips. It was over. Finally, after so much misery I'd get my taste of oblivion. No more disappointment. No more waking up in my own vomit.

I'd be gone. And the world would be all the better for it.

I went limp in the creature's embrace, a smile of surrender upon my lips. Its long arm dragged me closer. Close enough to make out bits and pieces of its misshapen form. Its body was a mass of corpses, knotted in a tangle of horror. Their bones were lashed together. Their skin hung from the creature like drapery, oozing black bile in viscous globs. A bald head near its shoulder gleamed back at me. Benny West.

"What took you so long, Danny?" he asked.

I grinned, my voice strangled by the monster's grip. "Just happy ... you found me ..."

A stench of decay engulfed me, so thick I could taste rot on my tongue. But I didn't mind. I thought it tasted beautiful.

The creature's maw yawned open, impossibly wide, lined with shattered fangs of glass that led to a gullet of spiraling, technicolor static. This close, I could make out more details of its crooked limbs—carved faces, scraps of flannel and denim—all knotted and fused together in a chimeric aberration. Pieces of townsfolk sewn into a patchwork of their sorrows.

Lucky ducks.

And there, molded into the creature's chest, was the severed head of Sheriff Milton. He stared back at me. Eyes clouded white, flesh sallow and peeling away. As I watched, the skin of his cheek flayed back further, revealing muscle and sinew working to form words.

"Thought ... I told you ... to stay inside ... b-boy?" His voice skipped like a scratched record, eyes flashing with digital interference. "You really are ... the du-dumbest ... fuck that ever lived ... "

"Don't I know it ..." I wheezed, grinning wildly.

And as the creature brought me into that mouth of flickering haze, another voice called out. This one from inside. I knew it well. It was the voice that lived at the bottom of every bottle – the one that beat me senseless for leaving the lights on when I was young – that picked apart my every flaw and made sure they stuck. It was shame. It was fear. It was self-loathing and denial. It was my deadbeat father and my witch of a stepmom. It was the abuse that rang inside my skull every time I dared to be less than perfect, every time I dared to be human.

It was me.

And it was right.

You might think this story has a happy ending. After all, here I sit, writing it out for you so obviously I escaped the jaws of that unholy thing. The hero survived, did he not?

Hell, maybe you think I even managed to save the day.

If you do, then I'd say you ain't been paying attention. I'm not the type of man who's cut out for that sort of business. Never have been. Fact is I was ready to go gentle into that good night. I would've gone raging too – I'd have probably hurt people to make them kill me. That's how badly I wanted to die.

I felt like an addict desperate for his next fix. Only my next fix wasn't in this life, and so I was aching to abort myself as quick as I could.

But Vanny wouldn't have it.

She'd heard my shouting from down below, heard that megaphone howl of Milton and Benny and she'd come running.

I remember it clear as anything – her up on that ridge, rifle against her shoulder, dark hair snapping in the winter gusts. "Danny!" she'd screamed. "Hold on, Danny!"

Bang! Bang!

The shots must've caught the monster in its eyes because those headlights dimmed, flickering and I saw what looked like two cracked television screens set within a head fashioned from Brayford's finest.

The next two rounds hit the creature in the chest, split Milton's nose into mulch. The monster stumbled backward, screeching in that electronic warble. It dropped me. I hit the ground and Vanny kept firing. Kept reloading. Firing more.

"Run, Danny!" she pleaded. "Get going, I ain't got much more bullets!"

But I didn't want to run. All I wanted was to die, to let that thing give me the only gift I ever deserved.

"Leave it be!" I bellowed. "Shoot me, Vanny. Please ... Just kill me instead ..."

I'll never forget the look she gave me after I uttered those words. Her heart looked broken in two. "Don't you talk to me like that, Daniel Ritchley! You're a good man!"

A good man?

No. That wasn't me. I was nothing but a dead end – the biggest fuck-up in a town rife with em.

More shots. The creature was being driven backward. She was doing it – Vanny Williams was saving my life for the thousandth time, watching over me for reasons I still couldn't fathom.

"I never stopped thinking about you," she shouted down, lowering the rifle to slip a few more rounds in. "Didn't realize until after Charlie and I broke it off but ..."

I didn't know if those were gunshots or my heartbeat. Suddenly, that hopelessness inside of me seemed to burn away. The monster's spell, its grip on me, was melting into nothing.

"I never stopped loving you, Vanny!" I shouted.

She tossed her hair over her shoulder. Fired three more rounds, gave me that trademark, magpie smile. "Danny Ritchly ... you're some kinda fool, you know that? I ain't ever stopped loving you either."

Her finger pulled the trigger but this time the muzzle didn't flash. She cursed. Her rifle jammed.

No.

The monster saw its opening, let loose a digital roar and barreled toward the slope. And I ran too. I tore across the snow, shouting my lungs raw, throwing myself in front of it and—

It leapt over me.

That shambling mess of corpses crashed against a birch tree in a shower of snow. The timber groaned beneath its weight. Its trunk snapped, but before the tree could fall the monster had already vaulted to the next. And the next.

"Vanny!" I shouted. "Get outta there!"

And she did. She turned, pounding toward her cabin and even got the door closed, but it didn't matter. The monster crashed down in front of it, started tearing her cabin apart like it were made of matchsticks. Bits of lumber flew over the ledge as I rushed toward the slope. I tried to scramble up, but it was useless – every inch I crawled I slid back another three.

Vanny screamed.

She screamed and she never stopped screaming. The monster took her, stole her away into the forest until her voice faded somewhere amidst the shifting trees.

I fell to my knees.

Frigid tears trickled down my cheeks. Vanny was gone. Dead. And it was all because of me – I'd led that thing straight to her.

***

Deputy Dawson found me just past sunrise, sitting in the rubble of Vanny's cabin, alone with my grief.

"Danny Ritchley?" he said, voice thick with disbelief. "The Hell happened here?"

I told him everything—told him about the headlights, Ryvel, the grotesque monster and what fate had befallen his missing Sheriff.

"He's part of it now, Dawson," I said in an empty voice. "Milton is. Same as Benny. Same as ..." Vanny's name hung on my lips. Somehow I didn't feel worthy of even speaking it.

Dawson heaved a sigh, running an exasperated hand over his boulder of a face. "Look, Danny. We go back to high school so ... let me give you some advice."

I looked at him, sensing an edge to his tone.

"You didn't tell me none of that just now. Not a word. What happened is you got drunk, stumbled outta your trailer and fell down a slope like a fool. That's it."

"That's not—"

He lifted a hand, cutting me off. "Trust me, Danny. Ryvel ain't the sort of tree you wanna be barking up. It ... It don't end anywhere good."

Dawson said the words with an air of finality, like this was the end of it. He helped me into his truck and was even kind enough to give me a lift down to the clinic. But he was wrong. I know what I saw out there. And I don't care what tree I'm barking up.

I think other folks know too – especially them researchers up at Ryvel. They've been watching me ever since I got back to my trailer. Surveilling. They've been driving by at all hours of the day, sunrise to sunset, and more than once I've spotted a man in a white suit going through my trash.

Even now, in the dead of night, they're here.

Maybe they think I'm asleep. Or maybe they've just given up all pretense of keeping a low profile. Don't know. All I know is I can see them through the cracks in my blinds—sitting out there, waiting patiently in my driveway.

Headlights in the dark.

AFTERLIFE SEQUENCE

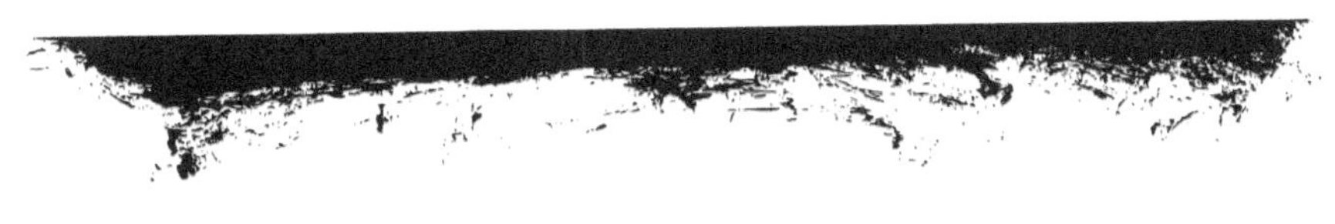

How does it work?

Death, I mean. How does it work? That was the point of the study– the trial. What happens when we die, where do we go, what does it feel like, and is it even worth the hassle? Is there a heaven? A hell?

We didn't know, but we wanted to. I suppose that's where everything went wrong, right out of the gate. We wanted to play God, or at least learn the rules of the game. To see behind the curtain for just a moment, if only so we could know what to expect when the lights went out and we said that final goodnight.

I'm telling you now, swearing to you that we never intended for things to go wrong the way that they did. The people that lost their lives knew what they were getting into. They signed releases. Paperwork. They *agreed* to let us do what we did, just so long as we promised to handsomely compensate their families. And we did. We held up our end of the bargain to the tune of 13 million dollars.

But things like this, they never work out the way they're meant to. I knew that. I did. I think that on some level all of us did, but the people who were funding us had no idea. They wanted results. *Be messy*, they said, *if that's what it takes. Do whatever you need to do to figure out what happens in the sequel to Life, and make it snappy because this funding is running on an hourglass, and that sand is slipping.*

So, we cut corners. We pushed people in ways that, in retrospect, were irresponsible. Dangerous. But we did it for the common good. We did it for *you* – for all of us, for the benefit of future generations who could look death in the eye without the horror of not knowing what came next.

It was a good thing. It really was.

The first death went smoothly. An older woman, 87 years old and dying of liver failure, was hooked up to our state-of-the-art equipment that had one job and one job only: to bring them back. To let them taste the cold kiss of death, and then tear their soul back into the land of the living long enough to give us a play-by-play of what happened while they were away. I know, I know. This has happened before. People have come back from clinical death plenty of times, haven't they? Sure. That's true.

But never after three days.

The three-day timeline was a tricky one because even though the corpse was dead, even though the cadaver was cold and beginning to cellularly decompose, we needed to keep it fresh enough to host life. Don't get me wrong, the life it hosted didn't last long, but it lasted *long enough*. I still remember the pulse of excitement that shot through the room when the old woman opened her eyes. Her first rancid breath drew applause.

"Agnes," Roger, our research lead said. He stood by her bedside, craned over her wearing a toque and gloves. "Can you hear my voice?"

The woman nodded. More applause. We watched the two of them from behind a layer of one-way glass, all of us in our lab coats while Roger communed with her breathing corpse in what was practically a freezer. Their voices carried over a loudspeaker.

"Where ... am I?" Agnes gasped, her throat trembling with the strain of vocalizing. "I'm ... tired."

"You're with friends," Roger said. "Safe."

Roger turned to us, grinning with a thumbs up. We'd successfully brought back our first subject, and not only was she alive – she was communicating. Lucid. He turned back to her, likely knowing we had a limited window to extract the information we needed.

"Do you remember the study you agreed to be a part of?"

Agnes' eyes opened wide, and her pupils seemed to jolt around like ping pong balls. "Death," she muttered. "Death."

Roger nodded, running a hand through her thinning hair. "That's right, Agnes. We wanted to know what happens to the soul after death, and you agreed to take that journey and return to us. You're the first human being to have done so. Congratulations."

I'll never forget what happened next. She gazed up at him, those rolling eyes and that absent voice, and she gripped the front of his shirt with a shuddering, frail hand. He leaned closer to her, no doubt thinking she wanted to speak into his ear.

"We belong ..." she said, her chest beginning to heave, "to them."

Roger looked at us, his expression confused. He shook his head. "Agnes, I'm sorry. To whom are you referring?"

Her legs jerked sideways, her spine arching as she began to thrash on the slab. Blood leaked from the corners of her eyes. Roger, concerned, attempted to hold her body so she wouldn't injure herself and compromise what little time she had left to communicate. He ordered more of us in. I hurried to his side with three others.

"We belong," she said again, and this time her voice was stronger, as though empowered by her agony, "to the ... forgotten ..."

Even with four of us on her, each holding a limb, she was rioting with a strength that could only be described as inhuman. It took everything I had to hold her scrawny blue wrist to the slab. Beside us the machine monitoring her vitals began to beep violently, indicating levels grossly out of range.

"What comes next," she hissed, and smoke began to drift up from her mouth, "is worse ... than any hell."

Before we could ask further – before we could subdue her and help her pass peacefully, she went still on the slab. Her limbs fell limp. Her buzzing pupils stilled. Her mouth ceased to smoke, and her head lolled to the side.

Agnes Mick had died for the second time.

We had her corpse carted to the morgue for an autopsy and discovered that her brain showed signs of hemorrhaging, her heart had partially ruptured in her chest, and most bizarrely of all, her vocal cords had been seared. As if something had lit them aflame.

Her results were ominous, to say the least, but we were intelligent enough to know that a sample size of one does not a conclusion make, and so we eagerly awaited our second subject. This one was a young boy named Jacob. He'd been struck by a vehicle in a hit and run and fallen into a coma. His parents never had an opportunity to say goodbye, and so they agreed to allow us to perform our study so long as they were there for his revival.

The process was similar to Agnes'. Jacob lay unmoving on the slab in the freezer room, wires and diodes hooked up to his chest and temples, a white sheet draped across him. By his side stood Roger, and both of the boy's parents, all of them clad in toques and gloves.

"Are you ready?" Roger asked.

"Yes," they said. We all waited behind the glass with heart-pounding anticipation. Roger clicked a few keys on the computer console, and the machine began its mechanical song. A moment later and the screen flashed green as it initiated its AFTER-LIFE sequence, filling Jacob's unmoving cadaver with a myriad of electrical pulses designed to shock his brain into functioning.

The boy's feet, dangling outside the white cloth, began to twitch. Then his fingertips. His mother and father looked at one another, grasping hands as they waited for their son to return to them. Hopeful tears leaked from the corners of their eyes, their lips mouthing silent words of affirmation as they prepared to say goodbye to Jacob.

Screaming filled the room.

It burst through the loudspeaker like an explosion, causing all of us watching to jump and scatter, our primal nervous systems fleeing while we attempted to uncover the source. But the source, I think, was always obvious even if we didn't want to believe it.

It was coming from Jacob.

He lay there, his toes and fingertips twitching as his mouth hung open in an ear-splitting scream, his mother and father crowding him in horror, doing their best to calm him. Assuage his pain. His confusion. His horror.

It's difficult to describe the sound of Jacob's scream. I'm hesitant to say it was human, let alone the sound of a nine-year-old boy. It was most similar, I feel, to a drowning sheep. It was an anguished bleating sound, one that seemed never-ending, and yet it told a terrifying story all on its own.

Eventually, Jacob's parents made the decision to pull the plug on their son. It was the second time they'd made the decision in a little under a week.

The last subject was the one that stuck with me. The one that haunts me to this day, and the reason I'm writing this now, sharing this with all of you. It was a woman named Charlotte. Young. Vibrant. In the prime of her life. Charlotte was an eccentric woman from a wealthy and educated family. She had spent her mid-twenties traveling the world, primarily across portions of South America as she researched content for her book *The Meaning of Life*.

A self-described shaman, Charlotte put great stock in the spiritual practices of different cultures. She'd participated in hundreds of rituals across dozens of tribes. She'd tried everything from peyote to DMT, leveraging any drug she could get her hands on that promised psychedelic insights. Despite the heavy usage, Charlotte appeared to be perfectly clear-headed and not at all negatively impacted – to put it simply, she was as healthy as could be.

That's why we found it strange when she approached our small project and asked to be included. When we informed her it was only for those suffering from terminal afflictions, she asked if she could be added to the list anyway. Sort of like an organ donor. We agreed.

Charlotte killed herself the following weekend.

Bullet through the skull. Quick and likely painless, though it's impossible to know for certain. Many times such acts of suicide last longer than the subject intends. Either way, we had our third volunteer, all thanks to the round narrowly missing her brain.

Charlotte's parents were initially opposed to the idea, but we informed them that we had her written, legal consent. They asked to meet us halfway, to be there when she returned. After the situation with Jacob, however, we disallowed them from participating in the trial. The science is new, you understand. It's possible that emotional catalysts like family figures may have an adverse effect on brains so far removed from life.

No, we said. *We'll bring her back and we'll tell you everything that she says, and that will be that.*

So they relented. No lawsuit. No drama. We were free to bring Charlotte back from death in three days' time, and that's exactly what we did. The scenario played out like the others before. The freezing room. The beeping machine. The diodes sprinkled across her body and the white sheet draped over her torso. Roger stood beside her, operating the machine while we monitored the readings. His fingers danced across the keyboard and the screen glowed with the words AFTERLIFE SEQUENCE INITIATED.

Once again we watched from behind the glass. Once again Roger waited patiently, a hopeful smile on his face. Twenty seconds passed and nothing occurred– not so much as a twitch of a toe or a flick of an eyelash. Charlotte's corpse remained every bit as dead as the day we carted her in. A minute went by and we still saw no sign of resurrection.

Roger looked back to the machine, shaking his head and he removed his gloves, evidently wondering if he'd hit a wrong key with his mitts. He began the sequence again. The machine buzzed and words flashed green across the screen once more, but Charlotte lay still.

"Elliot," he said to me, his voice ringing out over the loudspeaker. "Can you come inside and check this out? I think it might be malfunctioning."

I swallowed. I'd triple-checked the machine and made sure it was functioning to specification, just as it had the last two times. Still, I nodded from behind the two-way glass and opened the door to the freezer. As I stepped inside the—30 room, I pulled a set of gloves and toque from the wall and began my appraisal of the system. The wires checked out. The program was running to spec. All the diodes were in the correct place.

"I don't see any issues here," I said, shivering.

Roger frowned, looking back to Charlotte's cadaver. He placed his hands on his hips and cursed, wondering if somehow we'd encountered a dud. "Maybe some people can't be brought back," he theorized.

I opened my mouth to respond but something about Charlotte caught my eye. It was her lips. They were pulled into a thin grin, and black fluid was leaking from between them. "Have you … seen … it?" she muttered.

Roger and I exchanged looks and he slipped me a wink. "Well done," he whispered. "Now get back behind the glass." I obliged, not wanting to impact the experiment any more than I already had.

"Charlotte," Roger said. "Do you remember the study you agreed to participate in?"

She took a deep breath, and her body rolled upwards into a sitting position. This was new. Neither of the last subjects showed anywhere near that level of physical control. Her blond hair fell down around her as her cloth slipped onto the floor. "I remember … putting a gun to my head and pulling the trigger."

Roger looked back at us uneasily, as though unsure how to proceed. "Yes," he said after a moment. "Your parents were wondering if they had hurt you in some way or–"

"No," she wheezed, and her head snapped sideways to look at Roger. At the time I didn't think anything of it, but looking back there was something decidedly twisted about her eyes. Much like Anges' they were buzzing around her skull, her pupils darting about like ricocheting hockey pucks, but this time her mouth was a tight smile. This time she appeared to be in control. Aware. "I killed myself because I needed to know that my nightmares ... weren't real."

Around me, researchers were hastily recording details of her interaction – her words, her appearance, her biological readings. I gazed on in abject horror. I think that even then I knew that something awful was about to happen. I had that feeling, the one deep down in your gut that appears just before a car accident, or just before somebody's about to fall.

"And what was that?" Roger said, his voice breaking as he stood next to Charlotte's buzzing pupils. "What came next after you died?"

"Everything," she muttered, sweeping a leg off of the slab, "... that I feared." Her pale foot hit the linoleum floor with a dull slap. Then the other followed. She took a shaking breath and then pushed herself off of the table until she was standing naked in front of Roger. "What do you think happens after we die ... doctor?"

Roger looked sidelong at us from behind the two-way glass, his expression somewhere between nervous and fascinated. "I'm not certain," he said. "We all believe different things, I suppose. We were hoping you could answer that for us, Charlotte."

Charlotte laughed, I think. It's hard to say, but she threw back her head and started choking irregularly. "We believe ... believe ... *believe*..." she repeated the word as though tasting it. "We believe so many different things and we so desperately want them to be true, but the only truth ... is that we return to the forgotten."

The forgotten. It was a phrase we're heard before from Agnes. One in which I'd assumed it referred to human beings, like those who died in meaningless wars or in periods of widespread misfortune, and yet the emphasis that Charlotte placed upon it …

"The forgotten?" Roger repeated, taking a step back from Charlotte's hunched-over body. It was miraculous that she was standing at all, but that she remained living after several minutes was something neither of the other two subjects managed. "What are the forgotten?"

"Not what … but who." Charlotte reached out, placing a pale hand on either side of Roger's shoulders. We watched with our breath held. She lurched forward, planting her blue, decaying lips on his. They touched only for a second before Roger instinctively pushed her backward, causing her to stumble against the metal slab. She laughed again in that choking, rasping chorus, sliding onto the linoleum floor.

Roger rushed to her. "I'm sorry, I didn't mean to but–"

"Our minds are finely made," she wheezed, not seeming to care. "They evolved over … millennia to mask reality. To mask the bitter … bitter truth of the universe." She spat black bile onto the floor, wiping at her lips with a shaking hand. "You want to know what happens … when we die? We return to the abyss that birthed us."

The room around me began to murmur, some in interest, others terror. I merely watched on, my heart racing and my mouth dry.

"I put a bullet through my skull," Charlotte continued, "… because I had a vision of the end. I saw our makers, and they were dressed in … dying stars and empty space. They were hopeless. Empty. But just like us … they wanted medicine. A way to feel."

Roger knelt beside Charlotte as her voice grew quieter with every agonizing word. "We are their medicine," she rasped. "Our minds are primed for love, for joy, and for pleasure … and when we die, they feed on us. They leave our souls empty and rotting until we're rebirthed into the next human, a little less whole ... a little less complete." Once again that thin smile twisted its way across her blue lips. "... a little closer to putting a bullet through our skulls."

Roger waved at us, indicating that he wanted to make sure every second of this was being properly recorded. Then, he turned back to her. "What else can you tell us?"

"That we began with ... meaning. But as they fed ... and they fed, we grew emptier ... more incomplete. Collectively, the human soul ... withered." Black bile poured from her lips now. It streaked down her pale body, pooling around her trembling legs like blood from a butchered lamb. "Look around you. Do you feel ... the rage? The ... hatred and the pain? It's consuming the human race like a ... plague, and bit by bit ... we're getting worse. Not better. Soon we'll have nothing left to feel. No love ... no joy. Just ... emptiness."

Roger's mouth hung open. His voice stuttered as he attempted to formulate a response, to articulate why she must be wrong— at least, that's what I had hoped for. I'd hoped for *anybody* to stand up and say this was all a farce, and the experiment had been compromised and none of this could be true. But nobody did.

Charlotte reached up and gripped Roger by the front of his shirt. "If you want to know what comes next ... I can show you."

Roger looked at us then through the glass, his eyes wide with shock and fear. He looked at us one last time and I think he was waiting for somebody to shake their heads, to tell him that no, that was a bad idea. That he should decline. But we were all too shaken, I think. We weren't thinking straight.

So he nodded. He nodded and leaned into Charlotte, and then the lights flickered and the freezer and our observation room were both plunged into darkness. The blackout lasted for just a second. Maybe two. But it was long enough for everything to go wrong.

When the light returned, the glass was cracked and the machine was wailing a metallic tone. Roger lay in front of Charlotte's naked corpse, his head face-down in the pool of bile, smoke drifting up from his slack-jawed mouth. Charlotte's eyes were no longer buzzing. Her chest was no longer heaving. She had died for the second time. Roger had died for the first.

After that, our funding was pulled. Our donor abandoned the project and scrubbed his involvement from any and all corporate records. As far as the scientific community was concerned, the experiments never occurred, and the findings didn't exist. But I remember. I remember because there's simply no way I could forget the haunting look in Agnes' eyes, the hopeless agony of Jacob's screams, or the final message that Charlotte delivered in black bile on the linoleum floor.

It was messy and easy to miss. To the others, I think it must have looked like a common splatter, a simple side-effect of her legs spasming in the pool of dark fluid. But I know what I saw. The letters, though crooked and barely legible, were scorched into my memory like a cattle brand. They weren't so much a warning as they were words of advice– perhaps an answer to the question we set out to ask, and the question that Charlotte had set out to answer in her book.

The meaning of life, she wrote, *is to avoid the agony of death.*

THE ENTITY AND THE LAD

Alright, let me get straight into it.

I hate kids.

Like, I *loathe* them. My best friend has two kids – both bright, both courteous, both kind (bless their hearts), and both absolutely suck.

Oh, does that sound harsh?

Sue me. I'm running on three hours of sleep over here and I'm kinda on edge. My entire week's been a walk down insomnia lane, a non-stop barrage of ridiculous nonsense waking me up at all hours of the night.

I'm talking eggs splattering my bedroom window, ear-splitting renditions of Linkin Park (that always get the lyrics to 'Runaway' wrong), and strobe-lights beaming into my house that don't even match the beat of the music.

The weird part?

All of it's coming from the same place – the treehouse in my backyard.

You have to understand that when I bought this place the treehouse wasn't a consideration. It just wasn't. I was looking for a cheap property with a decent layout and potential to renovate.

What I wasn't looking for is a colossal pain in my ass. And yet here I am. I've been a homeowner for a little over a week, and I'm already ready to throw in the towel.

Initially, I thought my treehouse might've been annexed by some neighborhood twerp, but when I went out to investigate, I realized my situation was far more dire.

See, after I demanded the troublemaker show themselves, a ghostly apparition appeared. At first, I thought it was just a short ghost, but then I noticed the backwards ball-cap, Sum 41 hoodie, and the middle finger it was giving me.

The son of a bitch was a ghost kid!

Before I could grab the knucklehead by his ethereal collar and wring his translucent neck, he vanished.

Typical.

Fuming, I stormed back inside and fired up Craigslist. What I needed was somebody who could get this squatter off my property, and (ideally) book him into some kinda ghost-juvie in the process.

What I found was less than useless.

Seriously, have you ever tried putting out an ad for 'ghost removal'? Don't bother. The people responding are not society's shining stars. The first 'psychic' showed up in a sleeveless shirt with an open beer in his hand – a fucking Bud Light – and asked how many people the ghost had murdered.

Murdered!?

Buddy, if this ghost had a body count, I'd be contacting the FBI, not an alcoholic on Craigslist.

Somehow the next two psychics were even worse. The guy introduced himself as 'Crowley Mournfell' and his partner as 'Ravengloom Evershade' (DEFINITELY made-up).

They strolled through my house with EMF detectors, humming and mumbling to themselves in a language they probably thought was Latin. I tried telling them the ghost wasn't actually *in* the house, but they wouldn't listen.

"I feel a soul chained to this dwelling," Crowley murmured mysteriously. "There's great turmoil here, some unfinished business the spirit must attend to."

I tried asking what kinda unfinished business a fourteen-year-old could have besides mowing the lawn, and Crowley declared, "Alas! The spirit has ceased contact."

Ceased contact?

Excuse me? The brat doesn't get to make some vague allusion to *unfinished business* and couch-surf until the end of time!

Ravendark Gloomwhatever wasn't any better. She kept spritzing essential oils and rambling about crap like, "there's a strong aura in the bathroom," and "I feel a sense of melancholy in the kitchen."

Yeah, that 'strong aura' was last night's jalapeno burrito, and the 'melancholy' is the expired chicken I keep forgetting to take out of the fridge.

All in all, I was feeling pretty sour about paying these hacks three hundred bucks, but once they got to the treehouse, I realized it'd been worth every penny.

They started by wandering around with dowsing rods. Crowley sprinkled some salt here and there. Ravensorrow Sadgloom danced around with tears in her eyes. "There is grief here ..." she wept. "Crowley, I'm channeling *–ack–* so much pain ..."

Blegh.

It took all of three minutes for the ghost kid to get fed up.

SPLAT.

The little snot egged Crowley square in the face!

"Dude," he said flatly, losing his ethereal murmur. "Not cool. I just bought this jacket, bro."

One. Two. No—THREE more eggs pelted him in quick succession.

SPLAT. SPLAT. SPLAT.

"Ahh!" He ran around shrieking, ghost-eggs exploding and mucking up his obsidian hair (his words, not mine). Ravenwoe fell to her knees. She started pleading with the ghost kid to spare

Crowley (as if the little shit could be reasoned with), and then she too started getting showered in yolks.

"Save yourself, Doug!" she cried, scrambling from the tree.

Crowley (or Doug, I guess) booked it after her. I watched them dash across the yard, not even bothering to go for the fence and instead trampling my hedge.

Dicks.

In light of THAT failure, I decided to take matters into my own hands. After twenty minutes of YouTube research, I wheeled over to Wal-Mart and came back with a few choice items:

1. A Ouija board
2. Sleeping meds
3. Microwavable burritos (not relevant, but delicious)

That leads me to now.

I figure I'll kill two birds with one stone. First of all, I'll finally get some actual sleep, and second of all, I'm going to contact the little shit haunting my tree-house and give him a piece of my mind.

Here goes nothing.

I pop a sleeping pill, unbox my Ouija board, and make a collect-call to the afterlife. It only takes a minute for the kid to answer, and when he does it's with the typical teenage snark.

"what do u want"

Ugh.

I roll up my sleeves and get to work. I drift the planchette across the board, spelling out the words, "i want u out of my treehouse u fukin shit"

He doesn't take kindly to that. After a bit more back-and-forth, I tell him to vamoose before I come up there with a chainsaw and tear the whole tree down. Suddenly, he gets REAL cooperative. Spills the beans on everything.

Turns out, Doug and Ravendusk had actually been onto something with all that 'melancholy energy' and 'unfinished business' nonsense. The ghost (who I'll henceforth be referring to as 'Ghost Lad') lived in my house decades ago, right up until the moment a demonic entity crawled out from under his bed and gobbled him up.

"like it … ate u?" I asked.

"ya"

Oof.

I tell him that's super shitty, but also a pretty rad way to die.

Plus, it explains the weird stains on the wall (and why it's the only room that's hardwood and not carpet).

He goes on to say that his family fled for their lives, but first they hired an exorcist and chained the entity to the house. Nobody wants a demon moving with them, right? I make a point to apologize for his family's cowardice, but he tells me it's cool – they were just being pragmatic.

After a bit more chatting, he comes clean that he isn't so much loitering on my property as he is trapped here. Apparently, the entity did a nasty number on his soul, so when he floated up to the gates of Heaven, they told him to get lost.

Yeesh. Talk about picky.

Still, I've got a question I want answered. "dont ghosts haunt the same place they died or w/e?? y u in my treehouse"

"oh im sorry would u like 2 roommate with the demonic entity that devoured ur soul??? no that's rite I didn't think so"

Prick.

I let loose a yawn as I feel my sleeping meds kick in, and Ghost Lad (in typical teenage fashion), manages to take offense. "is my story borin u??" he Ouija's. "sorry that a demon scarrin my soul n murderin me dont exite u"

I tell him to chill, and that his story isn't boring me. I'm just exhausted thanks to his non-stop karaoke sessions and obsession with strobe lights.

He claps back that those 'karaoke sessions' are the only reason we're having this conversation in the first place.

"ud be dead if it wasnt for me"

I blink, staring at the Ouija board in disbelief.

Ghost Lad explains that this entity prefers to strike its victims while they sleep. That's how it got him. One minute he's dozing off, the next his leg is getting snacked on by an abomination from the pits of Hell.

He says all those karaoke sessions, strobe lights and eggs splattering my window were to jolt me awake before the entity could sink its teeth in.

Huh.

Suddenly, I'm feeling a bit embarrassed. My eyelids are getting droopy, and I'm realizing in my crusade for sleep I've made a fairly large blunder.

"sorry," I message. "gtg"

"y?"

"... took sleepin meds ... lol feel drowsy"

"WTF"

I get up from the table and realize I can't trust myself to stay awake. Already my world is spinning. To be safe, I'll probably just grab a hotel room for the night and come back tomorrow with Ravenshade and Doug.

No. Scratch that.

I'll call up Bud Light Guy. He clued into the mass murdering demon pretty much instantly, which as far as I'm concerned is some high-tier psychic shit.

Waving goodbye to Ghost Lad, I cross the living room and try to leave through the back door, but it's jammed. Yawning, I give the front door a try.

That one's not budging either.

Okay. The windows then.

...

Sigh.

They're sealed shut.

Frowning, I decide to give Ghost Lad a ring via Ouija. "hey... any ideas lmao"

"RUN!"

Yikes.

My vision is a slush of colors now. I'm running out of time and options, and as much as I hate to make a ruckus at this hour, I'm thinking it's time to go nuclear. I'm gonna grab a chair and whip that bitch through the living room window. Screw the HOA.

Before I do though, I'm leaving this testament. The next people who move into this house deserve to know what lives here and, God willing, get a better price than I did.

I'll give you an update if I manage to survive.

If not... Well, just remember that the next time something wakes you up, it might not be the nuisance you think it is – it might actually be a friendly neighborhood Ghost Kid trying to save your goddamn life.

Which reminds me, I need to save mine.

Toodles!

I AM HAPPY!

"I am happy." I say it into the mirror, brows furrowed and mouth pulled into a tight smile. My fingers clutch the edge of the bathroom sink. Something tugs at the corner of my mind. A thought, maybe. It's tempting me to peek at it, begging me to acknowledge it and push it out into the light of day, but I can't.

I won't.

My mother calls me from the kitchen. "Are you ready for school?"

"Yes," I call back. "I am."

I take another few moments to stare at myself, to burn the image of how happy I am into my memory – just in case I start to forget.

It's a big day, after all.

—————

The station wagon chokes and sputters as it pulls into the school. I'm in twelfth grade and I have no idea what I want to do with my life, but that's okay. It's normal. Nobody does. Nobody except for

Maggie Taller and Adam Wallace. They're going to get married and have children and live happily ever after.

They're going to be happy.

I crack the car door, look out over a sea of faces. Some of them are staring back at me. Some of them are snickering. One of them is Maggie Taller, and she's waving, all red curls and dimples, so I wave back. My stomach does a front flip.

"Have a good day," my mother says. Her face twists with an expression that resembles a smile, but isn't. There's not enough play in her cheeks. She forgets to engage her eyes.

"I will," I reply. I use the same smile that I practiced earlier. It's much better. When I look back to the steps, Maggie Taller is gone.

I lurch out of the car, dragging my bag out of the back seat. It's heavier than usual. It takes a lot of effort to get it on, to get it slung over my shoulders, and for a moment I'm terrified my mother's going to get out and help.

"Honey ..." she says.

"It's fine," I grunt. "I've got it."

And I do. I barely even lose my balance, barely even stumble against the car. My mother's staring at me like she wants to cry. It's like she's afraid I'm going to jump off a bridge or slash my wrists or turn into my sister as soon as she drives away. "You know you can talk to me about anything, right?"

"I know," I tell her.

"Okay."

I hit the door with my hip. It closes with a thunk. My mother pulls out of the parking lot, and I catch tears trickling down her cheeks. They're the same tears she cries at night when she thinks I've gone to sleep, the same tears she cried when my sister killed that boy with her nails and teeth, but I am not my sister.

I am happy.

The mutters follow me to English class. Their voices are hushed, but still loud enough that I can hear. This is intentional. It's by design.

"... walks like a goof."

"... smells like a dead animal."

"... saw him staring at Maggie's ass."

"... teach him a lesson after school."

I listen to Mr. Yu discuss the significance of metaphor in literature. He spends the hour comparing Animal Farm to Twilight, berating us for being too dense to appreciate good fiction. He says it's our generation. We're no good. He says there hasn't been a good generation since his, and this whole class is proof of it.

He points a finger at me. Asks me to define the term 'metaphor,' and I do my best.

"Wrong," he tells me. "Are you blind or something? Do you need glasses? It's been written on the damn whiteboard since you walked in."

Somebody laughs.

More join in.

Soon even Mr. Yu is smirking, and I think it's the first time I've ever seen him smile. My eyes crinkle with tears. I want to bash my head against my desk until I can see my brains and then keep going until I can't.

"... kid's a dumbass."

"... gotta be retarded, right?"

"... no doubt."

"... looks like he's gonna cry."

I am happy.

The cafeteria is noisier than a car accident. That makes it perfect. Serene. There are so many voices here that I can't hear anyone talking about me. It's just words drowning out words.

I get a table to myself, take out my worksheet and try to come up with ten different metaphors for Mr. Yu. This is an assignment just for me. He needs to know that I'm not as stupid as everyone thinks.

His example sits at the very top of the page: a woman with a heart of gold. Reading it makes my chest ache. It makes me think of my sister, of the way she used to smile before the horror took her. It makes me think that someday the horror will take my mother, too.

I try to write, but it's hard. The words don't come easy. My eyes scan the definition of 'metaphor' over and over but my mind is all blank lines and empty space. It's like I can't think. Can't focus. I'm wondering where Maggie Taller is sitting today. I'm wondering if she is wondering about me.

Somebody bumps into my chair and drops something onto my table. It's a crumpled piece of paper. I look around but I'm too late to catch who left it. Or maybe I'm just too blind. Whoever they are, they've already vanished into the crowd of hungry students.

Maybe it was Maggie.

I smooth out the paper and my heart starts to race. There's something written on it. It's messy. It says YOUR DEAD. A stickman is lying beneath the words, surrounded by three other stickmen that are stepping on him, kicking him. His body is covered in red scribbles. The other stickmen are smiling while they kill him.

I am happy.

The bell rings and school is over. I gather my things and pull my backpack up and over my shoulders. It's heavy and awkward. It takes me three tries to get it right, but this time I manage without losing my balance.

Today is a big day.

I make my way off the school grounds, over the hill that leads to the forest path that runs along the little creek that sounds like spring. I make my way home. My legs are tired. They're practically numb by the time I get over the hill, but that's okay. It just means I'm getting stronger, that all the work I've been doing in the forest is going to pay off.

Voices trail behind me. They're speaking in hoarse whispers, vibrating with adrenaline.

"... pervert is gonna get what's coming to him."

"... believe it when I see it."

"... heard Maggie moaning about wanting what's *inside* of him."

"... fuck off."

The forest is full of people. There are joggers and dog walkers and mothers pushing strollers. A homeless man in a big coat asks me if I have any change, and I tell him that I'm sorry but I don't. He tries to spit on me.

"... lying gimp."

I take the same shortcut I usually do, the one that runs by the creek, but today it makes me nervous. There are so few people around. It's like no one wants to walk by the creek that sounds like spring, but then I think that maybe it's for the best.

"... I'll beat his ass, just watch."

"... sure, just like you said you'd fuck Maggie."

"... not my fault she's frigid."

"... she'd fuck him I bet."

Footsteps. They're rushing at me, and I can't turn around fast enough. A fist connects with the back of my head. I stumble forward. Two people rip my crutches away, and another fist slams into my ribs. I whimper. Cry out. My body hits the ground and someone's knuckles collide with my nose. My vision spins. I taste something bitter in my mouth, warm and thick. I try to get back to my feet, but my legs aren't cooperating. They never do. They're useless, just like the rest of me.

"Crippled fuck!" shouts a voice like gravel. "You think I was gonna let you get away with hitting on my girl?"

A face swims into view. It's a boy with a square jaw and broad shoulders, with eyes darker than tar and a head of black stubble. Adam Wallace. He spits in my face. One of his friends kicks me in the side of the head.

My ears ring.

This is getting out of hand.

I open my mouth, try to speak, try to explain that they've got it all wrong, that I wasn't flirting with Maggie but I don't get the chance. Somebody jumps on my stomach. Lands with both feet. All the air goes out of me, and I start to gasp. Wheeze. A sneaker connects with my mouth, splits my lip open and then another shoe slams my jaw shut. My teeth snap off the tip of my tongue.

Blood.

So much of it.

I'm sputtering, stammering as I roll onto my back. A boot plows into my nose. There's a crunch of cartilage and a snap of bone, and suddenly I'm screaming. It's pouring down my face now, the blood. It's spilling all over my lips and down my chin and into my hair and now I understand how the stickmen felt in that stupid drawing. My world is a red smudge.

I curl into a ball, try to protect myself as best I can but it's a losing battle. "P-Please ..." I sob. "Please stop ... I won't tell anyone, I promise..."

"... shut it, sped."

"... somebody's gonna see us."

"... take him into the forest."

Strong hands grip my ankles. Start to drag me away.

I'm being pulled, pulled off the little path that follows the creek that sounds like spring, pulled into the forest where nobody hears anything ever again. Adam stuffs a ball of fabric into my mouth. Something moist. Revolting. It smells like sweat and tastes like something worse.

"... bet you wish those were Maggie's panties, freak."

"... how do you like the taste of my ballsack, bitch?"

There's laughter in the air.

I close my eyes. Try to smile. I try to remind myself that I am happy because happiness is everything. Tears slip down my cheeks, or maybe it's just more blood. I can't tell. Something claws at the edge of my thoughts. It's begging me to acknowledge it, to push it to the surface but I know what that means, so I can't. I won't.

I am happy.

It takes a long time for them to drag me through the woods. They go deep enough that I lose consciousness twice. They go deep enough that I know nobody will ever find us or hear us or figure out what Adam and his friends are capable of.

"... how much further, man?"

"... screw it, drop him here."

My legs hit the ground with a dull thump. I loll my head sideways. It's the best I can manage because I think my skull is cracked, that maybe my brain is bleeding.

Death is in the air.

"... wish Maggie could see this."

"... she'd rat us out for sure."

"... never know, she's lowkey nuts."

"... heard she's into witchcraft."

Pressure. I feel pressure on my chest as Adam Wallace bends down, rests his knee on my sternum. There's an animal snarl on his face. His fingers wrap around my neck like cords of sausage. Start to throttle. Start to choke.

"... he's actually doing it."

"... fuck me, I thought he'd be too chicken shit."

Above me, the trees start to fade with the air in my lungs. I'm clawing at Adam. Rasping. The best I can do is leave scratches on his face, the sort that can't even annoy him.

"You think I was gonna let you cuck me?" he hisses. "You? A fucking cripple? C'mon. Not even *you* could be that fucking stupid." His voice is dipped in cyanide. Marinated in hate. My legs kick out, my whole body spasming as I feel my face turning blue. I wonder how long he's worked himself up to this, how much teasing it took to make him comfortable with murdering me.

"... taking too long, man."

"... use this."

"... gotta be home before dinner."

I hear a switchblade open. Adam looks up. Grins. He lets go of my throat, leans over to grab the knife and I take my chance. Start to crawl. It's the most pathetic scene in the world, which makes it a suiting end to my sideshow of a life. I'm crying. Begging them to let me go. I don't even make it the length of a park bench before Adam catches me. He grabs me by my backpack, wrestles it off my shoulders.

"... check his bag."

"... maybe he's got cash."

There's the growl of a zipper opening. Someone starts rifling inside my backpack, starts tossing out my school books and binder and whatever's left of my lunch. My heart pounds. Somehow I know their next words before they ever speak them.

"... the fuck is this?"

They toss my backpack away in disgust, and it rolls across the forest floor. Bags tumble out of it. Garbage bags. Adam and his friends start to gag. Start to retch.

"... full of dead animals, man."

"... kid's a fuckin' psycho."

Something thrashes in my mind, crashing against my weakening will. It's screeching. It's roaring at me to stop being such a coward and do something about this before it gets worse, but I tell it to leave me alone. That I am okay. That I am happy.

"... sick in the head."

"... deserves to suffer."

Strong hands grip my shirt, pulling me up off the ground. Knuckles find my face. Again and again. Someone's shouting at me about the dead squirrels and the dead birds and the dead rats in the garbage bags, and they're telling me that this is better than I deserve. Maybe they're right. One of my teeth cracks loose, scrapes the inside of my throat and I start to choke. Sputter.

"... kinda freak collects dead animals?"

"... gotta be a serial killer."

"... cripples can't be serial killers, dipshit."

"... shut it, let's hear it from him."

Adam rips the jock strap from my mouth, props me up against a tree. I cough blood onto my shorts. My vision's a watercolor slurry, but I can still make out their faces. Adam Wallace. David Cho. Pacing behind both of them is Suhky Raj. He's shifting restlessly, peering into the treeline like maybe he hears something or someone out there.

"Well?" Adam demands. "You gonna talk or not? Let's go, Jeffery-fucking-Dahmer, we don't got all day!"

"O-Offe ..." I rasp.

He smacks me upside the head. "Speak up, bitch tits. If I knew you were gonna be crying so much I woulda brought you a soother."

David laughs. Suhky's too distracted. Something's stolen his attention out there in the branches and leaves, and his eyes are darting around like mosquitos in his skull.

"They're … offerings …" I croak. "The animals are offerings …"

Adam presses cold steel to my throat. "Offerings, huh? You think you're some kinda wizard, freakshow?"

My voice sounds like road rash. "I need the offerings … to cure me …"

"I got the cure for you right here," Adam says, pressing the blade into my throat. I feel a trickle of blood down my neck. This is it. The end of the line. Piss leaks from the bottom of my shorts, and what's left of my teeth rattle in my mouth, terrified of what comes next.

"Yo!" Suhky hisses, gesturing wildly. "Drop the knife, Adam! Now! Quick!"

Something shifts. It's out there in the trees. There's a crunch of twigs and a shift of leaves like somebody's moving through them, and before Adam or his friends can even think to hide, a shape steps out from the forest. It's someone familiar. A girl that's been following us since we left school.

Maggie Taller. Adam's girlfriend.

Sukhy tries to step in front of her, tries to block us from view but it's a lost cause. Words tumble from his lips. Excuses. He's trying to explain to Maggie that what she's seeing isn't as bad as it seems, that it's just a few boys horsing around. Rough-housing.

Snick.

He's interrupted by a horrible, wet-sounding jab. Then another. There's a series of four slick rips, like a pen tearing through paper, or a knife plunging into skin. Suhky crumples.

"… Jesus, Maggie!"

"… what's wrong with you?"

"... you're fucking nuts!"

"... didn't I tell you she was nuts?"

David's staring at Suhky's corpse. His lanky arms start to shake, start to tremble as he takes one step backward, then another. Maggie stalks toward him. Her knife drips with the same stuff that's pooling under Sukhy's body, and it's a lot bigger than a switchblade.

"... fuck this, Adam."

"... I'm out!"

"... I'm fuckin' out, dude!"

David bolts.

He takes off, vanishing into the forest and he doesn't once look back.

Now it's just the three of us.

Maggie. Adam. Me – the forever third wheel. Adam's talking. He's saying words, circling away as Maggie marches toward him. I can't see them, but I can hear them. Adam's spinning up a story about how I was taking pictures of Maggie beneath bathroom stalls, about how I deserve every last bruise gracing my broken face.

"... kid's a freak."

"... but I'm taking care of it, babe."

"... all of this."

"... it's for you, babe."

Maggie answers, "I know."

There's a rush of movement, a song of shifting dirt. They're tangled up on my left now. Grunting. Panting. Their limbs smack and clap as they wrestle, leaves crunching beneath their ballet of footsteps, and it almost sounds like sex – or it would except for Adam's whimpering.

"... please Mags, don't–"

Snick.

Adam's words turn into a breathless stammer. He staggers into my periphery, and I see that he's trying to run but his legs look like spaghetti. Quivering. Useless. His white shirt is turning a darkening red.

Snick. Snick. Snick.

The knife slips into him, over and over. Maggie's walking him down, and she almost looks bored as she slips the knife between his ribs, into his abdomen, into all the soft spots she can find. He drops to his knees, crying, but Maggie doesn't stop. He keeps asking her why.

"Why, Mags?"

Snick. Snick.

"Why are you doing this?"

Snick.

"Why won't you stop?"

Snick. Snick. Snick.

Adam teeters. He looks like he's about to fall over, but Maggie wraps a hand around his forehead, pulls his head back to her chest and looks down at him. His eyes are rolling up in his skull. "Why?" he whispers. "Why me?"

She smiles. Touches her lips to his. "Why not?"

The knife slams into his throat.

Adam starts to gurgle. Choke. Maggie grips his scalp, sets her feet and then tears the blade sideways. His neck splits open in a fountain of blood. His head rolls forward. Nods against his chest. Adam Wallace hits the ground with a heavy thud, and he never closes his eyes.

Maggie bends down, wipes her knife on his jeans. Checks her watch. She heaves a sigh, turning to me, clicking her tongue and running a red hand through her redder hair. "This wasn't part of the deal," she tells me.

And it's true.

She makes her way toward me, reaches down, and I think she might help me up, but instead she starts throwing the dead animals back into my bag, one by one.

"You forgot the rabbit," she says. Her voice is like frostbite. Her eyes meet mine and they're an empty blue, colder than an arctic wind. "You realize that demon's going to kill you, right? Just like it killed your sister. Just like it'll kill your mother once it's finished making you into a corpse."

"I know," I tell her.

"You're running out of time."

"I know that, too."

She frowns, cups her hands on my cheeks, her long nails digging into my skin. "Then give it to me."

"I'm trying to. I swear that I am."

She pulls back with a sigh. There's something around her neck. A doll. It's hanging from a cord of braided hair, decorated in pins and needles, and if you squint hard enough it almost looks like me. "I told you three offerings, didn't I?" Maggie says, giving Adam's corpse a dismissive kick. "I count two and a bag of roadkill."

David.

We're missing David.

"I'm sorry," I tell her, coughing up a mouthful of blood. "He ran off. Over there, into the trees."

"Then go get him."

I look around, but I can't see my crutches anywhere. They're gone. Probably floating down the river. "How?" I protest. "I'll never catch up like this."

"Then don't catch up like that." She reaches for her neck, twists one of the needles on the doll.

Pain.

I feel pain rip across my chest. My toes curl. The creature inside my mind bellows, screaming like the last breath of the universe. I slam my eyes shut, groan and twist. I can't lose control. I can't because if that happens, then I'm not happy anymore. People will get hurt. They always do. "Can't you get him?" I whimper.

Maggie shakes her head, slowly, twisting the needle and ratcheting up the agony. "He's too fast," she says, emotionless. "And the spell is specific. It demands you sacrifice the final offering, otherwise your demon won't change hosts. It'll stay chained to you. Eat you up, and then it'll pour itself into your mother and eat her too. Is that what you want? To eat your mother like your sister did your baby brother?"

Maggie kneels next to me, runs a hand through my tangle of hair and grips it in her fist. She's smiling, but she's not. There's not enough play in her cheeks. She forgets to engage her eyes.

"… now or never."

"… stop, I can't do this."

"… sure you can."

The knife plunges into me. Once. Twice. It doesn't stop. I whimper, writhing against the tree as Maggie slams it into me with both hands. She's snarling. The thing inside of me is snarling too. Tears stream down my cheeks. My body starts to convulse, starts to tremble in a widening lake of my blood.

I am happy.

I am happy.

The knife sinks into me once more, and this time Maggie fishes it around my stomach. The blade twists. I scream. I scream and I thrash as something crashes against my mind. It's speaking in a language of razor blades, dismantling my consciousness and overwhelming my will.

It escapes.

It pulls itself over my bones, extinguishing my thoughts and whispering violence into my soul.

I am not happy.

And neither is it.

SLEIGH FATHER

I need to talk. Like, I *really* need to talk. The trouble is, I don't have anybody I can talk to. My family's estranged, my friends are all gone, and the authorities think I'm a lunatic.

It's just five days from Christmas, and I'm alone. Isolated. If I don't get this off my chest though, I'm afraid it's going to start festering in my mind like a decaying carcass; I'm afraid it's going to sink its teeth in.

So I'll talk to you. All of you. It's not perfect, but it will do.

My name's Terrance Sims. I'm sitting in my rocking chair, rifle draped across my lap, in bloodstained pajamas that still reek with last night's piss. I haven't slept in two days, and I might not sleep for two more. Last night something came down my chimney, and I think it's coming back.

But I'm getting ahead of myself, so let me paint you a picture. I live alone, up in the mountains where the pine trees are draped in snow, and the rivers are an icy blue. I could be a bit more specific, but I don't think it's warranted. Besides that, I like my privacy.

All of this to say, where I am isn't important. What matters is what I have to say.

I'm a researcher. Or at least I was, once upon a time. My funding has long been cut, and my job along with it, but I've stayed out here because I believed in the research my team was undertaking. It was revolutionary. It meant the possibility of bridging worlds, of seeing new forms of life.

Now I'm terrified that research has found me.

You've probably heard of monsters, or urban legends, of things that claw at our imaginations and lurk in the dark recesses of our minds. Perhaps you've even felt one. They wait there sometimes, prowling just beyond our vision, tearing at the fabric that holds our realities together. Desperate. Hungry.

My job was to study these beings. I was tasked with developing an understanding of not only what they wanted from us but how to gain access to their world: the place Beyond the Veil.

Needless to say, I wasn't successful. The organization I worked for, the Facility, poured millions into my ideas and wasn't forgiving of my failures. When my theories came up short, they cut ties with me – *he* cut ties with me.

"It's unfortunate, but it's business," Mr. Reid had said, feet on his desk, long hair pulled back in a ponytail. "Your failures reflect on me, Terrance, and they've become an accounting nightmare."

I had begged him. Groveled. It didn't matter. I was terminated along with my research, and when you're studying the kind of things I am, they don't want that information leaking out into the world. It's what they call a liability.

So I was blacklisted. Facility teams picked away at my reputation, whispering in the back corners of universities and at the water coolers of laboratories. My name became synonymous with paranoia and madness. I was a laughing stock among my peers. A joke.

It was the end of my life.

Only one person cared to associate with me afterwards, a junior colleague and a brilliant young man named Alexi Azimov. He believed in the research nearly as much as I did, and luckily for him, his name wasn't attached to the project.

When the Facility pulled the plug and dragged my name through the dirt, they simply moved him to a new department, and that was that. Despite it, he spent his vacation days returning to the mountain, assisting me with further study whenever he could.

Until last year, when even he abandoned me.

But now I've shown Alexi – I've shown Mr. Reid. I've shown the entire Facility how wrong they were because it's here. And so is he.

The Sleigh Father.

I'd always suspected he lived in these peaks, that his Bridge was buried somewhere amidst the snow. The evidence suggested as much. It was almost impossible to argue against and yet I'd nearly lost hope.

I'd spent years looking for him. Decades.

And last night, he found me.

I'd been logging the final readings on my temporal oscillator when the entire cabin quaked. My first thought was an avalanche. After all, a blizzard was howling outside. Screaming. But then another sound reached my ears – a dozen dull thumps, clattering upon the roof.

Hooves.

I froze. A trickle of sweat trailed from my brow. It couldn't be – could it? And then laughter. It cut through the night, a shifting maze of emotion and tone, jumping from guttural to smooth.

Ho ho hO!

My heart leapt into my throat. The ceiling creaked overhead as boots crunched over a carpet of snow. It's funny. Half my life had revolved around this moment, preparing for it, chasing it – and yet now that it had arrived, I couldn't move. I couldn't even think.

Chattering teeth sounded then, biting through even the din of the storm. It was them. Those creatures the Sleigh Father commissioned in the First Days: eight abominations. Chimeras born from the rearranged pieces of children, stitched together into an unholy form. Their agony was his fuel. His gateway.

He used the despair of those children to power his sleigh, that eldritch mechanism that allowed him to leap between dimensions.

This was it – his Bridge. Within my grasp. With a shuddering breath, I forced myself into motion, lifting my rifle from the wall and stalking through my lonely cabin, following the sound of the Sleigh Father's boots above.

HO hO ho!

The chimney. I could hear him lumbering toward the chimney, and so I leveled my rifle at the fireplace. A blaze crackled in the hearth. It cast the sparse furnishing of my cabin in an orange glow, tossing shadows across the wicker chairs and document-ridden tabletops.

The night became still.

Even the blizzard quieted, the screaming gale becoming less than a whisper against the window panes. My grip shifted on the rifle. I lifted it to my cheek, staring down the scope at the flickering flames as my pulse pounded in my ears.

"Go ahead," I muttered. "Slide down that chimney and see just what's waiting for you."

Yet even as I spoke my threat I hardly bought it. I'd spent years studying the Sleigh Father, deconstructing his lore and mythologies – and out of all the monsters The Facility had dealt with, all the terrors that haunted old emails chain and spread through panicked breaths, The Sleigh Father was the anomaly. He wasn't feared, but celebrated.

Santa Claus, they called him.

It was an error I traced back to the 16th century, originating from a young girl in central Europe. Her father had been abusing her. Tormenting her. One winter's night, while she lay at her father's feet, bruised and bloodied, a deep laughter sounded in the darkness. Jovial. Menacing. In her diary, she described a towering beast crashing down their chimney, setting upon her father in a ravenous hunger. It tore the man apart. Devoured him, body and soul, leaving nothing but his skull as a small parting gift.

To the girl, the beast was a savior.

Perhaps even a Saint.

And so she spread her tale, choosing her words with care. She described a jolly being, one laughing and hungry, that comes down chimneys and leaves gifts for children in its wake. The story would go on to become history. Then legend.

Now the legend has found me – looking to add another soul to its collection.

Seconds stretched into minutes as I waited, tucked quietly behind the corner of the wall, rifle in my arms, elbow steadied upon my knee. Once, we had contingencies for this. Plans in place that provided the means to incapacitate the Sleigh Father should he pay us a visit, but those plans involved government agents no longer in my employ. They involved expensive technology and complex spells. They were a last resort.

Snow tumbled down the chimney, the hearth responding with a sharp hiss of steam. Something heavy shuffled above. Him. Emotions swam inside of me. Regret. Fear.

Why had I stayed out here?

How could I have been so stubborn – so bloody arrogant to think I could manage The Sleigh Father on my own?

But I already knew the answer, didn't I? Gritting my teeth, a face swam into my thoughts – Donovan Reid. My old boss. It was his mockery, his careless dismissal of my life and future that drove me to this desperate act. It was because of him I had to risk everything to prove the existence of the Sleigh Father – that I had to salvage what scraps remained of my reputation.

I hated that man more than words can say.

And Alexi had known it, too. He'd worried that my anger at Reid was becoming a distraction, a point of disruption in our research.

"Try writing about him," he'd told me in a recent email. "It's psychologically proven that writing, journaling – anything can be a cathartic and healing experience."

"I'm not much for journaling," I responded.

"Then keep it simple. Write it in bullet points. A list of all the reasons you hate him – of all the ways you wish you could hurt him and make him suffer. Better to get it out of your head, Terrance. Those thoughts are poison."

And so I did. It helped ... a little, but for what Donovan Reid had done to me, no amount of new-age psychology could heal that anger. What I wanted was to hurt him myself. To see the pain in his eyes, and—

hO ho HO!

The laugh came high and low, husky and slick. A crunch followed it, like something digging into brick, and panic found its way into my bones. Dust and debris fell into the flames. The Sleigh Father's legend was explicit in his form of entry; if possible, it was always down the chimney.

A groan swept down the flue, followed by more pebbles and stones. Then, the cabin shook. A pulverizing cacophony filled the night like cannon fire. Rubble tumbled into the blazing hearth while the bricks of the chimney bulged outwards, crumbling as something massive shot down it. I barely brought my rifle on aim before a figure crashed into the flames.

Burning logs shattered with a thunderous crack, while wooden splinters ricocheted like blazing shrapnel. I swung back behind the protection of the hallway wall, rifle clutched to my pounding chest. The fire had died. Darkness filled the cabin.

A short distance away, boots groaned against hardwood, kicking past broken logs in the hearth. My finger quivered against the rifle's trigger. A piece of me, infinitesimally small, wanted to see him, wanted to flick on a light or blindly fire into the darkness. Anything to witness the monster that possessed my life for so long ...

No, I told myself. *It isn't worth it. Breathe, Terrance. Don't waste this moment, not after everything you've sacrificed to get here.*

The footsteps stalked past a frosty window, dragging something heavy in their wake. In the faint slivers of moon, I could just barely make out a shadow. The Sleigh Father. He was tall – inhumanly so. His neck was bent forward, stocking cap drifting against the high cabin ceiling. A cloak fell from his broad shoulders, sweeping across the hardwood and ... A great sack loomed beside him.

"NaUghTy or niCe?" he hummed with a discordant, tuneless melody.

My jaw tensed. The rifle in my arms shook, my whole body a mess of erupting anxiety. Was this monster speaking to me? Did he know I was here? Swallowing hard, I steadied the rifle, aiming toward the colossal figure's head.

I could do it now, I reasoned. Pull the trigger. I could slam a bullet into this monster's skull, and maybe it'd actually kill it. Nobody had ever tried as far as I knew.

Ho HO hO!

The Sleigh Father seemed to look at me then, a glint of bobbing light flickering to life in front of its face. "Careful with that," it rasped. "You'll take your eye out."

A freezing kiss of air swept over me, and all at once my fingers burned with the agony of frostbite. My rifle clattered to the cabin floor. "Wh-what do you want?" I stammered, fingers clutched tight to my chest for warmth. "I wasn't going to shoot I sw-swear it."

"NAugHty?" the monster sang. "Or NIce?"

"Nice," I said at once, my voice pleading. "I'm a good man. A scientist! I only wished to learn about you, to better understand your legend!" The words stumbled from my mouth like lemmings falling to their death. Ineffectual. Pointless.

The beast crept closer, and as it did, its silhouette vanished from the scraps of moonlight. All that remained were the creak of its footsteps. I listened intently to the burdensome echoes of boots on hardwood and the heavy scratching of coarse fabric being pulled across the floor.

ho Ho hO!

He was close. So close. I screwed my eyes shut, waiting for the inevitable—waiting to die. Warm piss spilled down my leg. "Please," I begged. "I'm a good man! I told you already that I'm only here to learn from you!"

The rumbling of footfalls halted, and in their place came a coarse rustle of fabric, like the creature was opening that sack.

"NiCe, yOu sAy?"

A dim light formed, radiating out of a burlap bag some five feet away. Behind its glow, I could make out a white, singed beard hanging over a red suit. The Sleigh Father's face was otherwise indiscernible amidst the suffocating shadow, save for one dancing speck of light.

"WoULd yOu LiKe a GiFt?" it asked.

My mind raced. Was there anything in the mythology that warned against accepting gifts? I couldn't recall. "Err – yes," I hazarded, in a small voice. "Yes, please."

It seemed unwise to refuse the creature.

hO ho Ho!

A thick, red-jacketed arm reached into the swollen bag. Something moved inside of it. Struggled. Muffled screams followed, and the great arm pulled back, clutching a man by his lazy ponytail. The man thrashed. Whimpered. Tears soaked his pale face.

"You ..." I said slowly.

"Who's there?" he whimpered.

I stared at the man in stunned silence. Was this real? It couldn't be. This felt too good to be true – like the finest Christmas present I could ever receive, and that meant there must be a catch.

"Hello?" the man called out. "Please! I have resources - more than you could imagine! I'm a powerful individual! Just get me the hell out of here, and I'll give you whatever you want - money, power, anything at all." His voice turned weak, broken. "Please … Please just get me out of here. I have a family."

I opened my mouth, a smile dancing upon my lips. Words. I tried to think of words but I felt too excited, too stricken with joy to properly organize my thoughts.

"NauGhtY," the Sleigh Father hummed. "So, sO NaUgHty."

I found myself nodding along. Yes, that man *was* naughty. The worst in fact. He was an abomination, one fit for disposal. He'd doubted me. Made a mockery of me, and torn apart the life I'd so carefully built across decades of study and sacrifice.

"Donovan …" I croaked, doing my best to keep my voice level. "Donovan Reid, isn't it?"

The light was faint between us – just that tiny orb that hung from the Sleigh Father's cap. Mr. Reid squinted. He studied the shadows I sat within intently, and then—

"That voice … I know your voice." He paused, eyes widening. "You … Did you used to work for me?"

A muscle twitched near my eye. "I did."

Mr. Reid seemed to catch the utter contempt in my voice. "Listen, buddy – whoever you are. I'm sorry. Obviously we've had our disagreements in the past, and I'm happy to work through them if—"

"You don't remember, do you?" I told him, marching forward so that my face was clearly visible. "You don't even fucking remember me?"

He blinked, confused. "I …"

"The Sleigh Father!" I snap. "I was the one studying the damn Sleigh Father – the urban legend you called nothing but a myth and waste of resources."

The Sleigh Father growled, lifting Mr. Reid higher off the ground. He fought against the monster's grip, his hands like an infant's beneath the gnarled, clawed grip that held him. A low laugh rolled through the cabin. The Sleigh Father gave Reid a gentle nudge, and the piece of shit swung back and forth like a pendulum.

"Je-Jesus Christ ..." he gasped, tears streaming down his cheeks. "It's you. Fuck. Look, man. You were right – holy shit were you right about all of this. He's real. Of fucking course he is! Now are you going to help me or—"

"Help you?" I interjected, chuckling softly. "You want *me* to help *you*?"

Donovan Reid whimpered. "Yes ... Listen, I'm sorry. Firing you wasn't personal, but we didn't have any results to show for the spending we were doing on the Sleigh Father project and the higher-ups demanded accountability."

"Accountability ..." I murmured, my knuckles cracking into fists. Rage surged through me. Violence. I wanted nothing more than to drive my fists into Mr. Reid's face, beating it into a bloody pulp and yet I knew that wouldn't satisfy me. Pain was too straightforward. What I wanted was to taste his fear.

"Please ..." he begged.

"Shut up," I hissed. "Of course I'm going to help you. What do you think I am? A monster? You think I'd ruin your life all because you made a simple, stupid mistake?"

In the quiet of the cabin, Mr. Reid's tears struck the floorboards like gunshots. He hardly sounded like the man I knew. If he weren't swinging in front of me with his obnoxiously ponytail and skin-tight suit, I'd almost have doubted my own ears. This Donovan Reid sounded weak. Cowardly. A far cry from the self-absorbed egomaniac that had driven me to ruins.

"If I'm going to help you," I told him. "I need you to do something for me. Okay?"

hO ho HO!

He nodded frantically. "Anything! Your research is back on the table– of course, it is. You're brilliant! Look at you. You saw this before any of us. You knew it was out there and—"

"What's my name?" I asked quietly.

His words, once thundering along like a rollercoaster, crumpled into a heap of verbal wreckage. "Sorry? Your name? Look, I'm not in a position to remember every employee's name. That was years ago! Be reasonable, man!"

The floorboards creaked as I took a hungry step forward. Suddenly I understood our situation. It was the entire basis of the legend – those unwritten words that belied the truth of the Sleigh Father's purpose. That singular concept, still celebrated to this day.

Holiday cheer.

He'd come tonight bringing me holiday cheer. A smile touched my lips. I snatched Mr. Reid's black tie from around his neck, pulled tight with everything I had. He stopped swaying in the Sleigh Father's grip. Started to choke. Gag.

"Are you ..." he sputtered. "Fucking ... crazy?"

And there – yes!

His face lost the fear, the concern, the anxiety and the false remorse. In their place was something familiar. Recognizable.

Malice.

"That's more like it," I said, my mouth pressed to his ear. "There's the psychopathic son of a bitch that ruined my life."

"NaUgHtY oR niCe?" The Sleigh Father stroked a claw against Mr. Reid's cheeks, smacking his lips hungrily.

My eyes met Mr. Reid's. He stared back with a smoldering hatred, his teeth clenched in fury. Yes, I thought. Show me all your disdain – all of your anger at being so helpless, so powerless before a man you once perceived as little more than a slave. A worker bee to do your bidding. My smile widened, growing manic.

"Naughty," I announced, surprising myself with the glee in my voice. "Donovan Reid is a terrible man, Sleigh Father."

Ho ho Oh!

"You!" Mr. Reid snarled. "You worthless, good-for-nothing shit-for-brains piece of dogshit! I hope you die slow! I hope this fat bastard rips you in–"

His voice became a panicked gasp as a great, red arm thrust him to the ceiling. Mr. Reid's brows furrowed. His legs kicked. The Sleigh Father grabbed hold of them, chuckling merrily.

"Don't!" he shrieked as the Sleigh Father held him out, horizontal. "I really do have a family and—"

His words became a scream as his torso split slowly in two. Blood poured from his gut. It spilled onto the cabin floor in a curtain of red, followed by the splatter of his innards, striking the hardwood like spoiled fruit. Then, with a guttural roar, the Sleigh Father slammed both pieces together, drenching me in an explosion of blood and viscera.

I stood there, heart shuddering. It was warm in Mr. Reid's blood. It felt warm and so, so satisfying to feel him dripping off of me, to know that in his final moments he'd looked at me understanding that he was the pawn and I was the king.

My tongue slipped across my lips.

I'd once believed the Sleigh Father as little more than a reaper – a monster hungry for souls, but I knew then I'd been wrong. Like the girl had been joyous to be freed from her abusive father, I'd been joyous to exact revenge upon my crooked boss. This monster didn't just feed on souls. Like Santa Claus, it fed upon joy too. Mirth. It appeared that the Sleigh Father needed both to be fully satiated. Consuming a soul without providing joy ...

Why, it'd probably be like a meal without seasoning.

I laughed, shaking my head in disbelief. How could I have missed that?

Ho ho HO!

The windows rattled. All around me, the cabin started to tremble, floorboards splitting and cracking like gunfire in the dark. It felt like it was being torn from its foundations. I steadied myself against the wall as a blinding light exploded from Donovan Reid's skull before quelling to a gentle gleam. It snaked around the cabin, revealing the full extent of the building's disarray.

Tables had been upturned, documents littered the floor, and the fireplace had become little more than a pile of bricks and a frigid breeze. Shafts of moonlight pierced through the hole in the ceiling the chimney once occupied, revealing Mr. Reid's scattered bones.

Then, the floating light passed across the Sleigh Father.

It revealed a behemoth, clad in crimson cotton with white trim. Two legs burst from the long red jacket, coated in coarse, black fur that ended in leather boots. As the light swam upwards, I caught sight of the creature's arm scratching at its barrel chest. Long, terrible nails curled from the tips of the monster's fingers – almost like claws.

"Thank you," I breathed, my heart finally slowing. "Thank you ... for all of this."

"TiS tHe SeaSon," it sang with a laugh.

The orb of light ascended towards its mouth, and for the first time, I saw the monster's face. It was human but mangled. Above its white shock of beard were two pieces of coal, seared into its eye sockets. The skin of its face was discolored, a pock-marked mess of swollen, blistered flesh that sagged around its skull, and its nose was little more than two slits, with the faintest impression of bone jutting from beneath.

Burns. His face had been burned beyond recognition.

As the tiny orb of light finished its ascent, it revealed the Sleigh Father's red stocking cap. At the end of it was a white pom, and it blinked. It was looking at me. An eyeball twinkled where the pom should have been, glimmering like a star in the night.

It seemed clear to me the creature meant me no harm, and so the researcher inside of me took over. "Can I ask you–"

The Sleigh Father opened its mouth, and a blizzard screamed from its jaws. I recoiled. My fingers turned brittle and numb, my entire body aching with the stabbing sensation of absolute winter.

Then the floating orb vanished. It sucked itself up inside the Sleigh Father's maw, and with it fled the cold. The monster clamped its jaws shut. Gulped. Swallowed. A moment later it let loose a deafening belch, followed by a merry, tuneless round of laughter.

The Sleigh Father turned. His lumbering footfalls crunched along the cabin floor, snapping pieces of Mr. Reid's bones as he made his way back to the demolished chimney. "MeRrY cHRiStMaS tO aLL," the Sleigh Father wheezed.

Even with my pajamas covered in blood and my cabin in ruins, I felt happy. At peace. For the first time in decades, I felt full of Christmas cheer – so much so that I even finished the rhyme for him. "And to all a good night!" I sang.

His boots stopped sharply. The hardwood groaned as the hulking monster glanced over his shoulder, that bouncing eye winking in the gloom. "MErRy CHristmaS tO all," he corrected, his voice now devoid of its previous whimsy. "I'll sEe YoU iN tWo NiGhts."

The joy shriveled up inside of me.

No...

No that wasn't how the rhyme went! My jaw fell open, my mind spinning as panic flooded my thoughts. Why would he come back? We already had what we wanted. Mr. Reid was dead. The Sleigh Father had his soul. We were satisfied – our contract, whatever this was, it was over!

"Hang on!" I spat, my voice cracking. "You don't have to come back. It's fine! Seeing you was enough! I just needed to know I wasn't crazy– that I was right!"

"NAuGhty," he hummed, "Or RighT?"

I blinked, not understanding. That wasn't the rhyme either. "*Nice*," I confirmed. "I'm not naughty – I'm nice! I'm a good person that was abused and taken advantage of, just like that girl you saved. Remember?"

hO ho Ho!

His laughter echoed around the ruined cabin. "NAughty aNd RiGht. I'll sEe YoU iN tWo NighTs."

He stepped into the remains of the ruined chimney, shafts of moonlight framing him through the broken ceiling. The edge of his mustache turned upward with a grin. Then he bent his knees low, taking a sharp breath, before leaping into the air.

The ceiling shook as he landed back atop the roof. Footsteps crunched through snow. Hooves beat restlessly overhead, their teeth beginning to chatter in anticipation.

Ho HO hO!

I heard the crack of a whip – the taut snap of reins being pulled and the ceiling whined as the sleigh began to move. Slowly at first, then faster. Soon, the eight abominations had broken into a gallop, their hooves stampeding overhead before vanishing in twos.

Through the frost-kissed windows, I caught sight of the godless creatures soaring away. They were monsters in the truest sense of the word, a tapestry of limbs chopped up and reassembled into beasts of burden. Some had six legs and one arm. Others, three heads and feet sprouting from their necks. All were the stuff of nightmares.

As the sleigh vanished amidst the clouds, I heaved a sigh. Wandered into my office. With the blizzard gone, the night felt uncharacteristically warm. Whether or not that was a consequence of the Sleigh Father's visit, I couldn't say, but I was thankful for it.

It made thinking easier.

I turned on my computer, and my face was bathed in a digital blue glow. My satellite connection was online. Good. My fingers rocketed across the keyboard, firing out a handful of emails to my contacts at The Facility.

To Whom It May Concern,

I've done it. I've proven the existence of The Sleigh Father, and not only that – but I've secured a means of apprehending him. He's assured me he'll be returning in two nights. If we're quick, we can assemble a strike team to ambush him. We can take his sleigh – his Bridge!

Terrence Sims

Finished with my emails, I leaned back with relief. It was hard to believe, but I'd finally done it. Cleared my name. I'd resurrected my reputation and executed the monster that murdered it in the first place. It had been a busy night for Terrence Sims. An important one.

I had no doubt the Sleigh Father would return for me, but so long as I had The Facility's resources, I knew we would be able to handle him.

My inbox pinged with the first response.

Good evening, Dr. Sims,

Thank you for bringing this matter to our attention. Do not contact us again.

Saanvi Patel

Director of Research: Artifact Division

I stared at the screen in confusion. Had they even read my email? I just told them I located the bloody Sleigh Father– that I found his Bridge between worlds!

Two more emails pinged in the corner of my screen.

Terry,

Please take care, and know that you're in my thoughts. I'm so sorry.

Anna Ling

Deputy Head of Research: Myth Division

My eyes scanned Anna's message three times, then again for good measure. Nothing about it made sense. If anybody understood the opportunity in front of us, it ought to have been Anna. She'd worked under me on the Sleigh Father project.

Yet she sounded ... remorseful. Did she think I'd lost my mind, maybe?

I clenched my fists, frustration mounting toward these thick-headed numbskulls. Here I was, sitting on possibly the single most significant discovery in the history of humanity, and they were brushing me off like a raving lunatic.

With a bitter glare, I clicked on the third email. It was from the Director of Research and Development – Mr. Reid's boss.

Good to hear from you, Terrance!

First off, I'd like to say we're recommending you for the Medal of Merit. Your work has been incredible, and dare I say... Nobel Prize worthy?

A smile crawled across my lips. There. This was more like it. The Director of R&D had always been a shrewd, and clever woman – it's little wonder she saw the potential of my opportunity where the others couldn't.

Of course, public awards are off the table until the Bridge has been secured. I imagine you're probably a little upset. It's a terrifying prospect, what's to come, but unfortunately, it was our only option. Dr. Azimov has been pivotal in getting this organized, and we're genuinely thankful for your cooperation in the matter. What's losing another thirty years of life when you'll be immortalized in history, eh?

I blinked.

Dr. Azimov? As in *Alexi* Azimov?

But Alexi abandoned the project ages ago. This was me – my achievement. My victory. Furious, I made to type up a sternly-worded reply, but before I could get the first word hammered in my computer pinged once more. New email. From Alexi Azimov, the lying snake himself.

Terry,

I hope you're well. I'd like to assure you that the Facility will be arriving at the mountain this evening. They'll be monitoring you from a safe distance, and when the Sleigh Father returns in two nights' time, they'll attempt to apprehend his Bridge.

My anger began to settle. Alexi might be trying to take credit for my work, but he'd at least dotted his Is and crossed his Ts about getting an ambush set up. That was good. There'd be time to clarify my achievements later – preferably with a Nobel Prize in hand. Kid was too ambitious for his own good. I chuckled as I kept reading.

Earlier this year, I discovered some lore. I thought it might help both of us. You and I. You see, old friend, I have come to realize that the Sleigh Father shares more in common with the Santa Claus myth than either of us recognized. All those weeks, months, and years of study and failed attempts to locate the monster were rooted in a singular problem: we were too focused on the science of it all.

The Sleigh Father is a being that transcends science, of course. An anomaly. A myth. So it was to that mythology I returned. Within it, I found the means to quell some of your suffering and offer you an opportunity to have a merry Christmas before you pass from this world.

My fingers gripped the sides of the keyboard hard enough that the plastic shell began to crack. I reread Alexi's words. Again. Again. *Before you pass from this world?*

What kind of terrible phrasing was that?

Trust me, Terry. It'll be better for you this way. Easier. See, I discovered that lists have the power to summon the Sleigh Father. They act as a sort of ritual. When one creates a list, the creature will sometimes deign them with their request – providing they want it desperately enough. Don't you see, Terry? It's our emotional energy that calls to the Sleigh Father! It feeds upon our joy and our sorrow, our wishes and fears. Isn't that fascinating?

I saw in your hatred of Mr. Reid a perfect opportunity, so I had you write a list of all those ways you wanted to hurt him. To make him suffer. Terry – I couldn't have asked for a better partner in this. I'm so happy to know I was correct in my theory!

My eyes scanned his words, and my teeth dug into my lip. That son of a bitch. That absolute piece of shit. I made to get up and grab a new piece of paper, one I could use to write Alexi's name on. I'd list it a thousand times. I'd scribble a thousand different ways I wanted him dead, and each would be more painful than the last.

But his email wasn't finished.

Of course, there's more to the Santa Claus mythology than simple lists. There are consequences. One such consequence is when somebody requests something selfish or sufficiently deplorable. It is the Naughty or Nice paradigm. It's what I was counting on tonight.

Your desire for Mr. Reid's death was selfish and, frankly, monstrous, Terry! You'll excuse my dry sense of humor, but it really was a 'naughty' sort of thing. I'm genuinely saddened to hear Mr. Reid passed with such brutality, but as the old saying goes: you can't make an omelet without cracking a few eggs.

Just know that you and Mr. Reid will be remembered for what you gave. Carpe diem, old friend. Thanks to your sacrifices, we might have a shot at defeating that crooked horror barreling toward us across the cosmos.

P.S.

If at all possible, draw the Sleigh Father as far from his Bridge as you can. Our team will have an easier time retrieving the sleigh that way.

Happy Holidays,

Alexi

With shaking fingers, I shut down the computer. Didn't even bother typing a reply. It's not like I had anything left to say, and I doubted Alexi would even care to read it. No. He'd already won his prize. He had my head on the chopping block, and once it rolled he'd achieve a level of professional success that even Einstein would envy.

That double-crossing rat bastard.

I stewed in my own rage for a long time – long enough that dawn crawled in through the cabin windows, and birds sang in the sunrise. Then I made a decision.

True, the Sleigh Father might be coming for me, and true I might not have a way out of here ... but I do have a way of burning the people down who did this. The Facility. Alexi.

And my way is through you. All of you.

The Facility is powerful, but even they can't stop a wildfire of public outrage. So here it is. My last will and testament – the true account of my final hours of life, and the research that brought me here.

I'm not asking to be deified. I'm not even asking for a street in my name. I just want people to know the real story about what happened on this mountain. You'll forgive me for not trusting the Facility to represent my posthumous contributions to this project. They've already spoiled my name once. Who's to say they won't keep dragging it through the dirt after I'm dead?

Words are cheap, and I know better than to trust emails from suits. So I'm begging you to spread this, far and wide. Tell my story the way it truly happened, warts and all. I'm not a perfect person. I'm not a madman either.

When the creature returns, I'll accept my death. I'll even lead the bastard away from his sleigh, just like that snake Alexi requested. It'll be my final contribution toward my life's work. A contribution that I hope might someday lead to a better world. After all, if The Facility manages to steal the sleigh, then it'll be a colossal boon in the war to come. If they don't...

Well, just be careful what you wish for this Christmas.

Some gifts aren't worth the price.

THE DEAD WORLD

It happened late. I suppose these things always do. The end of the world isn't exactly a rise-and-shine affair, you know?

It's a big decision, nuclear war. You think you're ready to drop the bombs, but then you figure it's probably best to sleep on it. Then you wake up and think maybe, just maybe, we'll first see how the day plays out. Maybe somebody convinces you not to press the button. Maybe the world gives you a reason it shouldn't go up in smoke – like the stock market, like the riots in the streets, like the futures of an entire generation.

Or maybe there are no reasons.

Maybe starting fresh is all that's left, and cleaning humanity off this rock is the only truly moral choice left to make.

Hell if I know.

All I'm sure of is that it's been a week since the blast. A week since I sprinted to my bunker, alone, forced to leave my family behind. If that sounds heartless, then just know it wasn't me who abandoned them. They abandoned me.

They were disbelievers. All of them.

They called me crazy for building the bunker. Called me insane for stockpiling canned rations ten feet beneath the dirt. I tried to explain to them that we were running out of time, that if they cared enough to open their eyes, they'd see all the signs pointing to nuclear war.

But did they care?

Of course not.

To them, it was just noise—the ramblings of a madman. I pleaded, I reasoned, I begged. But they wouldn't budge. They stuck their noses up at me all the way to the end.

When the air-raid sirens finally sounded, I tried to drag them to safety, but my wife refused to listen. She snatched up our son and daughter, her face contorted with hysteria. "Get out!" she shrieked. "Leave and never come back!"

So I did.

I left them there. There wasn't any time to fight her for the kids, to fight the kids who were wholesale convinced that I was a fraud. A liar. The bombs were coming and the bunker was over a hundred feet away, buried behind our farm.

I didn't have a choice, you understand? No choice but to run, so that's just what I did. I ran like the devil himself was on my heels, tears carving hot trails down my cheeks. The hatch clanged shut behind me, and then—

The world ended.

A low rumble, like the Earth itself was groaning in pain. Then another. And another. Each tremor ripped through me, shattering my heart into a thousand jagged pieces. My family was gone. Vaporized in an instant.

That was a week ago.

By now, I figure the worst of the fallout will have settled. It'll be just the fires that are left—hungry, relentless infernos with no one left to battle them. Soon, though, they'll exhaust their supply of fuel and they'll die too, leaving behind a world reborn in ash and shadow.

A dead world.

The dark truth is that the nightmare of nuclear armageddon takes place in three stages. The first is what people often assume to be the worst: the bombs. They think the explosions and the mushroom clouds are as bad as it gets, but they're wrong. At that stage you're either afraid or dead. That's it.

Stage two, though?

Stage two is when things get scary. In stage two, whole cities become funeral pyres, mile-high firestorms that boil blood and turn bones to dust. The sky splits open. It weeps black rain upon the earth, leaking into the DNA of every last person it touches, unmaking them from the inside out. Anybody that doesn't burn to death wishes they did.

But even this pales in comparison to the final stage.

The Dead World.

In the Dead World, the strings that tie us together are burned away. There are no rules. No customs. There is no humanity, just chaos, unbridled and relentless. Raiders prowl smoldering ruins, pillaging and murdering, taking whatever they desire and violating whoever they please. People are rounded up like cattle. They're butchered and eaten, treated like human livestock.

And this, my friend, is the stage we're entering now. I know it is.

How?

Because the raiders are here.

I can hear the soft patter of their footsteps above my bunker. They've come sniffing for supplies, for anything they can get their hands on that might keep them alive for another day, another hour.

Don't worry about me, though. My bunker's well-hidden. They won't find me. Not unless ... not unless the shockwaves swept away the leaves camouflaging my hatch.

I clutch the cross hanging around my neck, bring it to my lips. The metal is cold against my skin. I whisper a prayer, the words falling from my mouth like stones.

In moments like these, I'm almost relieved that my family's dead – relieved that they were atomized in the blast. The thought of what these raiders might do if they found them here ... it makes my skin crawl.

Above, voices murmur. A dozen, maybe more. Frantic. Desperate. My guess is they've broken off into groups. They're probably searching my farm for any surviving livestock, for any crops that managed to withstand the rain.

Fools. They're wasting their time.

By now, my cows and chickens will be long dead. My crops? Nothing but irradiated husks. There's nothing left of the farm but rubble and memories. And I'm glad to give it up because down here, I have everything I need. Down here, I'm safe. Secure.

BANG! BANG!

My body goes rigid, freezing up like a heart attack. They're at the hatch. Christ, they've found the hatch.

I scramble up the ladder, press my ear against the cold steel. Muffled movements. Harsh whispers. Someone barking orders.

BANG

I jerk back, ears ringing. No doubt about it. The bastards found me.

Shit. Shit. Shit.

The shouting intensifies. Movement becomes frenzied. I slink to the back of my bunker, fingers wrapping around my rifle. The magazine slides home with a satisfying click.

Calm down, I tell myself. *You're panicking over nothing. Even if they've found you, they can't get in. Not through three inches of reinforced steel. Not with bolt cutters, not with a welding torch. This bunker was built to withstand a nuclear—*

KERCHUNK

My heart punches my ribs. Metal scrapes against metal. Something's being attached to the wheel of my hatch. A carabiner? A hook?

"You sons of bitches," I snarl, teeth bared in the darkness.

An engine roars to life above. Something big. Industrial. Tires scream against dirt and my pulse races in time with the sound.

I raise my rifle, arms shaking, aiming at the bunker entrance. The hatch groans. It shudders. For a moment, I think it might hold.

Then it vanishes. Snaps clean off. Ripped away like it was made of paper.

Sunlight explodes into the bunker. I throw up an arm, squinting against the assault of brightness. My lungs burn as I suck in a mouthful of fallout.

"I'm armed!" I roar between hacking coughs. "I'll blow the heads off any—gack—asshole that wants to try me!"

Silence stretches for a beat. Two.

"Mr. Falton." A voice blares through a megaphone. "You're under arrest. Come out with your hands up."

I bark out a laugh. "Like hell I am! You think you're going to fool me with that crock?"

My finger squeezes the trigger. The rifle bucks against my shoulder. A warning shot screams through the open hatch.

Wings flutter frantically. Birds scatter from nearby trees, silhouettes dark against the too-bright sky.

"Come any closer," I shout, "and the next bullet's going in your head!"

"Understood."

Something small and cylindrical drops through the hatch. It bounces once, twice, rolls to a stop at my feet. My eyes widen. My hand reaches for my gas mask.

Too late.

It's already hissing, spewing smoke into my sanctuary.

The world begins to blur.

God help me, the world begins to ...

I blink awake, disoriented. My bunker is gone. Abducted. Fuck—I've been abducted by the raiders.

The room swimming into focus is small, claustrophobic. Beige wallpaper peels at the corners, its pattern a dizzying swirl that makes my head spin. A naked bulb flickers overhead, casting dancing shadows across a scarred wooden table. Across from me sits a man in a dark suit.

"Where am I?" The words scrape out of my dry throat.

"You're at the precinct." His voice is calm, measured. Too calm. "I'm Detective Vaneer. I'd like to ask you some questions."

I blink again, trying to clear the fog from my mind. The raider is clean-shaven, his hair slicked back like some noir film reject. He's twirling a wooden stick in a paper cup, three empty coffee creamers arranged in a perfect triangle before him. Next to us, a window with its blinds conspicuously shut.

This is a set. A stage. Elaborate, I'll give them that, but not enough to fool me.

"Questions?" I say, laughing. "You've gotta be kidding."

"Not at all." He lifts the cup, takes a theatrical sip. Is it even real coffee? Or just another prop in this sick pantomime? "What were you doing in the bunker?"

"Surviving," I spit back. "Same as you out here, just with a little more class."

"I see." He leans back, fingers drumming a beat on the table. His eyes bore into me, dissecting, analyzing. Good luck with that, pal. "Why'd you do it?" he asks.

I clamp my mouth shut. This is Manipulation 101. He's trying to coax me into a false sense of security, trying to loosen my tongue so I'll let slip the location of my other supply caches. It's so transparent it's almost insulting.

"What's the matter?" the raider asks, tilting his head like a curious predator. "Stage fright? Or was a week not enough time to dream up an alibi?"

I have to hand it to him—the guy's good. Probably an actual cop before the world went to tits up. It would explain the attention to detail in this little charade. It's almost sad how far he's fallen. Then again, most cops were always just thugs with a badge.

"Well?" he presses.

"I don't know what you're talking about," I say.

"The bombs," he snaps, his mask slipping. "You don't know about the bombs? Come on."

My eye twitches. What's his game here? Bombard me with so many conflicting narratives that I start doubting my own sanity? "Of course I know about the bombs," I spit. "I've known about them for a long time."

"How long?"

"Long enough to build a bunker and survive the blast," I say, unable to keep a hint of pride from my voice. "That answer your question?"

"Years, then."

"That's right. Years." I lean forward, a smirk tugging at my lips. "You had no idea, did you?"

His eyes narrow to slits. "Was I supposed to?"

"Anyone with half a brain could have seen it coming. The signs were everywhere."

"Just not your family," he says, voice soft but cutting.

My jaw clenches so hard I hear teeth crack. "What gives you the right to talk about my family?"

"Where are they?"

I curse under my breath. This operation is more sophisticated than I thought. They must have found my photo albums, read my journal entries. Now they're using my loved ones against me, trying to break me, all to rob me of a few crates of buried rations.

He snaps his fingers, the sound like a gunshot in the small room. "Hey—I asked you a question. Where's your family?"

"Dead," I growl. "They died in the blast, you insensitive prick."

The raider leans over the prop table, taps his finger on the surface. "Get specific. What blast?"

Rage boils inside me. I want to lunge across the table, wrap my hands around the asshole's throat and squeeze until his face turns blue. My family's earned their peace. Their rest. For him to desecrate their memory like this, to use it as a tool to extract information ... it's beyond cruel. It's evil.

"What blast?" he repeats, rising slowly from his chair.

I say nothing. I show nothing. I am a stone, weathering this storm of psychological warfare.

He stalks toward me, looming over me, his face inches from mine. "What. Blast?"

He can keep this up all he wants. I'm not some weak-minded civilian plucked from the burning streets. I'm smarter. More prepared. I've spent years steeling myself against this exact type of manipulation. Psychopaths like him are all the same—they feed on reaction, on engagement. If I stay quiet, stay neutral, he'll get bored and move on.

That's what I'm counting on. If I could survive the end of the world, then I can survive some third-rate cosplayer playing detective, too. All I have to do is—

He lunges forward, fists bunching in my shirt. His forehead presses against mine, a furnace of barely contained fury. His eyes ... God, his eyes are bleeding fire.

"Last chance," he growls, each word a tremor of rage. "What. Blast?"

I meet his gaze, ice to his fire. My voice drips with glacial indifference. "You think I was standing around counting how many bombs fell? How should I know which blast atomized my family? Listen to yourself for God's sake."

He recoils as if slapped, running a hand over his face. "Christ almighty," he mutters, "you really believe it, don't you?"

I say nothing. Sooner than later he'll tire himself out, and if I'm lucky he'll let me go. They won't resort to cannibalism, not yet. Too early in the game for that brand of desperation.

He stalks to the window, a caged animal in a suit. "You saw it when we cracked open your little doomsday box, didn't you?" His words lash out, probing for weakness. "The trees. The birds. How many nukes does it take to level a farm but leave the local wildlife untouched, huh? Those must've been some damn resilient bird nests. Best twigs nature can buy."

I squeeze my eyes shut, willing away the memory. The birds were a hallucination, nothing more. My mind's feeble attempt to shield me from the stark, radioactive reality. It's painfully obvious. What else could they have been?

The raider—no, the liar—studies me, head cocked. A predator assessing its prey. He clicks his tongue, a sound of false sympathy. "Okay, okay. You need something more concrete. How about this?"

There's a soft whir as he tugs the blinds' cord.

Sunshine floods the room. It's blinding, searing, impossible.

"How about some fresh air?" he asks, voice dripping with mock concern.

The window screeches open, rust flaking away like dead skin. A cacophony assaults my ears—a symphony of lies. Car horns blare. Pedestrians shout. Music swells, punctuated by the cheers and applause of a phantom crowd.

It's all fake. A soundtrack of deception piped in to break my resolve.

My eyes adjust, and I squint into the technicolor glow of a movie playing against the window. It's a film reel, it has to be. A moving snapshot of the old world—towering buildings, bustling crowds, vehicles belching toxins into the air. They've hidden a projector somewhere. Clever, but not clever enough.

"It took me a week to find your bunker," the liar says, circling back to his chair. He pulls a laptop from a bag, a fresh prop for this elaborate farce. "Had to dig through your digital footprint. Receipts. Bunker installation records. You covered your tracks pretty well, but not well enough."

Their operation is more sophisticated than I'd imagined. Clearly I wasn't alone in preparing for doomsday. These raiders, they've been pooling resources, crafting intricate mind games to break the survivors. To pillage our supplies alongside our sanity. Sons of bitches.

The liar clears his throat, a conductor about to lead his orchestra of deceit. "Let me paint you a picture, Mr. Falton. You tumbled down an online rabbit hole, the kind that preys on desperate people. You bought into the idea of an impending apocalypse. Why? Because it gave your life purpose. Secret knowledge. It transformed you from a nobody into a prophet, practically overnight."

He reaches for a folder, thumbing through pages of fabricated evidence. "Your specific flavor of crazy centered on psychic vampires. You built this elaborate fantasy where they'd infiltrated every level of society. According to your social media rant on December 12th, 2024, you claimed world leaders were in on it. You wrote—and I quote—'global nuclear holocaust is our only recourse to stop the psychic vampire threat.'" The folder slams shut like a gunshot. "You prophesied this so-called holocaust would begin on New Year's Day, 2025. Ring any bells?"

My body betrays me, trembling despite my best efforts. His words are poison, seeping into my mind, corroding my certainty. But I know the truth. I know.

"You're one of them," I spit, the words tasting of fear and defiance. "A psychic vampire. Bitter too, I bet, now that your food supply's been cut in half. Humanity's circling the drain, and you're starving– all of your kind are starving. Good riddance."

The liar's eyes harden as he opens his laptop. His fingers dance across the keyboard, and he turns the screen to face me.

It's my house. Or what's left of it. Just a wasteland of splintered wood and smoldering ash.

"See this?" His finger hovers over a corner of the image. There's something there– a mess of colors. Mostly red. A bit of pink. Whatever it is, it's in pieces, scattered across the wreckage of my home. "That's your daughter," he says, voice flat.

My jaw clenches so hard I taste blood. A black hole opens in my gut, bottomless and cold. Is this another lie? It has to be. Even if it isn't, I always knew there would be horror in the aftermath of nuclear war. Always. I also knew that horror would be a necessary price to pay to eliminate the vampire threat.

He taps the screen again, zooming in. This time, I can't stop the bile from rising. "We think this might be a piece of your wife's skull," he says, clinical and detached. "Could be your son's, though. Hard to tell when the bodies are in so many pieces."

"Enough," I rasp, my voice a stranger's. "I don't ... I can't ... "

"Oh, but we're just getting to the good part." He switches to a new image – the trees behind my house. Zooms in on a bush. There's something there, large and black.

My insides twist into knots.

"Recognize that speaker? The one you set up to blast those air raid sirens?"

This isn't happening. It can't be real. It's all an illusion, a sophisticated psy-op designed by psychic vampires to crack open my mind and feast on my pain. Of course. It's too elaborate for mere humans. No question about it anymore – he's one of them. A psychic vampire.

The vampire leans back, trembling with barely contained fury. He hates that I know what he is—hates that I'm making it so hard for him to feed because my mind isn't so easily led astray. Not like the rest of the bleating masses.

"Let me spell it out for you," he snarls, "since reality seems to be a foreign concept."

I say nothing. I'm smarter than that.

I'm smarter than him.

"You rigged your house with enough explosives to sink a warship," he tells me. "I'm talking about bombs planted everywhere from the crawlspace to the inside of your walls. You set the house to blow the day the nukes were supposed to fly. Why? Simple. You didn't want anybody finding your bunker – just in case the ICBMs missed your rural slice of buttfucker nowhere. If your family survived, they might lead others to your precious bunker. Raiders, psychic vampires, whoever. You weren't just scared of the world ending – you were terrified your family would drag you down with it."

A vein pulses in my temple. I force myself to breathe, to shore up my psychic defenses. This is textbook gaslighting. Psychic vampires always try to wear down their prey before feeding. But I won't break. Not after everything I've sacrificed.

He pulls out a leather-bound book with a cross hanging from the tail. My journal. "Found this in your bunker, Mr. Falton. Almost sounds like you actually miss them."

"Of course I miss them!" The words explode from me before I can stop them. Damn it. Another crack in my armor.

He smirks, knowing he's drawn blood. "I believe you," he says. "Those sirens were for them, weren't they? Your last-ditch effort to prove you were right. If they'd only followed you into the bunker, you could've been one big happy, paranoid family. But they refused your test of faith. So you killed them."

"Fuck you!" I roar, slamming my fist on the table. "You're nothing but a parasitic liar! You think I can't feel you probing my mind, looking for weak spots? You think I can't recognize a psychic attack when I feel it?" I try to spit in his face, but it barely makes it halfway across the table.

He shakes his head, almost sad. "I pity you, Mr. Falton. One day, you'll realize this fantasy world you've built doesn't exist. That you're wrong. I don't know if it's going to happen when I leave this room, or when you stand trial, or when the prisoner door closes in your face. Maybe it'll happen a decade from now when you wake up screaming. I don't know. All I know is that when that moment comes, whatever's left of your mind is going to shatter. You're going to realize the mistake you made. And after that? You'll wish the world really had ended."

The vampire moves to leave, then pauses at the door. "You know, I looked into your conspiracies. They're compelling, I'll give you that. All those authoritative sources, those intricate connections. That stuff about psychic vampires and the moon landing? For a moment, I almost bought it."

His brow furrows. "But then the cracks appeared. I realized it was all smoke and mirrors. A predatory illusion designed to hook people like you. Just enough science, just enough history to lower your guard. Then it reels you in, feeding you delusions of grandeur and paranoia disguised as purpose. It's always the same – aliens, monsters, grand conspiracies. Never anything mundane. It's like they're designed to entertain above all else."

With a final shrug, he's gone. I'm alone in this elaborate set, marveling at the projected cityscape, the crisp sounds of a world that no longer exists. It's impressive, really. The lengths they'll go to deceive me. But I'm not fooled.

I know the nukes fell. I know we beat back the psychic vampires and I know human civilization is in ashes. I also know that it's for the best. My family, if they were still alive, would be proud of me for doing what was right. They'd be proud of me for resisting a point-blank psychic assault. For staying strong.

I know that.

I do.

The only thing I can't quite figure out are the blinds. There's something about the way they dance up and down in front of the projection of the open window, the way I can feel the coolness of a breeze that's hard to explain. A fan ... maybe?

I frown.

Part of me wants to get up and check, just to make sure they're fake, but then I think how pointless it'd be. After all, I already know the truth.

CACKLE HILL

The ascent up the hill was a nightmare. Bramble blotted out the moon, smothering us in perfect darkness. We navigated by touch alone, Landon leading the charge with Wendy and me bringing up the rear. Thorns clawed at us from all sides. Our youth was our saving grace; had we been any older than thirteen, we'd have never squeezed through that labyrinth of branches. We couldn't even crawl. Instead, we slithered through the dirt on our bellies, like snakes beneath a barbed-wire sky.

"How much further, man?" I called out to Landon, my voice muffled by the underbrush.

"Not far!" he shouted back, enthusiastic.

Wendy groaned somewhere just ahead of me. "You said that twenty minutes ago, Landon."

"It'll be worth it," he promised. "We'll be talking about this night for the rest of our lives. I mean, breaking into the house of a dead cannibal – what's more festive than that?

"Gee," Wendy said, and I could almost hear her roll her eyes. "I don't know. Maybe dressing up? Going to a Halloween party? You know, the same crap the rest of our school is getting up to right now."

Landon's laughter echoed through the thicket. "Dressing up? C'mon, Wend. We're fourteen, not babies."

"Could've fooled me," she shot back.

"Not like it's tough to fool you, though, is it?"

I kept my mouth shut, having learned long ago that taking sides in their arguments was a losing game. Better to let them exhaust themselves. But twenty minutes later, they were still at it, trading snark like an old married couple. It was almost impressive.

Just when I thought it would never end, Landon's sharp intake of breath cut through the night. There was a frantic scramble of limbs, a snap of twigs. Branches crunched somewhere ahead, followed by his excited exclamation: "Holy shit, guys! Check it out!"

"What is it?" I asked, squinting uselessly into the gloom. "You make it to the house?"

"See for yourself," he called back. "And hurry! I'm dying of old age up here!"

Wendy and I pressed on, and soon the overgrowth began to thin. Slivers of moonlight pierced through the canopy. Before I knew it, I was dragging myself out of the maze of needles and stumbling to my feet.

My breath caught in my chest.

There it stood, looming before us – the house. It sat like a teetering tribute to the dead, perched atop Cackle Hill like a crown of rotting lumber. Its walls sagged inward, weary and ancient. Broken windows peppered its face, their jagged glass gleaming like hungry teeth in the moonlight.

"Whoa," Wendy gasped, spinning around on the weedy hilltop. "You can see just about the entire town from up here!"

She wasn't wrong. I gazed down at the sprawling vista below, where an army of trick-or-treaters marched along the streets. From this height, they looked more like pastel smudges than costumed kids. It struck me then how distant their world seemed from ours – as if we'd crossed some invisible boundary into a whole other realm.

"Forget the stupid trick-or-treaters," Landon said, fishing a flashlight from his jacket. "We're here to catch a ghost, remember? Stay focused."

Wendy cocked her head, skepticism etched on her features. "We're here because you won the coin toss. Besides, you know ghosts aren't real, right?"

Landon flicked on his flashlight. "Guess we'll find out, won't we?"

He strode up to the house's battered doorstep, the drooping porch groaning beneath his weight. His thick fingers wrapped around the knob. Twisted. A stubborn rattle echoed, but the door didn't budge.

I couldn't help but laugh. "You're kidding, dude. After all this, it's locked?"

He gave the knob another futile twist before frowning and stalking over to one of the broken windows. Peering inside, he called out theatrically, "Hulllllloooo, Mr. Cackle? Open up. Your food's waiting."

"You're such an ass," Wendy hissed. "You know Cackle really did eat like a dozen different kids, right? They probably died horrible deaths."

"Duh," Landon said, chuckling. "That's the joke, Wend. Congrats on figuring it out."

"Maybe we can get in through the window," I suggested, trying to diffuse the tension.

Wendy shook her head. "And get cut up on all that glass? No thanks."

"We'll just cover the glass with our jackets," Landon began. "It's what people do in–"

A low groan filled the night, stealing our attention. We turned to see the front door swing open with a rusty whine, as though pushed by an unseen hand.

"Still don't believe in ghosts?" Landon asked, shooting Wendy a smug look.

It took her a second to find her voice. "Of course not," she sputtered. "You don't think I know when you're screwing with me? It's obvious the door was never locked. Try harder, Landon."

"Sure, Wend," Landon said, poking his head inside the doorway. "Definitely opened that door with my telekinesis."

"See any dead cannibals?" I asked with a nervous smile.

He shook his head. "Nope. Coast is clear."

The three of us ventured inside, Landon leading the way. Cobwebs draped every inch of the ceiling like grotesque chandeliers. The floor was littered with old beer bottles and tattered magazines – remnants, I guessed, from a time before the hill's bramble had grown too thick to traverse. A narrow, threadbare carpet covered the rotting floorboards, beckoning us deeper into the decrepit mansion.

"What a dump," Wendy muttered, recoiling as a rat scurried past us into a baseboard.

"What a *haunted* dump," Landon corrected, his voice tinged with excitement.

We turned into a wide doorway, entering what must have been the dining room. A long, rectangular table dominated the center, surrounded by high-backed chairs. Each step was punctuated by the crunch of broken ceramic – old plates and cups that'd been scattered across the floor. Dust coated everything. It hung in the air like a spectral mist as we made our way to the far end of the room.

We paused beside a shelf laden with black-and-white photographs. Wendy lifted one of the frames, her voice hardly a whisper. "This is him. This is Erich Cackle."

I leaned in, squinting at the photo, and felt ice skitter down my spine. Something about the photo made my skin crawl. Maybe it was the skeletal gauntness of Cackle's cheeks, or the waxlike quality of his skin. Perhaps it was the emptiness in his eyes. Or maybe it was the girls flanking him, his long arms draped over their shoulders like gnarled branches. They seemed so scared. So quietly terrified to be standing next to him, like they wanted to cry out for help but couldn't.

"Those are probably girls he ate," I croaked, my stomach turning at the thought.

Wendy shook her head, her voice heavy. "Poor kids."

"Kids?" Landon scoffed from behind us. "Those girls look about our age. Matter of fact, the one on the right is kinda cute. I know I'd–"

Wendy's elbow found Landon's ribs before he could finish his sentence. "Gross," she seethed. "That's just about the most insensitive – LANDON!"

I spun around to find Landon nonchalantly flipping a carving knife in his hand. "What?" he asked, feigning innocence.

"Where did you find that?" Wendy demanded, advancing on him.

"Where else?" he said, backpedaling. "The table. But look – the knife's got these dark stains on it. I'm thinking they might be blood." He ran a finger over the blade, rusted beyond recognition and probably duller than a spoon. "Could be one of the knives Cackle used to carve kids up before he ate 'em," he added with disturbing enthusiasm.

Wendy snatched it from him. "Could be a decent way to get tetanus, idiot."

He laughed. "Relax, Wend. I'm pretty sure we're vaccinated against that."

But Wendy was livid, her freckled cheeks flushed with anger. "You're being so disrespectful I can't even right now. People died here, Landon. Real people."

Landon stuffed his hands in his pockets, adopting a mock-solemn expression. "Sure, but they're long gone. I mean, it's been ages, hasn't it? Even their bones have probably decomposed by now. What is this place anyway, like a hundred years old?"

"A hundred and thirty," I offered, recalling a snippet from the town newspaper. "And you're right. Cackle didn't do much to preserve the remains he buried on the hill. Most were never found."

Wendy shot me a reproachful look. "Ian."

"What?" I said, taken aback.

"Don't encourage him."

"I wasn't!" I protested, hands raised defensively. "The house is old, Wendy!"

Landon planted his hands on his hips, fixing me with a stern look. "Yeah, Ian. Very irresponsible of you to have fun with your friends. You oughta know better at your age."

"Oh, please," Wendy groaned. "Grow up, Landon."

"You grow up," he countered.

Wendy stuck out her tongue. "I'll probably end up with gray hair next year thanks to putting up with your crap."

"Yeah," Landon chuckled. "That's called karma, Wend. And you'd deserve it."

"Oh, I'm gonna kill you for that–"

BANG.

My head snapped sideways. The sound had come from the hallway to our right, but I couldn't see anything down there. Just drifting dust and shadows.

"– like to see you try."

"Watch me."

"Hey!" I interjected loudly. "Did you guys hear that?"

They paused, blinking at me. "Hear what?" Wendy asked.

"That loud bang," I replied. "Just now."

Landon's eyes lit up. He hurried over, his round face bright with excitement. "Weird sounds are textbook ghost stuff. Where'd you hear it?"

"From down the hall," I muttered, taking Landon's flashlight. I swept it across the dark corridor, but there was no sign of whatever made the sound. The hallway was empty save for a broken vase atop a small table and a pair of double-wide doors at the far end.

"It's probably just rats," Wendy suggested. "I've already seen half a dozen running around. Wouldn't be surprised if they heard us arguing and got spooked, knocked over that vase."

I bit my lip. "No ... this didn't sound like a vase breaking. It was loud – like a firecracker, or a gunshot. You guys really didn't hear anything?"

Landon shook his head. "Nope."

I swallowed hard, the hair on the back of my neck standing on end. Suddenly, I felt deeply uneasy. It reminded me of how my dad described being stalked by a mountain lion while hunting – that prickling sensation of unseen eyes watching from somewhere in the woods.

"Okay," Wendy said, clapping her hands together, her voice tinged with exasperation. "This place is the worst, and it's lowkey freezing. I'm sick of picking spiders out of my hair, and I'm pretty sure we're one aggravated rodent away from catching the plague. Why don't we call it here?"

Landon groaned, his shoulders slumping. "Come on, Wend! It took an hour just getting up here, and you already want to leave?"

Wendy had a point, though. The temperature *had* plummeted in the last few minutes, and even our breath was fogging in front of our faces now.

"I'm with her," I said, pulling my jacket tighter around me. "Let's head out."

"One more room?" Landon pleaded, his eyes wide with a childlike desperation. "Please, guys? It'll be like five minutes."

Wendy and I exchanged tired looks. "Your call," she told me, her voice resigned.

I looked back at Landon, my best friend since first grade, and felt a tug on my heartstrings. He'd been so excited to spend Halloween up here. It was all he'd talked about for a week straight.

"Fine," I grumbled. "Five minutes."

Landon punched the air in triumph. He plucked the flashlight from me and practically danced down the hall, toward the double-wide doors at the far end.

"Where are you going?" I called after him.

"You said you heard a bang from down here, didn't you? Well, let's investigate." He gripped the handles of the double-wide door, then pulled them open with a performative flourish.

I doubled over, retching. A stench wafted out of the room, more awful than anything I'd ever encountered. It was rancid, grotesque – like a noxious blend of manure and putrid meat. I pinched my nose, fighting the urge to vomit.

"You okay?" Wendy asked, concern written on her face.

"That smell ..." I choked out. "It's *terrible*."

Landon blinked, a smile tugging at the edge of his lips. It was as if he was trying to figure out if I was screwing with them – if between this and the bang, I was attempting to convince Wendy that ghosts were real.

"Oh yeah," he muttered, clearly playing it up. "So terrible. Surprised you don't smell it too, Wend."

"I'm not joking," I said seriously, glaring into the room with watery-eyed revulsion. "I really do smell something. You're telling me you can't? It's like somebody bottled up a thousand of your farts and left them out in the sun, Landon."

"Why is it always my farts?" Landon said with mock indignation. "Is this a fat thing? It's a fat thing, isn't it?"

Wendy jabbed a finger at him. "Nope, it's a *you-stink* thing."

"This is fat shaming," Landon announced.

She shook her head. "Nuh uh. Just Landon shaming."

"Grow up, Wend," he said, folding his arms haughtily. "Honestly. You're going to give me gray hair."

"Save it, guys," I muttered, sweeping past them into the bedroom. It wasn't half the mess I expected. Compared to the rest of the house, it looked almost tidy. There weren't any old beer bottles here. No torn-up magazines. Just a big bed in the very center covered by moth-eaten curtains, their surface speckled with black spots of mold.

As I stepped further into the room, the stench grew stronger, more nauseating. Something about this place felt wrong – more wrong than anywhere else in the house. And as my eyes adjusted to the gloom, I couldn't shake the feeling that we weren't alone.

"Look for anything cool," Landon instructed as he marched toward the bedside closet. "Priority is any kind of cannibal paraphernalia, but I'll settle for a nice belt buckle too. Anything to show off at school, really."

Wendy rolled her eyes, wandering toward a nearby bookcase. She examined the leather spines with forced interest, stifling a yawn. That left the far corner for me. There wasn't much there but a dusty old mirror covered in cobwebs, but it beat staring at the wall.

I drifted over, the floorboards groaning loudly beneath my feet. Something strange happened as I approached – the closer I got to the mirror, the colder the air became.

"Hey!" Landon shouted from the bedside closet. "Where do you guys think Cackle kept all his cannibal shit? It's just a bunch of ugly shirts in here."

"Cannibal shit?" Wendy echoed, exasperated. "What do you even mean by that?"

Landon's head appeared between the closet doors. "You know, like knives or skulls or something. Souvenirs."

Wendy made a face. "Jesus Christ, Landon."

"What?"

"Nothing. It's just … you're disgusting."

"Oh, I'm disgusting?"

"Uh huh. Ian's not asking for the bones of dead people, is he?"

"Ian's too lost in his own eyes to care about anybody else," Landon said cheekily. "Isn't that right, buddy? You must really like your own reflection, huh?"

"It's not my reflection," I murmured, running my hands across the mirror in morbid fascination. "Come check this out. This mirror is freezing – like way colder than anything else in the room."

Landon practically tripped over his feet rushing over, his flashlight bobbing up and down. "That means it's haunted, dude," he said with wide-eyed reverence. "Nice find."

Wendy strolled over behind him. "I don't know about 'haunted', but it is a pretty mirror. A bit dreary, though, and probably too big for a souvenir. Sorry, Ian. Guess you'll have to settle for one of Landon's skulls."

Landon mumbled something inaudible, not paying attention. He was staring at the floor, pressing his foot down on one of the noisy floorboards around the mirror.

Creak. Creak. Creak. Creak.

"Do you mind?" Wendy snapped, glaring at him. "That's so annoying, dude."

But Landon's usual retort was nowhere to be found. Instead, his expression brimmed with curiosity. "There's something under here," he said. "It's hollow. See?" He gave the floorboard a couple kicks and from somewhere below came a faint echo.

"Yeah, it's called a basement," Wendy said, unimpressed.

"Cackle's house didn't have a basement," I muttered, recalling an old history lesson from sixth grade. "They canvassed the place pretty good in the years since his death, and the house was built on bedrock ... There shouldn't be any rooms below us."

"Well, there is," Landon said, his eyes gleaming. "Which means Cackle had a secret lair no one knew about – until tonight." He lifted his sneaker and smashed it down on the loose floorboard. It bent. He brought his foot up to try again, but Wendy grabbed his arm.

"Don't!" she snapped. "You're gonna cut up your whole ankle like that. Go find a hammer or something. God."

Landon took a breath, nodding to himself. 'Yeah, good call. I'll be right back."

Without another word, he brushed past us and out of the room, flashlight bobbing merrily. His footsteps whimpered along the twisting hallway before fading entirely. Wendy and I stood alone in the dark.

"We should've gone with him," she murmured. I could just barely make out her silhouette beside me, faintly lit-up by shafts of moonlight filtered through the cracks in the boarded up window. "He's probably gonna break a leg tripping over a beer bottle or something."

I chuckled. "He'll be fine. Besides, you know how Landon gets. Once he gets an idea in his head, there's no talking him out of it. Stubborn as hell."

She sighed, a smile in her voice. "True."

"So what's the deal with you two?" I asked, seizing the moment.

"What do you mean?" she said, her tone suddenly guarded.

"Just that it's obvious you're practically in love with one another, so why all the arguing?"

Even in the dark, I could see Wendy bristle, crossing her arms defensively. "Uh, what? I don't love Landon, Sherlock. We've just been friends for so long I've got no choice but to hang out with him. It's kinda sad, really."

I laughed. "Yeah. Such a tragedy, Wend."

"I'm serious."

"Okay. I definitely believe you."

"Could be worse," she chided, tucking a strand of hair behind her ear. "I could be in love with that broken old mirror like you are."

I ran my finger across the mirror's surface for what must have been the hundredth time. "It's just strange that it's so cold … I mean, it feels like it just came out of the freezer. Don't you think that's weird?"

She shrugged. "No weirder than anything else in this house."

"Yeah," I muttered. "Maybe."

We waited for what felt like forever. I started pacing back and forth, stealing nervous glances toward the mirror as I wondered what was taking Landon so long. Meanwhile, Wendy sat cross-legged on the floor, humming to herself and tracing lines on the dusty hardwood as if she didn't have a care in the world.

My thoughts started to race.

I couldn't shake the memory of that loud bang I'd heard earlier, or the feeling of being watched by something unseen in the house. Something malicious. Hungry. I'd dismissed it as superstition, but now that Landon was out there alone, I kept coming back to that thought. What if something really had been watching us? What if it had found Landon?

"That's it," I blurted out, my conscience tearing me up inside. "Let's go look for him. It's been long enough."

Wendy narrowed her eyes, as if trying to figure out if I was pulling her leg. "Why? It's only been like five minutes."

Five minutes? That didn't seem right. "Are you sure?" I asked.

"I've literally been timing him," she said, lifting her watch as proof. "See? Five minutes and fourteen seconds, and it's a pretty big house. Takes time to explore. Listen, Ian, are you feeling okay?"

I swallowed hard. "Why wouldn't I be feeling okay?"

She gave me a look. "Are ... are your parents fighting again?" she asked, her voice laced with concern.

"My parents?" I said, shaking my head in confusion. "No, they aren't fighting. What are you talking about, Wend?"

"I'm talking about the fact that you've just spent the last three minutes ignoring me," she replied, her brow furrowed. "You just stood there, muttering to yourself in front of that stupid mirror. Clearly, you're going through something."

What?

No. I was pacing back and forth, worrying about Landon because–

Footsteps.

Breathing.

Coming from outside the room, stalking down the hallway toward us. My pulse quickened. A wave of dread washed over me as I squinted into the gloom, wondering why I couldn't see Landon's flashlight glow as the footsteps neared.

"Landon?" I called out, my voice trembling.

No answer. A dark shape appeared at the entrance to the room. It was hunched forward. Panting. It stepped inward, moving through a shaft of moonlight, and I breathed a sigh of relief as I recognized our friend's silhouette. But Landon's dusty hair was more tussled than usual. His expression, more vacant.

"What took you?" Wendy demanded, getting to her feet. "Dick move leaving us in the dark like that."

Landon looked down, and something struck me as off about him. He shook his flashlight. The batteries rattled inside, and a bright beam spilled out, illuminating the room before quickly flickering and dying. "Out of batteries," he muttered. His voice was cold, distant. It was like all the joy had been squeezed out of him, like he'd been hollowed out.

Don't trust him, a voice whispered in my ear.

I spun around, heart smashing against my ribs. "Jesus!" I exclaimed, scrambling backward into Wendy.

She shoved me off. "What's gotten into you, Ian?"

"A voice," I sputtered. "I just heard this voice and–" My eyes swiveled around the room, searching for the source of the guttural, raspy whisper, but the culprit was nowhere to be found. It was just the three of us and that mirror.

The mirror.

I took a step toward it, feeling some haunting, inescapable magnetism. It was like an event horizon drawing me in. Swallowing me. The floorboards creaked as I moved across them and – there, something in the reflection. A strange, unnatural glint.

A face, staring at me through hollow eyes.

"Look!" I shouted, pointing madly. "There's someone in the mirror!"

Wendy bent down, examining the mirror with skepticism. She tapped the glass. "Um, yeah, Ian. That's called a reflection. It's you."

"It wasn't my damn reflection!" I snapped, terror scratching at my insides. "It was a man. He had these gaunt cheeks and waxy skin and—" My mind reeled, the image from the dining room photo flashing before my eyes. "It was Cackle! I just saw Cackle in the fucking mirror!"

Wendy's gaze darted between Landon and me, her eyes narrowing with dawning comprehension. "Ah. Okay. I get it. This is you two trying to scare me, isn't it? How long have you guys been practicing your little script—one week, two?"

A hand closed around my shoulder, fingers digging into my flesh with bruising force. Landon. "Yeah," he muttered, his voice an unfamiliar rumble. "We'll need to do better than this if we're gonna scare her, Ian. Let's show her the basement."

"Basement?" I stammered, weaseling away from him, my heart thundering.

He stepped onto the creaky floorboard, the wood groaning beneath his weight. A hammer dangled at his side. "Sure. You can even go down first."

I shook my head vehemently, backing away. "No way. I'm fine sitting right here, thanks. Go do your serial killer safari on your own—I'm officially no longer interested."

Landon's face contorted into a pout, his voice suddenly flat and lifeless. "I'm too fat, though. Look at me. I'll hurt myself if I drop down there."

"And I won't?" I said, exasperation mingling with fear.

"You're tall and skinny," he said, his eyes glinting strangely in the dim light. "You might even be able to touch the ground."

"I'm not that much taller than you, and it doesn't matter because I'm not doing it. Do it yourself or we're leaving."

Wendy sighed, her breath a ghostly whisper in the stillness. "Screw it. I'll do it."

I gaped at her, shock coursing through me. "What do you mean *you'll* do it?"

"I mean ..." Her cheeks flushed, visibly embarrassed. "I know Landon's wanted to do this trip since forever, and I've kinda been a drag all night so ... I'll drop down. It's whatever anyway. Not that big of a deal."

An uneven smile spread across Landon's face, transforming his features into something almost unrecognizable. "Gee, thanks, Wend."

"Don't mention it," she said, taking a shuddering breath. "But after this, we're even. Hand me that flashlight by the way – I brought spare batteries. Somebody had to." She plunked four AAs inside and turned it on, filling the room with a soft glow. "Just promise you'll help me back out of there, okay, you guys? I'm not good with cramped spaces. Claustrophobia. And if I start crying you can't tell anybody *ever*."

"Cross my heart," Landon said, his tongue slipping across his lips. "You really are the best, Wend."

She blushed.

"Wait," I said through clenched teeth, my resolve hardening. "I'll go."

Wendy lifted an eyebrow, surprised.

"I'm not claustrophobic or anything, so it's not gonna traumatize me," I said, hating the idea of Wendy suffering for my ridiculous fears. She was right anyway. There wasn't any such thing as ghosts, and here I was spinning myself into a panic over my own dim reflection in a mirror. "But after that we're leaving," I said flatly. "No more rooms. No more exploring. Back down the hill and out of this dump."

Landon nodded. "Of course."

He positioned himself above the bent floorboard, lifting the hammer high. It came down with a deafening crack that seemed to reverberate through the very foundations of the house. The rotting wood splintered easily under the assault. He brought it down again. And again. He continued to smash away, his expression morphing into something gleeful, almost ravenous, as though he were taking some bizarre pleasure in tearing up the floor.

"That should do it," Landon gasped after several minutes, his breath coming in ragged heaves. He sat back on his heels, gazing hungrily into the jagged hole he'd carved in the floor. Wendy brought the flashlight over, peering down into the pit with narrowed eyes.

"Doesn't look too deep," she said quietly. "Probably deep enough that we'll need some kind of rope to get down there, though. Sit tight. I'll have a look around, see if we can tie together some of Cackle's old shirts or something."

"Great," I said with a near-total lack of enthusiasm. Wendy's light bobbed away, leaving me in darkness with Landon. His presence felt off, like a familiar painting hung slightly askew. Was something wrong with him, or was my imagination just running wild in this stupid house?

"Sorry about earlier," I offered, hoping to ease the tension. Landon didn't respond, rocking slightly on his heels. The quiet was unsettling, broken only by Wendy's distant rustling.

"I don't know if this will work," her voice carried from across the room. "These shirts are falling apart in my hands."

"Landon?" I tried again, squinting uselessly in the dark. "You okay? Listen, if you're—"

My words cut short as Landon's hands connected with my chest, shoving me backward with unexpected force. I stumbled, teetering for a moment before falling into the black void behind me.

Pain exploded through my body as I hit the ground. My ankles twisted unnaturally, and I felt something give way with a sickening pop. A scream tore from my throat, raw and involuntary. Tears welled in my eyes as the reality of my injury set in.

"Ian!" Landon's voice came from above, suddenly full of concern. "Are you okay?"

I could only respond with another cry of pain. Wendy's light appeared, illuminating their faces peering down at me.

"What happened?" she demanded.

"He pushed me!" I managed to gasp out between waves of agony.

Wendy's tone turned venomous toward Landon. "Are you kidding me? What were you thinking?"

Landon's response was a flurry of denials. "No, it wasn't like that! We must have bumped into each other. Ian, I'm so sorry! We'll get you out, I promise!"

I groaned, the pain radiating from my ankles in sickening waves. Judging by Wendy and Landon's faces above, I'd fallen maybe seven or eight feet, but the awkward landing had done its damage. My ankles were a mess, clearly fractured. Walking was out of the question.

Gritting my teeth against the agony, I tried to drag myself forward across the dirt floor. There had to be another way out—a ladder, stairs, anything. But after a few feet, my body rebelled. White-hot pain lanced through me, and I collapsed.

"I can't move," I whimpered, hating how weak I sounded. "Guys, I'm really messed up down here."

Wendy's voice floated down, tinged with worry. "Just hang on, okay? There's got to be a ladder around somewhere. I'll find one."

The glow of her flashlight disappeared, leaving me in near-total darkness with Landon. The silence stretched.

"Thanks a bunch, asshole," I finally spat out. "Why'd you push me? What the hell is wrong with you?"

Landon kept silent, a looming silhouette against the dim light above. Something about his stillness sent a chill through me. It was as if he only spoke when Wendy was around, maintaining some façade of normalcy. Alone with me, he seemed ... empty.

A rhythmic sound cut through the silence. *Smack. Smack.* The sound of something hitting flesh. With a jolt, I realized it was Landon, slapping a claw hammer against his palm.

"If this is some sick joke, you can stop now," I said, my voice cracking. "You win, okay? You've scared the shit out of me. But I'm really hurt. This isn't funny anymore."

Smack. Smack. The sound continued, maddeningly steady.

"Why won't you talk to me?" I shrieked, panic rising in my throat. "You're supposed to be my best friend!"

BANG.

The sound echoed through the crawlspace, identical to the racket I'd heard upstairs. But this time, it was close. Too close.

"Hello?" I called out, my voice small and trembling.

A dull thud answered me, followed by a shuffle. The sound of movement. Of hands and knees dragging across dirt. And then ... breathing. Heavy, ragged breathing, drawing nearer in the dark.

"Who's there?" I stammered, cold sweat breaking out across my skin.

Silence was my only answer.

"Landon!" I yelled, desperation gripping me. "There's someone down here! Please!"

But Landon remained mute. I screamed for him, for Wendy, my voice growing hoarse. And then, bizarrely, Landon began to hum. The sound grew louder, drowning out my cries, all while that steady smack, smack of the hammer continued.

Panic overtook me. I tried to drag myself backward, but my hands met cold stone. I was trapped. The shuffling, the breathing—it was getting closer. My fingers scrabbled through the dirt, searching desperately for anything I could use as a weapon, but it was just dust and pebbles.

And then—my hand closed around something. Long, metal. A screwdriver.

"Ian! You okay?" Wendy's voice rang out like a lifeline.

"Get me out of here!" I screamed. "There's someone down here, and Landon's gone crazy!"

She blinded me in the glare of the flashlight. "That's odd," she said, her tone strangely disconnected. "What would someone be doing down there?"

My mind reeled. "How should I know? Just help me!"

"Hey," Wendy said, her voice now distant, dreamy. "Remember that face you saw in the mirror earlier? I think ... I think I see it too."

Tears streamed down my face as the sound of crawling grew louder. Closer. The air thickened, warm breath ghosting across my skin. Whatever it was, it was right on top of me, about to—

CRASH.

Wood exploded inches from my head, showering me with splinters. I scrambled sideways, my heart pounding as I registered the ladder's legs where my skull had just been. The old wood groaned under new weight.

Wendy descended first, her movements jerky and unnatural. Landon followed, landing with a dull thud that sent vibrations through the earthen floor. Relief washed over me, quickly replaced by a growing unease as I noticed their vacant expressions.

"Christ," I gasped, struggling to catch my breath. "You nearly bashed my brains in!"

Landon's gaze swept past me, his eyes glassy and unfocused. "So this is the secret lair," he murmured, his voice unnaturally flat. "See anyone else, Wend?"

Wendy's flashlight sliced through the gloom, revealing a labyrinth of wooden beams jutting from the dirt floor. Shadows danced between them, hinting at twisting corridors that seemed to defy logic. The light caught something white—animal bones scattered among the beams. My stomach knotted.

"Nope," Wendy replied, a note of disappointment in her voice. "Guess Ian was making it all up."

"Making it up?" I sputtered, gesturing at my mangled ankle. The bone jutted at an angle, stark against the darkening bruises. "Does this look fake to you?"

Wendy's eyes, usually warm with concern, now rolled dismissively. "Still going on about that? We heard you the first dozen times."

"Such a crybaby," Landon chimed in, his words dripping with disdain. "A little time in the dark, and he's blubbering like a toddler."

They laughed—a hollow, empty sound that echoed off the dirt walls. I stared at them, my mind spinning. These weren't my friends. They wore familiar faces, but everything else—their voices, their mannerisms, the cruel glint in their eyes—made my skin crawl.

Wendy drifted between the wooden beams, her movements fluid and dreamlike. "It's endless down here," she breathed, her voice tinged with an unsettling wonder. "Like a never-ending maze. Isn't it beautiful?"

"How much you wanna bet Cackle buried his victims here?" Landon's voice trembled with a sick excitement. "This is probably where he butchered those kids."

Wendy's eyes lit up with an inhuman gleam. "Ooh, yes. Should we go looking?"

"Don't—" I choked out, panic rising in my throat. "Please, don't leave me alone down here."

"Why not?" Wendy asked, her head tilting sharply.

My chest heaved as I fought for words. "Because ... because I'm terrified. There's something else down here with us, and I ... I just want to go home."

Wendy knelt beside me, her face inches from mine. Her eyes were bottomless pits, devoid of any warmth or recognition. Her lips moved like she was speaking, but no sound came out. Then she stood, turning to Landon who lurked at the edge of the darkness. His lips were pulled back in a rictus grin, but his eyes remained dead and vacant.

"Let's go," Wendy said, taking his hand. "I want to see where the children died."

They melted into the shadows, the light fading until the crawlspace turned pitch black. My skin prickled with goosebumps, my throat parched and tight. I wanted nothing more than to wake up from this nightmare, to be home with my friends—my real friends. But I knew somehow that Wendy and Landon were gone. Whatever wore their skin now was something else entirely. Something cold. Unfeeling.

Inhuman.

Time stretched endlessly. "Guys?" I called out, my voice weak. How vast was this underground anyway? "Please come back. I ... I just want to leave."

A sound.

My heart leapt into my throat, pain forgotten in a surge of adrenaline. It was that breathing again. Ragged. Heavy. And this time, it wasn't just close.

It was right next to my ear.

I lashed out blindly with the screwdriver, slashing through empty air. "Get away from me!" I snarled, fear and rage mingling in my voice.

The darkness made no reply.

"Wendy! Landon!" My voice cracked as I screamed into the nothingness. "Get back here – something's fucking breathing on me!"

A voice.

High-pitched. Childlike.

Run, it told me. *You must run.*

I scrambled backward until my spine pressed against a wooden beam. My heart raced, breath coming in short gasps. I felt like prey, cornered and helpless. Wendy and Landon had to have heard me by now. I'd been yelling myself hoarse ...

Another voice reached my ears.

Landon's.

Low and quiet, it seemed to come from just around the bend where they'd disappeared moments ago. He'd turned off his flashlight. Without it, I couldn't see a thing.

"Now that we've got him here," Landon whispered, "I think I'll bash his brains in. Tenderize them. Then, I'll give you the first bite."

"No," Wendy's voice echoed, seeming to come from everywhere at once. "I want to cut him open and see how much I can eat before he dies."

"Greedy," Landon hissed.

"I thought the whole point of bringing him here was so we could take our time?"

"It was, but I wanted to play with his brain, not stir up his guts." Landon grunted, his footsteps shifting on dirt. "Where did you put the saw?"

My body shook uncontrollably. Panic overrode the pain in my ankle as I lunged for the ladder. I grabbed the highest rung I could reach and hauled myself up with a strangled groan.

The wood splintered in my hands.

I crashed back to the dirt floor, my injured ankle twisting beneath me. A scream tore from my throat. In the faint light from above, I saw my bone pressed fully from my skin.

"Help!" I shrieked, praying somebody might be walking by Cackle Hill. Maybe they'd hear me. Maybe they'd come rushing up and burst in and—

No. It was pointless. It was far too late for anyone to be out walking, and even if they were, how could they possibly reach me?

It had taken us an hour to fight through the brambles. I didn't have an hour.

I wasn't sure I even had a minute.

Footsteps approached, accompanied by soft humming. A figure emerged from the gloom. Wendy.

"He's kinda cute when he squirms," she said, her voice dripping with a perverse glee.

Something glinted in her hand as she tapped it against her leg. A saw. Rusty and wickedly sharp.

"Wendy," I pleaded, my voice trembling. "This isn't you. Please, I'm hurt. I need help."

She didn't respond. Instead, she took a jerky step forward, her head snapping to the side, her body moving like a puppet on strings. Her tongue slithered across her lips, splitting them into a manic grin.

Landon appeared beside her, his face eerily illuminated by faint slivers of moonlight falling from the hole above. He slapped his hammer against his palm in a steady rhythm, humming along with Wendy. Their voices were discordant, detached. Empty.

Just like their eyes.

I knew then that my friends were gone – something had crawled beneath their skin and stolen their faces. Something ancient and hungry.

"Let's savor this, Ian," Wendy purred. "You and me. Let's try to enjoy this moment as much as we can, okay?"

"What ... what does that mean?" I whimpered.

"He'd like an example," Landon said. "Go on. Don't be shy, Wend."

Wendy's tongue lolled from her mouth, sweeping across her teeth. Then she lunged.

I screamed as the saw bit into my shoulder. She worked it back and forth, tearing through flesh and muscle. Blood soaked my jacket as agony consumed me.

"Stop!" I howled, thrashing beneath her.

But Wendy—or the thing that had been Wendy—only stared at her handiwork with manic delight. Madness danced in her eyes as she tried to saw my arm clean off.

My free hand, still clutching the screwdriver, moved on pure instinct. I swung with all my remaining strength. There was a wet, sickening pop as the tool sank into the side of Wendy's head.

Her mouth fell open in shock. The maniacal gleam in her eyes dimmed, then vanished. For a moment, she swayed above me. Then she collapsed forward with a soft groan. Tears poured from my eyes, mixing with the river of red pouring from her skull. I gagged, choking on the coppery tang as I tried to push her off. But Landon was faster. He scrambled on top of her lifeless body, driving the air from my lungs.

"Don't you ever fucking relax?" he snarled.

I twisted and writhed, but it was useless. Even if I hadn't been injured, the combined weight of their bodies was too much.

"Your friend wants me to tell you it'll be easier if you close your eyes," Landon said, raising the hammer. "But I disagree. I like seeing the lights go out."

The hammer crashed down on my forehead. Pain exploded through my skull as my vision blurred. Landon's outline became a haze of shadows. Smells, sounds, and the nauseating taste of blood all swirled together in a maelstrom of insanity.

Through the haze, I saw Landon lifting the hammer again, ready to finish me off. My hands scrabbled desperately through the dirt, searching for anything I could use to defend myself. My fingers closed around something small and sharp.

As Landon swung, I thrust my arm upward. I felt the object sink into flesh. Landon's eyes went wide with shock.

But gravity's a cruel mistress.

The hammer fell through the air, striking my face with a dull crunch.

Darkness swallowed me.

I awoke to blurry lights and muffled sounds. The room appeared sterile. White. My head throbbed with each heartbeat, and nausea roiled in my stomach. As my vision slowly focused, I became aware of a familiar presence nearby.

"Oh, baby!" My mother's voice, thick with worry and relief. "You're awake!"

I tried to speak, but my throat felt raw, as if I'd been screaming for hours. Maybe I had. The memories were there, just out of reach, like shadows flickering at the edge of my vision.

My father's face swam into view, his usual stoic expression cracked with concern. He muttered something about getting a nurse, and then he was gone, the swinging doors marking his exit.

As a nurse in light blue scrubs bustled in, checking monitors and scribbling notes, I struggled to piece together what had happened. Cackle Hill. The house. The mirror. Landon and Wendy. A crawlspace that seemed to go on forever.

"How do you feel?" the nurse asked, his voice oddly distant.

"Like I'm still dreaming," I mumbled. The words felt wrong in my mouth, as if they belonged to someone else.

He nodded, unsurprised. "You've suffered considerable physical trauma. You're lucky to be alive."

Lucky. The word echoed in my mind, bringing with it a surge of unease. There was something important I needed to remember, something just beyond my grasp.

A new figure entered the room – a woman in a dark jacket with eyes that seemed to look right through me. "Ian," she said, her voice gentle but firm. "I'm Detective Reeves. I need to ask you about Halloween night."

Halloween. The word sent a jolt through me, fragments of memory flashing behind my eyes. The old photographs. The creepy mirror. The voice –

"Landon and Wendy," I croaked. "Are they okay?"

The room went eerily still. My mother let out a choked sob, quickly stifled. The detective's face remained impassive, but something in her eyes shifted.

"Ian," she said carefully, "what's the last thing you remember?"

I closed my eyes, trying to focus. "We were in the house. There was a crawlspace. Something was down there with us. It – " I stopped, a chill running through me. "It wasn't human."

The detective exchanged a glance with my parents. "Shouts for help were heard up on Cackle Hill around midnight. We found you in that crawlspace, Ian. Along with Landon and Wendy. They … didn't make it."

The words hit me like a cement truck. Memories crashed over me – the sound of a saw cutting flesh, Wendy's face twisted into a grisly smile, Landon's hollow eyes as he raised the hammer.

"No," I whispered. "That's not possible. They were – it wasn't them. Something was inside of them."

Detective Reeves leaned in closer. "Ian, we found evidence that suggests … violent activity. Your fingerprints were on a screwdriver and a nail, both of which were used as weapons. Can you help explain that?"

I shook my head, my thoughts a whirlwind of confusion and horror. "I was defending myself. They were trying to kill me. But it wasn't really them, you have to understand. It was …" My voice drifted away, lost in what felt like some awful nightmare.

The detective's voice softened. "There's more, Ian. Both Landon and Wendy showed signs of … consumption. We found traces of them in your system."

The nausea intensified. I gagged, my body instinctively trying to curl in on itself – but something was wrong. I couldn't feel my legs. Or my arms.

Panic surged through me. I tried to sit up, to look at myself, but my body wouldn't respond. The heart rate monitor beside me began to beep rapidly, its frantic rhythm matching the terror pulsing through me.

"What's happening?" I gasped. "Why can't I move?" The detective took a deep breath, her face etched with concern. "Ian, I need you to try to stay calm. Whatever happened in that house, it ... it took parts of you."

With trembling hands, she pulled back the sheet covering me. I looked down, expecting to see my body, but instead...

Nothing.

Where my arms and legs should have been, there was only empty space. Burned flesh, cauterized. Stitched.

A scream built in my throat, raw and primal. The heart monitor shrieked, its steady beep replaced by a constant, high-pitched wail. My vision swam, darkness creeping in at the edges.

"No, no, no," I moaned, my eyes fixed on where my limbs should be. "This isn't real. It can't be real."

My mother rushed to my side, her tears falling onto what remained of my chest. My father turned away, his shoulders shaking with silent sobs. The nurse hurried to adjust something in my IV, likely a sedative to calm me down.

But how could I ever be calm again? I was a torso, a fragment of a person. Memories flooded back – the saw biting into my flesh, the sickening crack of bones, the burning pain as my limbs were torn away.

"Ian," the detective's voice cut through my panic. "If you know anything about who or what did this, you need to tell us. Other people could be in danger."

"You wouldn't believe me if I told you," I rasped, my gaze drawn to the mirror hanging on the far wall of the hospital room. For just a moment, I thought I saw a face there – gaunt and hungry, with eyes like teeth. Smiling an empty smile.

"Try me," the detective urged. "We've got a psychopath on the loose and we need a lead. Badly."

I looked at her then. I looked at my mother, my father – the nurse. All of them stared at me like they were waiting for me to point the finger at some satanic cult, or some escaped asylum patient. None of them wanted to believe the truth. None of them wanted to accept the fact that the man who fed on me was already dead.

He'd been dead for over a hundred years.

HIS CROOKED GOSPEL

12, October, 1991

The forest is nothing but a black smear. I can hardly see my handlebars, but that's fine because I've biked these woods my entire life – all twelve years of it. I could ride this trail with my eyes closed if I had to. And I pretty much do.

My bicycle bucks and jolts, shuddering as we rattle across the wooden bridge, and I shudder along with it. If I'm being honest, I feel a little uncomfortable.

Maybe even frightened.

There's something in the air tonight. A chill. It's the sort that crawls up your spine, that carries with it the deep-rooted knowledge that something about your surroundings is deeply wrong. It's that unsettling sensation of being watched.

Pursued.

I stand up and ride harder. My lungs burn with every push of the pedals but I can't shake the feeling that I need to get out of these woods and fast. Visions of serial killers claw at my mind, but I bury them with gritted teeth. As if I need more fuel for my stress. After all, I'm racing towards an altogether different horror – watching my sister die in slow motion.

She's not doing well. Are your mother and father home?

No, ma'am.

Can you get here to be with her? I'm afraid she doesn't have long.

Yes ma'am. No matter what.

Hope. My big sister Hope is dying in a hospital room while I'm out here jumping at shadows. Tears sting my eyes, shame burning hotter than my screaming muscles. She deserves better than a coward for a brother. Hope deserves someone who—

Thunder.

It cracks the sky, rumbling like the bass of infinity. A gale slams into me from behind. It's a battering ram of wind, ravishing the forest like a tempest. Branches snap like bones, ricocheting through the air as shrapnel. One slashes my cheek. Another nearly blinds me. I cry out, one hand flying up in defense, the other desperately trying to steer. This is madness. It's like a tornado crept up on me in the dead of night. It's like–

My eardrums bleed. The thunderclap grows louder, more deafening. It's as though the whole forest is shaking now, like the ground might split in two and swallow me whole. My bike protests beneath me, metal groaning as I fight to keep us upright.

A flash of white.

Then another.

I wonder if it's lightning, if the storm is right on top of me but then my world blinks away, turns into nothing but a ringing void. I'm hollering. Shouting. I can't see a thing, and then I feel my seat jerk out from under me as I lose control of my bike. My spine twists as my body careens through the air. I brace myself for a broken arm. A sprained ankle. I brace myself for the crunch of gravel meeting my face, but it never arrives.

Nothing does.

For a while, it's like I'm just floating there – like gravity's unable to finish what it started. I wonder if I've died and this is limbo, or purgatory, or the worst heaven anybody's ever imagined, but then my world reappears. It happens slow. It starts as a blurry smudge, but soon graduates into a shifting mess of pine trees.

"Help!" The word tears from my throat. "Somebody help!"

It's useless.

Nobody can hear me. I know that because I'm too far away. I'm watching in horror as the forest fades from view, watching as the trees turn into matchsticks below. My heart is racing like a Formula One engine, and I keep telling myself this isn't real because it can't be.

I'm floating.

Up and up, high into the coal-black sky. Stolen by a beam of light.

———

Present Day

That was a long time ago. Thirty years, give or take. A lot's changed since then, but the nightmare's remained the same. I have it almost every night. I dream about that flash-bang glow, that cosmic roar and that gut-churning dread of being eaten by the sky.

I dream about things that don't exist. Of things that have no right to.

My name is Isaiah Mitchell, and I'm a boogeyman. Only I don't hide in closets or haunt old houses. I'm the type that boomers rant about while watching the evening news, the type that tinfoil hats point to when things go wrong. I'm what you might call a Man in Black – and that means I'm well connected.

I know things. I'm privy to information that the President couldn't eavesdrop on if he tried, and so when I tell you that something big happened last night, I'm not talking about the stock market dipping a couple percentage points or the Saudis slashing oil prices. I'm talking about a disaster. A reality-warping cluster-fuck that's got me questioning my own sanity. One that'll have you questioning yours too.

Don't believe me?

Let's put it to the test.

I'm going to tell you a story. It's about me, but it's also about you – really, it's about everything in the universe, right down to the last atom.

It takes place across sprawling starscapes over endless eons. It's about an alien race, a renegade heretic and a fallen god unable to outrun its own, miserable humanity. It is the story of the greatest man to ever live, and how his search for meaning may soon cost us everything.

It goes like this.

---

12 October 1991

"Hello?" My voice echoes in the void as I scramble to my feet, rubbing my eyes.

The shadows are thick enough to taste. It's the forest all over again, only worse. I stumble forward, arms outstretched, desperate for any hint of my surroundings. My palms connect with a sur-face—cold, smooth. It almost feels like metal but it's too soft, too malleable.

Footsteps.

I shrink backwards, instinctively seeking somewhere to hide before remembering I don't even know where I am. My head is spinning. Pounding.

I'm wondering if I've been drugged, and I think that's proba-bly the only explanation. People don't float into the sky. They just don't. And that means I'm hallucinating, which means whoever kidnapped me knows a thing or two about stealing kids, which means they're a professional, which means they're a ... What's the term?

Serial killer.

Yeah, that's it.

A riot of sound slams into me. I clap my hands over my ears, teeth clenched in agony.

It's that same otherworldly bass from the forest, except now it's all around me. Throbbing. Inescapable. Another bellow joins the cacophony, higher-pitched and coming from the opposite direction. They pulse in a rhythm, almost like some counterfeit Morse code.

Whatever they are, they've got me surrounded.

"Please!" I beg them, voice breaking. "Just let me go. I swear I won't tell anybody!"

Static crackles. It's followed by a sharp squeal of microphone feedback, then the buzz of modulating frequency. "COMMUNICATION CALIBRATED," a robotic voice announces. "SUBJECT IDENTIFIED AS HOMOSAPIEN. TERRESTRIAL LOCATION: NEW MEXICO. LANGUAGE MODEL: ENGLISH."

There's a pause, it's long enough that I can hear my pulse rushing through my veins. *This is it*, I think. *I'm going to die.* Stuff like this doesn't happen to kids who live to tell the tale.

The voice speaks. "CAN YOU UNDERSTAND US, HOMOSAPIEN?"

"Um, yes ... " I croak.

"COMMUNICATION LINK ESTABLISHED. PROCEED WITH—"

"Sorry," I interject weakly. "Can you ... maybe turn on the lights?"

"THE LIGHTS?"

"Yes, please." The way I see it, the only thing worse than being murdered is being murdered in the dark.

An electronic hum fills the air. It's followed by a flicker of illumination. I blink as a warm glow floods the chamber, and my stomach coils into knots. I'm standing in a labyrinth of vats—massive glass containers filled with murky, bubbling fluid. Tubes snake out from them. They're converging on a console with a holographic display and an array of bizarre dials.

"IS THIS LEVEL OF LUMINANCE SUFFICIENT?" the voice inquires.

I whirl around, and my breath catches in my throat. In front of me is something that doesn't exist – *can't* exist. It's ten feet tall. Maybe more. It's got teeth like a shark, claws longer than my forearm, and a freaking *tail*.

"You're a monster ..." I stammer. "A dinosaur!"

"INCORRECT," another voice interjects. "WE ARE THE CHOSEN, LIFEFORMS FROM A DISTANT GALAXY THAT HAVE COME TO SAVE YOUR SPECIES."

This new voice belongs to another creature, identical to the first—all fangs, claws, and scaled skin. They converge in the center of the vat maze, their enormous eyes fixated on me. Each eye contains countless pupils, expanding like living ink blots.

"I've been abducted ..." I gasp, struggling to breathe. "Aliens are real ... and I've been abducted ..."

"CORRECT," the alien with deep gray scales confirms. Its counterpart, shimmering in soft teal, looms beside it. Gray's arm illuminates with a holographic display, which it studies intently. "READINGS INDICATE HEIGHTENED CORTISOL LEVELS AND INCREASED ADRENAL FLOW. SOURCE: FIGHT OR FLIGHT RESPONSE. DETERMINATION: IRRATIONAL. YOU HAVE NEITHER THE OPTION TO FIGHT OR FLEE, HUMAN. COMPLIANCE WITHOUT FURTHER PHYSICAL STRAIN WOULD BE OPTIMAL. DO YOU CONCUR?"

I gape at them, words failing me. What is this? The alien equivalent of my Miranda Rights?

"HUMAN?" Gray prompts, its multitude of pupils pulsing impatiently.

"Look, I know what this is about," I stammer, crossing my legs and inching away. "You're going to probe me. I've seen the movies, but I just want you to know that I'm a lousy specimen. There are way better people to probe. Michael Keaton, for instance. He was awesome in Batman and I bet you he's–"

"INCORRECT," Teal booms. "WE ARE COGNIZANT OF THE CONCEPT YOU REFERENCE, BUT DO NOT ENGAGE IN SUCH PRIMITIVE BEHAVIOR. WE SEEK MERELY TO HARVEST YOUR DNA." Its claw taps one of the bubbling vats. The murky fluid clears. A man floats within, his lower half dissolved, intestines drifting freely in the viscous liquid.

"Jesus Christ!" I choke out.

"UNLIKELY," Teal rumbles. "THIS SPECIMEN WAS PROCURED MERE DAYS AGO, 3,213 KILOMETERS WEST OF NAZARETH."

"I mean you're ... you're k-killing people!"

Teal lumbers across the chamber, its massive form leaving fleeting indentations in the strange, self-healing metal floor. It rests a clawed hand on the computer console. "YOUR CON-CERN IS UNWARRANTED, HUMAN. YOUR ABSENCE WILL BE ACCOUNTED FOR. A CLONE WILL ASSUME YOUR LIFE, PREVENTING FAMILIAL DISRUPTION AND DISSOLUTION OF SOCIAL ORDER."

It's almost too much to wrap my head around.

No, scratch that. It's *way* too much to wrap my head around.

"So, let me get this straight," I say, fighting the rising nausea. "You're going to kill me to ... what? Save the world?"

"WE WILL DECONSTRUCT YOU TO ENSURE HU-MAN SALVATION," Teal corrects.

"You ... You're ..." My words crumble into incoherence. The room starts to warp, my vision blurring. My chest constricts, and a piercing ringing fills my ears. "No …" I plead weakly. "Don't do this …"

I stumble, crashing against another vat. A woman floats inside who's seen better days. Pieces of her skull have been eaten away, the wrinkles of her brain now visible beneath.

"SPECIMEN'S HEART RATE IS CRITICAL," Gray announces, but the words barely register. I don't even notice as Gray approaches, seizing my wrist and pressing a device into my palm. A brief sting, then an icy chill spreads through my hand.

I look up at Gray, my vision tripling. Nausea and delirium overwhelm me. "What did you do …" I mumble, but even as I speak, I wonder why I bothered asking. Suddenly, everything feels … fine? No. Better than fine. What was I so worked up about anyway? It's just a couple of giant space monsters and some floating corpses. No biggie.

"YOU HAVE BEEN ADMINISTERED A SEDATIVE," Gray explains.

"Oh," I reply, a dopey grin on my face. "Cool."

Gray keeps tapping at the display on its forearm, keeps talking all official and serious. "CORTISOL LEVELS REDUCED. ADRENAL RESPONSE SUPPRESSED. BIOMETRIC READINGS INDICATE SUITABLE LEVELS OF SUGGESTIBILITY. VERDICT: PROCEED."

"AFFIRMATIVE," Teal says from the main console.

"You guys need to, like … chillax," I giggle. "Like, you're *super* uptight." My eyes drift closed, and I'm lost in bliss. It's like floating on a sun-warmed lake, my heart overflowing with all the love in the world. This must be paradise. If only my sister could experience this before she dies …

"PULSE QUICKENING," Gray says sharply.

Hope. My sister. My dying sister, alone in that sterile hospital room, wondering why her little brother abandoned her.

"SEDATION EFFECT DIMINISHING," Gray warns, its tone urgent. "READINGS AT 98%. 94%. EMOTIONAL IN-

STABILITY APPROACHING CRITICAL LEVELS. HOR-MONES IN FLUX. HARVEST VIABILITY STATUS: COM-PROMISED."

"Hope …" I gasp, the haze lifting. "You have to send me back! I need to get to the hospital, say goodbye to my sister. Please! She's dying, and she needs me!"

Gray presses the device to my other hand, another wave of artificial calm washing over me. "INVALID CONCERN," it drones. "YOUR CLONE WILL BE AN EXACT REPLICA, RETAINING ALL MEMORIES. IT WILL SEAMLESSLY CONTINUE YOUR EXISTENCE. CONCLUSION: YOUR EXPIRING SIBLING WILL RECEIVE APPROPRIATE SUPPORT BEFORE DECOMPOSITION. IS THIS SATISFACTORY?"

"No!" I groan, fighting the double dose of sedative with everything I've got. "I never agreed to this, so just put me back! Find somebody else!"

"IMPOSSIBLE," Teal growls from the console. "INSUFFICIENT TIME. WE MUST HARVEST YOUR DNA TO AID IN HUMAN SALVATION. HE IS COMING."

"Who is coming?" I demand.

Teal's enormous eyes narrow, its myriad pupils contracting to pinpoints. "INVALID QUERY. INFORMATION TOO SENSITIVE FOR DISSEMINATION."

"REBUTTAL," Gray interjects. "CLONE'S MEMORY CAN BE ALTERED. CURRENT BIOMETRICS INDICATE IMMENSE EMOTIONAL DISTRESS, COMPROMISING HARVEST SUCCESS BY 34% AND RISING. SOLUTION: PERMIT SUBJECT TO COMPREHEND PURPOSE OF SACRIFICE. OUTCOME: EMOTIONAL CLOSURE AND ENHANCED PROBABILITY OF PROJECT SUCCESS."

Teal turns back to the console. "REBUTTAL ACCEPTED. PROCEED."

Gray crouches before me, its scaly digits pressing against my temples. "PREPARE FOR DISORIENTATION," it warns.

"YOU WILL EXPERIENCE PHYSICAL DISCOMFORT RESULTING FROM HYPERSTIMULATION. AFTER, YOU WILL COMPREHEND THE HORROR THAT AWAITS YOUR SPECIES IN THE DARK."

Present Day

I bolt upright, gasping. Another nightmare. The same crap that's haunted me for three decades now.

Except ... it wasn't, was it?

I rake my fingers through my graying hair, gulping air like a drowning man. My trembling hand seizes the water glass on the nightstand, nearly spilling it. This dream was different. Vivid. I saw things that I've never dreamed before, things that felt closer memories than hallucinations. And yet—

Bzzz. Bzzz.

My phone vibrates angrily. I fumble for it, my hand shaking so violently I almost drop the damn thing before it reaches my ear. "Whatisit?" I grumble, voice thick with sleep.

"WhAt iS iT," a female voice mocks. "Do me a favor and go fuck yourself, Mitchell. I've been tearing my hair out for the last two hours while you've been off in dreamland banging Dolly Parton."

I heave a sigh. My boss, Lisa. Charming as ever.

"Dolly Parton?" I mutter, rubbing my eyes. "Isn't she pushing eighty now, Lis?"

"How the hell should I know?" Lisa snaps. "Point is, she's a babe. You'd screw her. I'd screw her. The whole world—"

"Are you drunk? Hell. Who am I kidding—it's 3 AM on a Saturday. Of course you're drunk."

"Christ, if only," she says, and I can almost hear her scowl. "Listen, are you sitting down right now?"

I yawn cavernously. "Safe to assume since you just woke me up."

She gives a humorless chuckle. "Yeah, about that—pretty much nothing is safe to assume, not anymore."

Lisa launches into a rapid-fire briefing. Her words rattle through the speaker like automatic gunfire. From the background chatter, I gather she's addressing more than just me—probably briefing a team of stone-faced government types as she power-walks down some sterile hallway.

"Got all that?" she asks after ten minutes of nonstop verbal diarrhea.

"I think so."

Something about a shitstorm. Something about an F-35. Apparently, the Air Force shot down a UAP an hour ago, which is how we say UFO these days to avoid getting laughed out of the room. And of course, it had to happen in New Mexico. My backyard. This calls for a liter of coffee. Probably two.

I stumble into the kitchen, set a pot brewing, and stay on the line while Lisa continues barking orders at her underlings.

I don't care what it takes, Mallory! Make it happen! Do I look like I'm fucking laughing, Douglas? O'Riley, if you publish this I swear to God I'll tear off your dick and—

One cream. Two sugars. My spoon clinks against the mug as Lisa's voice blares through the speaker. "Mitchell? Still there?"

She rattles off coordinates. I take a swig of scalding java, barely registering the burn on my tongue. My fingers punch the numbers into my laptop, bringing up the crash site of the so-called UAP.

I spew coffee across the screen.

"Did I just hear you throw up?" Lisa asks.

"No."

"I did, didn't I?"

I wipe the screen clean with my bathrobe sleeve. "You sure you got those numbers right?"

"Am I sure?" she says, incredulous. "Yes, I'm bloody sure. I've been gnawing my nails for the past hour, Mitchell. My manicurist is gonna think I've taken up meth. This isn't some Chinese spy balloon—this is the real deal. A genuine fucking UFO. So suit up and get ready to launch. I've got a bird on the way."

The microwave clock blinks 3:34 AM. My stomach growls in protest. "Can you give me ten minutes for breakfast?"

Click.

The line goes dead. Figures.

I take a deep breath, try to rationalize this. There's gotta be some mistake here. Some error. The coordinates Lisa gave can't be accurate because they're not pointing to some barren stretch near Roswell or Eglin. They're pointing to a forest. A cluster of trees with a rickety old bridge and a winding dirt trail. They're pointing to a place where I used to pedal my bike as a kid.

Outside there's a drumroll of helicopter blades.

Time to go.

I bolt upstairs, throw on my suit, and hurtle out the door, still wrestling with my jacket sleeve. A half-eaten cheese bagel dangles from my teeth. I board the chopper in a daze. We rocket towards the crash site like we're trying to outrun a cruise missile, and I can't even bring myself to finish the bagel. I'm feeling sick. Woozy. I'm watching the lights of the countryside drift by and it occurs to me that from all the way up here, in the dead of night, those lights almost look like stars.

I'm wondering how long it'd take to snuff them out. I'm wondering how long it'd take to burn a whole galaxy to ashes, or crush a universe in the palm of my hand.

Things to consider.

The closer we get to the crash site, the worse my thoughts become. They're spiraling, bordering on obsessive. I'm tangoing with darkness. Radio chatter comes through the com line in a gargle of static, and I catch bits and pieces. They're talking aliens. Extraterrestrials. They're talking about things that don't exist, and the whole time I'm just trying to control my bladder.

I'm drowning in hypotheticals.

What happens, I wonder, if I lose my mind between here and the crash site? What's the protocol for that? Do they pull me from the mission? Do I get the night off? The week?

"Everything okay, sir?"

It's the co-pilot. She's turned around in her seat, looking at me like she's worried I'm gonna make a mess on her deck. "You look a bit queasy," she says. "Not much of a frequent flier, I'm guessing?"

My muscles work overtime to yank my mouth into a smile. "I'm fine. Not thrilled to be working on a weekend, but what can you do, right?"

She grins. "Tell me about it. I'm Kennedy, by the way."

"Isaiah," I manage.

"Nice to meet you. The guy in the chair next to me is Johno."

Johno offers a casual wave.

"How much further to the crash site?" I ask, fighting to keep my voice steady.

Kennedy furrows her brow. "Ten minutes, give or take. Maybe twelve. All depends on whether Johno here grows a pair and stops piloting this bird like my grandma." She gives him a playful jab on the shoulder.

Johno chuckles. "Can you believe I've gotta fly with this witch? God help me. She'd be better off on a broomstick."

They share a laugh. I try to join in, try to blend in, but the whole time I'm thinking about how dry my mouth feels, how badly my hands are shaking in my lap. The longer I'm spending in this helicopter, the more I'm coming undone. It's the memories, I think. The memories of my nightmare that are trickling into my thoughts like psychic cyanide.

I'm remembering what I saw in my dream. Awful things. Things more terrible than words can describe, and with each passing moment those things seem less impossible and more inevitable. The radio buzzes. It keeps buzzing, keeps bombarding us with transmissions about advanced metal alloys, about non-human technology.

"Nearly there," Johno announces. "Eight minutes to touch down."

Five.

Four.

"Holy ..." Kennedy breathes at the three-minute mark. "Are you two seeing this?"

It's impossible to miss. There's a plume of smoke rising from a forest on the edge of town, and all amongst the branches are the ghosts of dying flames. Beyond the canopy, a constellation of industrial lamps traces a miles-long path from a checkpoint at the woods' edge to its heart, following a swath of devastation through the trees.

"What the hell is that?" Johno asks, his voice tight.

Kennedy leans forward, her face pressed against the cockpit glass. The blood drains from her features, leaving her ghostly pale in the dim light. "That's ... that's not one of ours," she whispers, her words barely a breath.

"Sure isn't," Johno mutters, his knuckles white on the controls.

I lurch from my seat, wedging myself between them to peer down. My jaw clenches. Below us stretches an ocean of splintered lumber, and at its center lies something colossal. It's the size of an aircraft carrier, its surface rippling and shimmering, reflecting the glow of the flickering fires as if forged from liquid metal.

"Son of a bitch," Kennedy breathes. "I thought all that radio chatter was bullshit, but this is the real deal, isn't it? That's a goddamn spaceship."

Johno only manages a shaking nod.

I try to speak, to offer some explanation or reassurance, but my voice fails me. As we circle above the metallic leviathan, a chill runs down my spine. I realize we've just crossed a threshold– the kind there's no coming back from because that thing that we're looking at doesn't belong to this world. It belongs to me.

To my nightmares.

But as hard as I try, I can't seem to wake up from this dream.

The Recall

Gray's scaly fingers connect with my temples, and static crackles across my skull. I'm convulsing, frothing at the mouth, choking on my own breath. I'm pretty sure I'm going to die, but then—poof. It all vanishes.

After that, I'm just falling.

Plummeting through the atmosphere of my own mind, I crash into a dimension beyond myself. Beyond everything.

Images flash.

They spin up like a cosmic film reel, bombarding my consciousness from every angle. They're everywhere. Inescapable. Weirdly, it's as if I'm inhabiting these moments, every sensation—sight, sound, smell—collapsing into a singular, overwhelming experience.

Gray called this 'disorienting.'

I think he might have undersold it.

Then, just when I know I can't take another second of this chaos, it decelerates. The visual hurricane calms from a Category 5 to a 3.

Moments float to the surface. Others sink out of sight.

Like a sponge, my mind starts absorbing information, everything from quantum physics to the lyrical discography of Shania Twain. Knowledge becomes trivial. As soon as I want to know something, I just reach out and take it.

It's pretty sweet.

But something catches my attention. A series of lights shimmer in my lake of thought, gleaming jewels beckoning to me. They're what I'm after. I don't know how I know this. I just do.

I sort of know everything now.

So, I reach out. Touch one.

Big mistake.

Information pummels me. It carpet-bombs my mind, blowing up my consciousness and making the last round of hyperstimulation feel like I was watching paint dry. I think I'm disintegrating. It's maybe the worst thing I've ever felt, and yet in the madness of it all, the entire history of the cosmos unfolds before me.

I see it.

All of it.

Gray and Teal? Not monsters. They're members of an alien race called the Vytar. Their technology makes ours look like sticks and stones, and I guess they've existed for billions of years. Holy hell. They've accomplished mind-boggling feats in that time—everything from mastering faster-than-light travel to creating edible rocks, and of course, mapping the entirety of the cosmos.

They've been busy with a capital B.

And that's just scratching the surface. The revelations don't let up, they keep coming and coming. I see their sprawling civilization, their gargantuan spaceships bristling with awesome guns, their High Council and ...

And then I see tragedy.

I watch as the Vytarian race makes two terrible discoveries. First, they learn they are alone in the universe. Second, they discover their entire species is dying.

How? Let me explain.

Near the edge of space, a Vytarian research vessel discovers life, only it's not the intelligent kind. Far from it. This life is microbial, viral, and it infects the Vytarian explorers. They're quarantined.

Observed. And you know what they discovered about this strange, alien virus?

They discovered it was pretty great.

In fact, it's just what they've been looking for. Before long, Vytarians across the cosmos are lining up to be infected. Within a century, their entire species are carriers. It jumps between them like the common cold. They don't mind, though. Not one bit. Why? Because this virus comes with a satisfaction guarantee—biological immortality.

Now there's a deal.

The trouble is, these Vytar don't work like humans do. They don't mate, make babies, sleep, wake up, and do it again. No, these Vytar lay eggs. And only certain members of their species lay eggs. And what's more, they only lay eggs during a specific molting period at the end of their life cycles.

See what I'm getting at?

Immortality or laying eggs. Pick one. You can't have both if you're the Vytar. But by the time they figure this out, this virus has infected every last colony of their civilization. Unable to reproduce, their population enters freefall. It develops what's known as an existential crisis, and if there's one thing civil society hates, it's dealing with an existential crisis.

Trust me.

I know everything now.

Anyway, tempers flare. Emotions run hot. Things are said that maybe shouldn't have been, and that brings us to the crux of the Vytarian dilemma: war.

And lots of it.

Whole worlds erupt into conflict. Galaxies become battlefields, and entire solar systems are laid to cosmic ash.

If you thought nuclear weapons were bad, consider what happens when a moon is kicked out of orbit into the surface of a planet. It ain't pretty. Hell, as the fighting escalates, the stars themselves become weapons. The Vytar discover that if you can just push one toward instability ...

Well, *boom.*

There goes the neighborhood.

This penchant for galaxy-brain problem-solving decimates their population to mere billions. Over a millennium, the Vytar plummet from an intergalactic empire to a handful of clans clinging to a single world in some backwater system

Still with me? I know it's a lot to process, but trust me, it's crucial.

So, the Vytar essentially self-destruct, obliterating each other out of sheer frustration. The survivors, traumatized by the horrors wrought by their technology, swing hard towards spiritualism. Cults sprout like a fungus. Various sects compete, but one ultimately devours the rest: The Way of the Chosen. These guys peddle the ultimate snake oil—an end to Vytarian suffering. No more existential dread. No more war. No more planetary billiards with moons.

It's a good sales pitch. All the Vytar need to do is swallow their three-step program:

1. EMBRACE YOUR SUPERIORITY! You're the universe's only intelligent life, so own it!

2. ENDURE THE ENDLESS! Immortality is your final test. Buck up and find a hobby!

3. ACHIEVE COSMIC NIRVANA! Survive until the heat death of the universe and attain rapture! *Terms and conditions apply. Limited availability. Nirvana will be offered on a first-come first-serve basis.*

Believe it or not, it's a smash hit.

The Vytarians flock to The Way in droves, desperate for purpose and a break from their all-consuming rage. Within a decade, The Chosen seize control across all colonies, unifying the warring factions and establishing an uneasy peace. Sounds great, right? The catch: all non-believers must be exiled. It's for the greater good, they claim. The only way to prevent future conflict.

And maybe they're right.

After all, this is a species that knows how quickly disagreements can spiral toward interstellar armageddon. So, dissenters are given their marching orders. Here's a spacecraft, some supplies, now scram. Live however you want, wherever you want—just not on Vytar. It's not exactly "Kumbaya," but there are worse ways to run a theocracy.

Among the exiles is a scientist known in collective memory as the Heretic. It's an apt name, almost poetic given what his destiny has in store for him, but we'll cross that bridge when we get to it.

The Heretic fancies himself a philosopher. He ponders the big questions, like what happens after the Vytar kick the bucket and intelligent life vanishes from the universe. He concludes that it's curtains—not just for the Vytar, but for the universe itself. After all, if there's no consciousness left to perceive it, does the universe even exist? To the Heretic, this lights-out scenario is a bit of a bummer, and if there's one thing the Heretic won't stand for, it's bummers.

So, he rolls up his sleeves. Gets to work.

The Heretic hatches a plan. It's not exactly foolproof. Hell, it's barely even sane. The odds of success are astronomical, and it's definitely skirting some ethical boundaries. But it's a plan nonetheless.

It's simple. Straightforward. The Heretic reasons that the Vytarians are the universe's sole sentient beings, facing extinction due to incurable sterilization. It's inevitable. Inescapable. So what's left on the table?

Just one wildcard play.

The Heretic charts a course for a distant star system, one with a promising sun and a goldilocks planet ripe with potential. He sets his sights on destiny.

And that is where our nightmare begins.

Present Day

The helicopter touches down in a clearing that shouldn't exist. I step out to find a forest that's broken, smoldering, one that's cleaved in two with a cloud of cinders in its wake. This isn't how I remember this place. Not at all.

I remember a wooden bridge over a lazy creek, and tall trees that–

"Mitchell!"

Lisa.

Of course it's Lisa. She's barreling towards me, phone glued to one ear, her free hand slicing through the air like a metronome gone berserk. "Mitchell! Over here!" She's bulldozing through a sea of personnel—stern-faced government types in crisp suits and military fatigues. They're swarming everywhere, a thousand different tasks underway, all of their voices breaking with anxious unease.

At least I'm in good company.

Lisa squeezes past a square-jawed general, doubling over with her hands on her knees, gasping for air. "What the hell took you so long?" she wheezes. "It's been hours!"

I glance at my watch, puzzled. "It's been thirty minutes—twenty-eight, actually."

She smacks her forehead. "Shit. Time dilation."

"Time what?"

"We've discovered that time operates differently inside the UAP," she explains, waving off my confusion. "Look, it doesn't matter. Just follow me. I'll fill you in on the way."

We take a surreal stroll through the newest gully in America. The ground is a minefield of UAP fragments—pieces of soft metal that hazmat teams are scooping into clear bags like the world's worst Easter egg hunt. My stomach is in my throat. A shadow passes overhead, and I look up to see helicopters unfurling a massive tarp across the forest canopy.

"That's to keep the satellites out," Lisa explains, gesturing skyward. "The last thing we need is China getting wind of this—or God forbid, Google fucking Maps."

"Feels like we might be a little late on that," I mutter.

Lisa wags a finger in my face. "Don't you start with me. The Pentagon is already breathing down my neck, as if I didn't get here as fast as humanly possible." She contorts her face, mimicking the Secretary of Defense. "WhAt exaCtly did we shoOt doWn? Is iT ChinEse? ArE we goiNg to wAr?"

"If you think that's bad," I say, "just wait until the media wakes up. Or worse, the kids with smartphones."

She groans, running a hand through frizzy, chestnut hair. "Don't remind me. I should've kept on as an accountant. I'd still be in bed right now, thinking of all the ways I could jump off a bridge tomorrow – you know, like a normal person. But no, I had to follow my dreams. Fuck me."

As we push deeper, the smoke thins, revealing a shape through the hazy veil—the colossal silhouette of an oval craft smoldering amidst the devastated trees. It's breathtaking. Large enough to pass for a football stadium and round enough to sell the illusion.

"So this is it," I mutter, suddenly light-headed. Woozy. I fumble with my tie, loosening it with a desperate tug, but it does little to free whatever's stuck in my throat.

"This is it," Lisa confirms with a nervous chuckle. "A bonafide flying saucer. I mean, geez. You'd think these aliens never heard of a bad cliche."

Memories crawl up from my psyche, but I wrestle them back down. I keep telling myself that there's gotta be more to this. Some other explanation. Maybe this is some other alien spaceship, and my dreams really are just dreams.

"What do you need?" Lisa asks, studying me.

"Huh?"

"You look like you're going to throw up, so what do you need? Dramamine? Gravol?" She glances around furtively, then reaches into her jacket, pulling out a flask with a mischievous wiggle. "A dash of liquid courage, perhaps?"

"I don't drink."

"Never been a better time to start."

"I'll pass."

"Well, I won't."

She lifts the flask to her lips, takes the kinda swig that'd make my deadbeat father lift an eyebrow. A trickle of whisky runs down her chin. Finally, she comes up for air, wiping her mouth with the back of her hand before tucking the flask away. She exhales sharply, the scent of bourbon hanging in the air. "Right. So before we jump inside that circus, I want you to take a few deep breaths. Get your shit together. We've already had a couple ... uh, *incidents*."

"Incidents?" I ask, warily.

"Oh yeah, big time. You do yoga at all?"

I shake my head.

"Well, you should. It's great for shit like this. Kills stress like nothing else. I can get you a discount at my studio, but only on Tuesday and Thursdays – and no Hot Yoga. Interested?"

"I'll consider it. You mentioned incidents?"

"Oh, right." She starts ticking them off on her fingers. "So far, we've had two Marines piss themselves, one lieutenant hurl all over what I'm like *ninety* percent sure was some kind of alien artifact.

And—oh god, Mitchell—somebody shat their fucking pants. No lie." Lisa laughs weakly, her face suddenly pale. "Can you believe that? I mean, Christ. Now the whole UAP reeks of chili dogs and somebody's chipotle-ringed asshole."

I grimace. "Spare me the details next time, Lis—that's disgusting."

"No, a fart is disgusting, Mitchell. This ..." Lisa shivers, her eyes glazing over at the memory of it. "This was something else entirely. Anyway if I didn't warn you, you'd figure it out the second you walked in. That stench is *lingering*."

"Fantastic," I mutter.

We halt at a checkpoint. Lisa flashes her badge, and I follow suit. A sergeant with a crew cut, looking like he'd rather be anywhere else, takes them, scans them, and then delivers the standard spiel through a stifled yawn. No photos. No touching. No running. No yelling. No wandering into sections the hazmat teams haven't cleared for contagions, and absolutely no pocketing alien technology as souvenirs.

It's just *No*, all the way down.

Finally, he finishes his rundown and takes a deep breath. "One more thing" he adds, giving the knife-hand gesture to a row of porta-potties. "If nature calls, I'd answer it now. We've had some *incidents*."

I give Lisa a sidelong glance. "So I've heard."

Lisa slips me a smirk as we pass the checkpoint. The entrance to the UAP is tough to miss– it's the gaping hole the F35 left in its hull when it blew it outta the sky. There's a makeshift ramp leading up to it. We pass throngs of people coming and going, each of them more ashen-faced than the last.

"You sure you're good?" Lisa asks.

"Peachy," I tell her.

"Uh huh. You don't look peachy."

"Weird. Look harder."

She exhales, exasperated. "Look, Mitchell. I'm not trying to be a bitch. I just want to make sure you're prepared."

"Prepared for what?" I say, folding my arms.

Lisa's teeth worry at her lower lip, her entire body thrumming with barely contained energy. "Nothing," she chirps, unconvincingly.

"Lis ..." I groan. "Spill it."

"Bodies!" The word explodes from her face, eyes alight with ghoulish glee. "They've got fucking *bodies in vats*, Mitchell. It's insane! Total X-Files shit. Honestly, you're gonna love it. Or hate it. I don't know. Either way, there's not enough therapy in the world for you to get over this. You're in for a lifetime of nightmares – guaranteed."

She slings an arm over my shoulder, steering me towards the shrouded entrance. "That means no more Dolly Parton for you."

The Recall

The Heretic paints life in his image, and Earth is his canvas. His first brushstrokes are behemoths – colossal reptiles that roam a primordial world, but these are rough drafts of his grand design. He studies them. Learns from them. He leverages them to unravel the enigma of complex intelligence, but fate has other threads to weave.

A surveillance drone drifts by the Earth. A Vytarian relic. It's charting a repeating course, one set long before the Vytarian War, and now it's relaying its data to the last colony in existence. The Heretic's vessel crackles with an incoming transmission – a collect call from twelve billion light years away.

"Hello?" he answers.

It's the Chosen High Council. They aren't pleased. To them, the creation of life is a sacred honor reserved for their deity, The Distant One, and so the Heretic has their attention. And not in a good way.

Cease this, they order.

I can explain, he tells them.

Don't bother, they growl.

Please listen, he pleads.

But the line goes dead, leaving only the hum of distant stars. The Heretic's mind races with calculations. Two weeks, he estimates. He has two weeks before The Chosen arrive to execute him, and so he flees to a neighboring star system.

The Chosen arrive. They search for him, but find nothing. Before they leave, though, they decide to clean up the Heretic's blasphemy. They redirect a passing asteroid toward the Earth, obliterating it in fire and ash.

Time marches on. Years bleed into centuries, and centuries into millennia. The weight of his loss hangs heavy on the Heretic's conscience, driving him back to Earth. He seeks closure, a chance to pay respects to the life he condemned.

So he returns. And his sorrow becomes hope.

Life, in its stubborn persistence, has flourished. It's thrived, evolved, and adapted. Yet, the creatures that now inhabit Earth aren't the offspring of his colossal prototypes. Instead, they're the descendants of the tiny mammals he created as their sustenance.

These new beings – humans – captivate the Heretic. Their powerful brains, dexterous hands, and upright gait mirror his own Vytarian form. He watches, fascinated, as they form rudimentary societies, birth the first stuttering languages, and craft primitive technologies. In these fledgling humans, the Heretic sees the future stewards of the universe.

If only The Chosen weren't looming.

The Heretic knows they'll return, realizing their genocide was incomplete. This time, they won't hold back. Earth will be reduced to cosmic rubble, floating amid crystallized blood.

So the Heretic gets to work. Strategies whir through his mind, each more desperate than the last. He has but one ship, no weapons – the odds seem insurmountable.

Then, inspiration strikes.

Humans have an edge: adaptability. Swift evolution. They could potentially match the Vytarians' intellect given time, but time is a luxury the Heretic can ill afford. Another surveillance drone could drift past Earth any day now, and so he needs to act – intervene. Spike humanity's gene pool. Rig the results. He'll need to give his children more than a push– he'll have to throw them down the evolutionary stairwell if they have any hope of matching the Vytarians.

So he devises a solution.

It starts by forging a man, one shaped from the genetic clay of thousands. Each strand of his DNA will be carefully selected, isolating the potential for runaway evolution. But he won't just be a human. No, his flesh is to be interwoven with the Heretic's own Vytarian essence. Enough to unlock the Collective Recall, to flood his mind with eons of cosmic memory. The man will become a living catalyst, a walking singularity. His genes will then spread through humanity like a virus of metamorphosis, each generation leaping forward, their minds racing ever faster toward a terrible apex.

Project Runaway.

That's the name the Heretic gives it, and he believes in his hearts that it will result in the liberation of humanity. He believes it will bring about the salvation of the universe.

And in this, he has made the worst miscalculation since the dawn of time.

Present Day

"Watch your step," Lisa warns.

We push through a forest of plastic tassels, blinded by the glare of industrial work lamps. We're standing in a circular chamber, a hub with corridors spiraling outward like the spokes of an alien wheel. The spacecraft is a hive of activity. Personnel in biohazard suits and military fatigues swarm around us, buzzing with urgency and barely-contained panic. Teams seal off entrances with sheets of plastic wrap while other teams are scribbling labels, scotch-taping them above the doorways labeled A through G.

"Take it in," Lisa says, closing her eyes and breathing deep. "We're inside a UFO – a real one. Makes you feel like Agent K, or Dana Scully, or–"

"Yeah, I get it," I mutter.

I sulk forward, the heel of my shoe sinking into the soft metal with every step, almost like I'm walking over a mattress. I hate how familiar it feels.

Lisa jogs to catch up. "Hey Mitchell?" she says.

"Hm?"

"Anybody ever tell you you're a total drag?"

"Most people, yeah."

"Great. Just making sure."

We head down a corridor labeled D. Lisa explains we're looking for somebody named Major Luca. Apparently Luca called her a few minutes before my helicopter touched down, said she had something big to show us. Something 'crazy.'

"By 'crazy' do you mean corpses in vats?" I ask.

"Nope. I mean bodies," Lisa tells me.

"Bodies?"

A nod. "Apparently of the *non-human* variety, if you can believe it."

I feel the color drain from my face.

We venture deeper, twisting through corridors D2, D4 and D7, and each corridor feels worse than the last. My heart is pounding like a war drum. I nod mechanically as Lisa rattles off details about the UAP, about what the teams we're passing are up to, but internally I'm having a breakdown. The further we get into the spacecraft, the more I'm wondering how much of my dreams were dreams.

The more I wonder if all I am is just some clone with a badge.

"What did the bodies look like?" I hear myself ask, voice hoarse. "The dead aliens, I mean."

Lisa's laugh is sharp, pointed. "No clue. I'd put money on little green men though. Fits the whole flying saucer motif, don't you think?"

"Yeah," I manage, swallowing hard. "Suppose it would."

Lisa gets a call over the radio. It's the Pentagon. Apparently we've got an ironclad alibi to deal with the journalists, something banal enough to keep them far from the crash site. As for the public, we're going to feed them some freshly plucked political controversy– something juicy enough to keep them distracted. Fighting. But I'm too deep in my thoughts to catch specifics. I'm caught up in my own mind, recalling a memory that was meant to be a dream.

I'm remembering him.

The Runaway.

And the more that I remember, the more I want to forget.

The Recall

The first time the Runway opens his eyes, he's twenty years old. The jungle around him pulses with life—a kaleidoscope of green pierced by shafts of gold. His naked skin prickles under the gaze of the sun, its ultraviolet rays baptizing him in fire and sweat.

He has no instructions.

No guidance.

This world is entirely new to him, and in his stomach flutters the first ghosts of adrenaline. The Runaway rises to his feet. His first step is a stagger, a graceless lurch that sends him sprawling into the lush undergrowth. Pain, that most ancient of teachers, introduces itself. It's harder than it looks, walking when you've never done it before, but eventually he gets the picture. For him, it gets easier by the second.

After only an hour, the Runaway has learned to run. To sprint. He's dashing through the ferns, leaping from tree to tree with a grace bordering on simian. His stomach howls—a cavernous emptiness demanding to be filled. Food. He must find food. But what to eat in this verdant labyrinth?

By his third hour alive, the Runaway has learned to forage.

By his sixth, he has learned to die.

He writhes upon the ground, every nerve screaming as his body wages war against a toxic feast. The berries burn his stomach. They make his tongue swell and his skin glisten with a fever sweat.

But as the seconds march on, his agony fades. His cellular structure begins to realign, his enzymes mutating, and within moments, the poison has become his fuel. He gets back to his feet. Reborn. The Runaway takes his first breath, a whole new creature – subtly improved by evolution's kiss.

Twilight paints the jungle. The Runaway collects wild game from his crudely-made traps. The Heretic, observing from afar, marvels at his creation so easily tapping into the Collective Recall.

The Runaway's hands move with ancestral memory, skinning his catch and kindling fire as if he'd done so for a thousand lifetimes.

A week passes, and the Runaway learns what it means to *be* food.

A pack of wolves ambush him while he sleeps. Their eyes gleam in the night. Saliva drips from their gnashing jaws. Their throats rumble with a promise of violence, their paws padding ever closer as their haunches lift into the air, ready to lunge.

But the Runaway is unconcerned. A week is a long time for a man like him, and by now he has well learned how to handle his fear, how to subdue it. Command it.

Now his fear serves him.

His muscles tense, his hands flexing into calloused fists. He follows the gray beasts with his eyes, watching as they prowl nearer and nearer. The large one, he thinks. The large wolf will engage first, and then the rest will follow. But only if he permits it.

The Runaway strikes first.

He darts forward, his feet leaving a cloud of dirt in his wake. By the time the first scatter of dirt falls, he's already brought his fist down on the alpha of the pack, his blow connecting with its skull in a crack of thunder. The colossal canine stumbles. It whines. The others draw back, pupils wide as the Runaway grabs hold of the patriarch's jaws, pulling them apart with everything he has.

Another crack of thunder.

A dying yelp.

The remaining wolves scatter, fleeing into the trees as their champion hits the ground. The Runaway's message is clear – he is the predator, and they are his prey.

As weeks bleed into months, the Runaway's evolution accelerates beyond all comprehension. At six weeks, his body is a masterpiece of efficiency. Nutrition is rendered an afterthought, with only a handful of berries sustaining him for days on end, his cells multiplying every iota of their energy. By ten weeks, oxygen itself becomes optional. His lungs, once slaves to the rhythm of breath, rest for hours at a time. He plunges into the ocean's depths, racing with sharks in the midnight zone, plucking delicacies from the seafloor as casually as one might pick apples from a tree.

On the anniversary of his awakening, the Runaway transcends even the specter of mortality. His DNA, once bound by the cruel arithmetic of cellular division, now replicates flawlessly. Age becomes a concept as foreign to him as death.

Five years pass, and the universe bends to his will. Atoms dance at his command, reality reshaping itself at his merest whim. To him, the laws of physics are little more than suggestions. He soars through the sky on wings of thought, peers into the minds of lesser beings as easily as one might read a book.

He has become a god in flesh, the most powerful entity to ever grace existence.

And as the Heretic watches this, he feels no fear – not even a phantom of concern. The Runaway has proven himself to be kind. Compassionate.

As the decades roll by, the Runaway's appetite for violence diminishes. Even the savagery of his fellow human beings—their bloodlust and petty cruelties—becomes too much for him to bear. He retreats from their world, seeking solitude in nature. Yet humanity, in its endless thirst for meaning, continues to seek him out. They scale treacherous peaks and hack through dense jungles, desperate for a glimpse, a touch, a word spoken from the mouth of this miracle.

Some fall to their knees in worship. Others spit curses and threats.

To the Runaway, they are one and the same—lost children, fumbling in the dark. Their instincts, once his own, now seem as foreign as the language of ants. He has evolved beyond them, becoming something else. No longer kin, but a distant observer.

Yet for all his power, for all his transcendence, there is turmoil within him. A deep loneliness. It gnaws at him, reminding the Runaway of his mortality. His human core. He seeks answers in meditation, sometimes sinking to the ocean floor, other times soaring among the clouds to escape the chaos of the world. And it's during one such meditation, suspended between heaven and earth, that the Runaway turns his gaze to the stars.

He wonders if there could be others out there. Others like him.

And like an answer to a prayer, he sees it. A figure, reptilian and humanoid, encased in a shelter made of polished ore. It drifts amid the rings of a gas giant—Saturn, though the Runaway doesn't yet know this name. The creature stares back through a curious device, its gaze piercing lightyears.

In that moment, the Runaway makes a decision. It's a decision that will change the tide of history – that will give birth to the suffering of billions, that will risk the destruction of everything that ever was. But the Runaway is unaware of these things. He knows only that he is lonely, and that he does not wish to be.

And so he flies.

It is not a simple journey, reaching this creature in the stars. The Runaway presses up against the Earth's atmosphere and his body is incinerated, but like a phoenix, he is reborn from the ashes. Stronger. More resilient.

On his second attempt, the Runaway breaks through the atmosphere only to discover a new challenge. The vacuum of space. Yet this vacuum has its benefits. It offers him the sort of silence that allows him to center his mind, to focus in new and more profound ways, and so as he sets his sights on Saturn he begins to pick up speed.

Soon, he's not merely flying– he's blazing across the solar system, a comet of potential racing toward fate. In the span of a month, he traverses distances that would take conventional spacecraft years.

And then he arrives.

The Heretic's ship hangs before him, a metallic bubble in a black ocean of asteroids. The Runaway reaches out, rapping his knuckles against the hull.

THUNK

THUNK

The ship's exterior shimmers, becoming transparent. The reptilian being he'd seen from Earth bows its head in greeting, then ushers him inside.

"HELLO," the being rumbles, in the ancient tongue of man.

The Runaway studies this strange creature, his mind working to decipher its unfamiliar sounds. When he responds, it's not in the language of man, but in the deep, resonant bass of Vytarian. "Hello," he begins, the word feeling strange on his tongue. "Your language is ... curious. But I believe I can master it. Tell me, who are you? Why have you been observing me?"

The being—the Heretic—sees no point in deception. After all, the Runaway could pluck the truth from his mind as easily as picking a flower. So he lays bare everything: the extinction of the Vytarians, humanity's cosmic inheritance, and the Runaway's pivotal role in it all.

"Do you have any questions?" the Heretic asks, his tale concluded.

"Many," the Runaway replies, his voice a mix of wonder and trepidation. "Above all, why do you fear me?"

"I do not."

"You do," the Runaway insists. "I see it reflected in your thoughts ... Along with hatred. Disgust."

The Heretic pupils pulse with resignation, his shoulders sagging under an invisible weight. "Of course. I should have anticipated this."

The Runaway tilts his head, curious.

"The fear, hatred, and disgust you perceive ... none of it belongs to me," the Heretic explains. "What you sense are echoes from the Collective Recall, a shared knowledge passed down by my people. The emotions you're perceiving are actually those of a religious sect, felt by those who follow the Way of the Chosen."

The Runaway's face contorts into a mask of bewilderment. "These Followers ... they view me as a monster? An abomination?"

The Heretic hesitates, choosing his words carefully. "Not exactly. To be precise, they do not think of you at all. To safeguard my work I was forced to sever my connection to the Collective epochs ago, but echoes of Chosen dogma still remain. To them, my work is blasphemy. And you, my child, are the apex of that blasphemy."

The Runaway ponders this. "You say I'm destined to guide humanity's evolution. Is that all I am to you? An instrument?"

The Heretic reaches out, gently clasping the Runaway's shoulder. He smiles—an expression he learned from his study of humans—and speaks softly. "I am a barren creature, ravaged by a virus that has stolen the future of my people. My biological imperative can never be fulfilled. Reproduction is beyond me." His pupils blot with fragile emotion, splashing like raindrops in his eyes. "No, you are not an instrument." With slow, awkward, yet earnest movements, the Heretic initiates the human ritual of embrace. He wraps his arms around the Runaway, holding him close.

"You are my legacy," he whispers. "You are my son."

12, October, 1991

A gasp escapes me, sharp and sudden. My eyes snap open to find Gray standing before me, his alien pupils pulsing like living ink. In that moment, a tidal wave of realization crashes over me. His name isn't Gray. It's Wor. And he's ancient—70 million years old. The same goes for his companion, not Teal, but Kez. Both are devotees of the Way of the Chosen.

"Did you see?" Wor's voice resonates, no longer filtered through a digital translator. The thought transfer has unlocked something in my mind; I can understand the Vytarian language, make sense of the vibrations that previously just seemed like low bass.

I lean forward, my heart racing. "Yes, but ... there's more, isn't there? What aren't you telling me?"

Kez's neck twists unnaturally as he fixes us with a stare. His pupils expand and contract rapidly—a reaction I now understand to mean *I'm pissed*. "Enough," he growls. "Prepare for genetic deconstruction, human. We are done here."

"No!" The word erupts from me, a thunderclap that shakes the ship. I'm startled by the power in my own voice, suddenly aware of the raw force behind Vytarian speech.

Clearing my throat, I try again, this time with measured control. "No. Look, if you want to liquefy me into some kind of ... cosmic soup, fine. I get it—salvation of humanity and all that. But you have to prove it's worth it. For all I know, you could be blowing this whole thing outta proportion."

The Vytar exchange glances, a silent conversation playing out in their pupils. Wor's shrink to pinpricks—he's nervous, conflicted. "Further revelations may invite ... excessive distress," he says carefully. "I had hoped a glimpse of cosmic history would suffice."

"Well, it didn't," I retort, crossing my arms. "So let's do this again, and this time don't skimp on the details."

"Invalid request," Kez interjects. "Such knowledge is beyond your capacity to bear."

I frown, my gaze ping-ponging between them. "It's him, isn't it? The Runaway. He's the source of all this—your fear, your mission to 'save' humanity. I might not have all the pieces, but I'm not blind. Your eyes are going haywire like a pair of busted TVs. He's the problem, right? You haven't had any luck dealing with him."

Wor and Kez remain silent, their downcast expressions speaking volumes.

"Look," I press, inhaling deeply. "I'm human too. In a way, I'm like The Runaway—just less ... well, terrifying. But maybe there's something in those visions that only another human could make sense of. Ever think of that? What if I can spot something you've missed? Isn't that a chance worth taking?"

The Vytar fall quiet, locked in a staring contest. Their pupils explode with emotion, a fireworks display of alien feeling. Kez turns away abruptly, letting loose a guttural warble as he throws his arms up in exasperation.

"What's eating him?" I ask.

Wor approaches cautiously, casting a glance at his companion. Kez hunches over the console, radiating disagreement.

"Kez ... he worries for your mind," Wor explains softly. "Your tale of Hope, your dying sister—it affected him deeply. He fears that showing you the rest of The Runaway's story might shatter your consciousness beyond repair. There will be no perfect clone. Your sister will find no solace in her dying moments."

I watch Kez fiddle with the console, frustration evident in every movement. A wave of empathy washes over me. Maybe I've judged him too harshly. After all, he was just looking out for my sister.

Then again, he still wants to turn me into DNA soup.

"This feels important," I say to Wor, clenching my fists. "If the fate of humanity—of everything—is really at stake, then I think Hope would want me to help however I can." I force a smile, trying to hype myself up with false confidence. "Besides, I can't imagine it's *that* bad."

"You are right," Wor tells me, his hands resting on my temples. "It is much worse than you could ever imagine."

The Recall

Images riot past me. A torrential downpour of cosmic memory. I'm falling again, spiraling out of my body and mind, plummeting into the collective history of the Vytarian species. Millennia flash by in heartbeats. Epochs become blurs. My very consciousness strains under the weight of it all, like a white-hot sphere of mental energy growing redder with each new detail, each fresh revelation.

And then it cools.

The maelstrom of history coalesces, focusing like a lens zeroing in on a singular moment. Once again I'm observing the spacecraft orbiting Saturn's rings, a fragile bubble of life amidst the vast, indifferent starscape. Within it the Heretic and Runaway stand frozen in time, their words poised to rewrite the very nature of existence.

"They've come for my world before," the Runaway murmurs, his eyes flickering as he sifts through the Heretic's memories. "I see it now—the great lizards, wiped from existence. Their strike was cataclysmic, bringing the planet to its knees, making molten gold scream from its wounds. If they return ..."

"Yes," the Heretic confirms, his clawed hand pressed against the observation window. In the inky void beyond, a green speck—Earth—floats, magnified by digital overlay. "Should they come again, they will ensure nothing remains but cosmic dust. Your very existence terrifies them, for you are beyond their comprehension."

The Runaway's brow furrows. "What if I could make them understand? If I were to journey to the realm of The Chosen, to prove I'm not some instrument of destruction, would they forgive you then? Would they spare my world?"

The Heretic's pupils contract to beads, a display of grim concern. "I fear not. A millennium of peace couldn't sway them to trust you. It goes against their very nature. In their eyes, you will forever remain a false god."

"False ... god?" The Runaway echoes, the words alien on his tongue.

"Yes. A pretender."

The Runaway's eyes narrow, a spark igniting within them. "If I am a false god, then what is the true one?"

The Heretic taps a finger against his temple. "It would be simpler for you to see for yourself."

The Runaway's expression hardens, his jaw set with determination. The Heretic feels a cool whisper as his son's consciousness slips into his mind. The Runaway's eyes become slits, his lips pressing into a thin line as he delves deeper and deeper into the vast ocean of the Heretic's knowledge.

Suddenly, he recoils, sucking in a sharp breath.

"Him ..." the Runaway gasps, his eyes wide with a mixture of awe and terror.

The Heretic kneels, placing a comforting claw on his son's trembling leg. "Yes. The Distant One. He is the deity of The Chosen, the purported omnipotence that exists just beyond the reaches of the universe."

"In the Edge ..." the Runaway whispers, his voice quivering with a cocktail of fear and excitement. He turns to the Heretic, his eyes alight with a feverish curiosity. "Have you ever visited this place – The Edge?"

"Never," the Heretic says, shaking his head. "It is a realm beyond reach. Countless Vytarians have embarked on pilgrimages, but none have returned. If the universe can be called hostile to life, then The Edge ... it harbors an active, implacable malevolence toward it. All who seek it are consumed."

The Runaway falls silent, his gaze drifting back to the star-speckled void. Even his unfathomable mind seems to struggle with the weight of these revelations. Moments stretch into minutes, minutes into hours. The Heretic attempts to speak, sensing a shift in his son, but the Runaway remains unresponsive, motionless, his eyes unblinking.

At last, the Runaway's lips part, his voice barely a whisper. "I should have realized long ago that these humans were not like me. And nor, for that matter, are you." A tear escapes the corner of his eye, followed by another, and another, until they cascade down his cheeks in a quiet river. The Heretic, recognizing this display of human sorrow, moves to comfort his son, but the Runaway shrinks from his touch.

"I was born of humans," the Runaway says, his words fracturing under the weight of his grief. "I was shaped by them. Their genetic influence torments me, driving me toward this ... inescapable need for companionship and connection. But these humans ... they offer nothing to sate this hunger – their experiences are too limited to grant me wisdom, their perspectives too narrow to afford me knowledge. My mind expands with each passing moment, my capabilities growing beyond measure. I sit before you, evolving still, and yet ..." His voice breaks. "I would throw it all away to be like them."

He turns, locking eyes with the Heretic. "Why?" he pleads. "Why did you make me this way, Father?"

The Heretic's voice is brittle, shattered by the suffering in his child's words. "I am sorry," he says, the words feeling wholly inadequate. "I never meant to burden you with such an existence. If it were in my power, I would take away your pain in an instant."

The Runaway turns away, his knuckles cracking as his hands clench into fists. He raises an arm, wiping away the tears with a swift, angry motion. "Perhaps," he says, his voice low and determined, "you already have, father."

"My child?" the Heretic asks, confusion in his tone. "I don't understand your meaning."

"Connection," the Runaway explains, rising to his feet. He leans his forehead against the cold surface of the observation window, staring out into the abyss. His dark hair falls across his hollow eyes. "I will find it, Father. Someone like me. Someone who truly understands what it means to exist without limitations, to stand above all other forms of life, unburdened by ignorance."

An uneven smile slips across his lips. "I will find God."

12, October, 1991

My consciousness crashes back into me like an asteroid impact. Every nerve ignites, electricity coursing through my limbs in violent spasms as something powerful holds me down.

Wor.

My vision swims into focus, and I see him looming above me, gripping my shoulders. His eyes are wide with a mixture of concern and fascination. Behind him, Kez hovers anxiously. Both of their pupils are pulsing like strobe lights.

"You saw?" They ask in perfect unison, their voices thrumming with urgency.

I take a breath, my muscles relaxing and mind slowing as the effects of the Collective Recall leave my psyche. "More ... more than before," I croak. "The Runaway ... he went in search of God ... or The Distant One. Is that right?"

Wor nods solemnly. "Yes. The Runaway sought out the Distant One in the Edge. I apologize for the abrupt extraction. Your biometrics indicated extreme stress. How do you feel, human?"

"Fuzzy," I mutter, blinking away the last vestiges of disorientation. "But I'm okay, I think." I look up at the Vytar pair, suddenly aware of the tension crackling between them. "Is everything alright?"

They exchange loaded glances. Kez huffs, a sound like grinding boulders, before stalking back to his console. His clawed feet click ominously against the metal deck. Wor's eyes, by contrast, are wide with barely contained excitement.

"We extracted significant data during your Recall," Wor explains, practically vibrating with enthusiasm. "This could prove invaluable to our mission, exponentially increasing humanity's chances of survival."

"That's ... that's incredible!" I exclaim, a spark of hope igniting in me. "So, does this mean you're scrapping the whole 'turning me into human soup' thing?"

"Oh no," Wor says gleefully. "Your genetic material has become even more valuable. By combining it with the neurological data harvested during your Recall, we can dramatically accelerate the development of our countermeasure."

The spark of hope in me gutters and dies. Maybe it's the lingering effects of the sedative, or perhaps I've simply reached my limit for cosmic disappointments, but something inside me snaps, and I round on Wor, my voice trembling with barely contained fury.

"So that's it? I get *this* close to understanding the biggest asshole in the universe, and instead of answers, you're just going to liquefy me? That's my reward?"

"Human—" Wor begins, but I cut him off, my emotions boiling over.

"No. *You* listen. I've been nothing but cooperative. If what you're saying is true—if my 'data' has actually helped turbo charge humanity's salvation or whatever—then don't I at least deserve to see how the Runaway's story ends? Don't I deserve to see what I'm throwing away my life for?"

"Listen, human!" Kez thunders, startling me. I turn to find him fixing me with an intense stare. "You will enter the Recall once more."

I blink, caught off-guard. "I ... I will?"

"Yes."

Wor's pupils shrink in unease. "But Kez–"

"Enough," Kez interrupts, his own pupils flaring. "The human has aided our efforts at great personal risk. We offered closure. It is time we delivered." He takes a deep breath, his booming voice softening as he addresses me directly. "However, you must understand the gravity of your request. There exists a possibility you may not emerge from this Recall. The experience could destroy your mind entirely."

Fear claws its way up my throat.

Wor begins to pace, agitation evident in every movement. "Kez, consider the implications. Another Recall could compromise our ability to harvest the human's DNA. After our recent discovery—"

Kez cuts him off, his tone curt and final. "When the Heretic created these humans, he did so believing that one day they would choose their own destiny. Perhaps that day has come."

Wor turns back to me, desperate. "Your last Recall provided us with invaluable data. If you go back … if your mind fractures … we may lose our best chance at saving humanity from the Runaway."

I shift uneasily, feeling like a rope in some cosmic tug-of-war. Both Vytar are staring at me intently. It's like being offered the series finale of the most important show in the universe, but told that watching it might doom all of humanity. The weight of the decision is almost paralyzing.

"And if I can handle it?" I ask, carefully weighing each word. "If I survive another dip into the Recall … is there a chance you could extract even *more* useful data? Could I maybe accelerate this 'salvation' even more?"

"Unlikely," Kez replies.

"But … not impossible, right?"

His pupils pulse slowly, and I recognize the wry amusement. "Correct. There is a slim possibility that additional data could further accelerate our countermeasure's development. However, consider your sister, Hope. If your genetic material is compromised, we cannot produce a viable clone. She will face her final moments without the comfort you wish to provide."

It's true. The thought of Hope dying alone, thinking I'd abandoned her, is almost unbearable. And yet … I know my sister. Hope wouldn't want me to pass up a chance to save the universe, no matter what it cost.

I take a deep breath, steeling myself.

"Do it," I tell them. "Show me how this ends."

The Recall

My mind catches fire.

I feel my consciousness fracture and split, shuddering beneath an unbearable force. For the third time, I descend into the Collective Recall, and this time I know I can't take it. My thoughts begin to burn up. My memories ignite, scorching to ashes as they're blown into the void.

I'm losing time.

Losing all sense of self.

My name. What was it again?

Isaac? Ian?

No ... Something else.

My birthday. How old am I?

Fourteen? Forty-eight?

Christ. I'm watching myself fall to pieces from the inside out, and it's terrifying. I'm forgetting who I am. What I am.

Human?

Vytarian?

WHOAMI

And then it stops – all of it. The cacophony of panic, the missing memories and the impossible fear, it all fades to black.

No, not black.

Space.

I'm gazing out across the canvas of space. There's a ship there, a gleaming craft floating beyond a planet with rings, and suddenly, piece by piece, the memories come back. This is Saturn. The ship belongs to the Heretic.

And I'm here to investigate – I'm here to learn, at last, how this ends.

I peek within, and the Heretic paces relentlessly, his mind a storm of unease. The Runaway is gone, vanished in pursuit of God, The Distant One, or the Edge. Whatever he's after, he's nowhere to be found.

The Heretic is worried. He does not think of his creation as volatile, as threatening, but if it were to make contact with the Edge – that place where the laws of physics become unknowable and violent, then there's no telling what will happen. The consequences are unfathomable. No, he must intercept his child before he reaches the outer limits of existence.

He must stop the Runaway at all costs.

But his ship, advanced as it is, lacks the capability to track him. His options are limited. He knows what must be done, yet it scares him for there will be consequences, but perhaps not worse than the consequences of inaction.

With trembling hands, he contacts The Chosen.

They have the resources he needs, commanding the vast fleet of surveillance drones scattered throughout the cosmos. If they grant him access to these, perhaps, just perhaps, he can locate the Runaway in time. He might persuade his child to remain within the bounds of our reality.

The communication channel crackles to life. The Chosen's fury is immediate, palpable even across billions of lightyears.

"What have you done?" they thunder, their collective voice resonating with rage. "Your arrogance has doomed us all!"

"It was never my intention," the Heretic pleads, his voice quavering. "If we act swiftly, we can intercept him before he reaches the Edge. There is still time to make this right."

"Remain where you are," they order.

The Heretic complies, for he is no fool. He knows his reckoning has arrived. This is a disaster millenia in the making, and now he must face it head-on.

The Chosen descend upon him like avenging angels, imprisoning the Heretic for his sins. They deploy a fleet to intercept the Runaway, and they nearly do – but he breaches the Edge just as they near. They watch in horror as he vanishes beyond the furthest reaches of the universe, trespassing into the realm of eternity itself, into the domain of their God.

Months become years, years become decades.

The Chosen torture the Heretic. They demand he tell them everything he knows about the Runaway, and he does, holding nothing back save for the birth of the human race. That is a secret that he cannot reveal. Humanity must endure. He believes they may yet be our only hope against the Runaway.

Decades stretch into centuries. The Heretic languishes in chains, buried in a lightless prison beneath the surface of a dead world. The Chosen, nervous of the Runaway returning, keep the Heretic alive. They believe they may yet need him.

A hundred years pass. Then nine hundred more.

On the thousandth anniversary of the Runaway's blasphemy, a scout ship reports an anomaly near the Edge. Space there is behaving strangely. It's a phenomena they've seen only once before, when the Runaway stepped beyond the Edge to find God.

Alarms ring. They echo across every Vytarian military vessel, and The Chosen High Council convenes an emergency session. They know well what this means.

He is returning.

The Runaway is emerging from the Edge.

A Vytarian armada materializes, a swarm of gleaming vessels poised to intercept the Runaway. As they converge, a collective gasp ripples through the Recall—the Runaway has changed. Gone is the human form; in its place floats an entity both familiar and alien. Its body, now sallow and elongated, twists in impossible geometries. Eyes, once windows to a human soul, have sunken into abyssal voids.

Images cascade through the Collective Recall, searing themselves into the consciousness of every Vytarian. The Heretic, summoned before the High Council, trembles as he beholds what his creation has become.

"This ... this is not him," he whispers, his voice cratering. "This is not my son."

"Then what is it?" they demand, their pupils pulsing with fear and trepidation.

But if the Heretic knows, he does not speak of it. He watches in detached horror, his whole body trembling as a thousand military vessels surround the Runaway. Yet his son does not flee. He floats idly just beyond the Edge, unbothered by the building threat around him.

"Surrender," booms the flagship, "or we will be forced to open fire."

"Fire," the Runaway answers, his words echoing across the universe. "You know nothing of fire."

With a twist of his wrist, the Runaway unleashes a nightmare. A thousand warships shatter like glass, erupting in cerulean and obsidian flames. Video feeds blink out one by one, leaving only static in their wake. A lone surveillance droid, distant and unnoticed, captures the unfolding carnage. It beams the footage to the High Council and the Heretic, who weeps silently, drowning in despair and regret.

But the High Council has had one thousand years to prepare for this. They are not yet finished. As the last of the warships burn to dust, they reveal a ring of planets surrounding the Runaway. These planets have come a long way. They have been carted from distant solar systems, distant galaxies, and they have come here for one reason.

To become dust.

With the flick of a switch, ancient engines roar to life. A hundred worlds lurch forward, accelerating towards their target. Their surfaces quake, their molten cores churning with building momentum. One by one, they collide with the Runaway, burying him beneath a solar system, the resultant shockwaves shaking the galaxy.

Light-years away, the High Council watches with bated breath. The Heretic, however, doesn't dare to look up, for he knows this god-like display of force is nothing compared to a god itself.

As the last of the planets impact the Runaway, as the last of their fire and fury fades to scattered rubble, he is revealed to be a mangled corpse. His torn carcass floats between the debris. Pieces of him are scattered millions of miles apart, and these images are shared across the Collective Recall. Vytarians rejoice, proclaiming the fall of the false god, the unseating of the pretender from his crooked throne.

Their celebration is short-lived.

Slowly at first, then with increasing speed, the fragments of the Runaway begin to coalesce. Shattered limbs slam together, skull fragments fuse, and from this cosmic jigsaw emerges an abomination that defies comprehension. Nine arms writhe from a twisted torso perched atop three mismatched legs. Its bulbous head, draped with wisps of white hair, houses a dozen eyes, each swirling with a vortex of cosmic abyss.

The Heretic's hearts sink. This ... thing before them is no longer his child, no longer alive in any recognizable sense. It has transcended life, death, and everything in between.

It is something new.

Something less.

But the High Council is not convinced. A thousand years is a long time, and it's longer still for a race as advanced as the Vytar. They have suffered wars that have ended solar systems, turned whole galaxies into wastelands, and so they are no strangers to violence. This Runaway? He will learn his place, one way or another.

Those planets were never meant to end the monster. No – they were merely an opening salvo. A distraction to give the High Council time to prepare their real weapon.

And now the fuse is lit.

In the static-laced feed of a distant drone, the Heretic watches as a red hypergiant star begins to pulsate. Tendrils of plasma lash out from its swollen surface. It throbs. Hums with building energy. This is it – the most powerful weapon in the Vytarian arsenal, and they're triggering it on one of the largest stars in all the universe.

Supernova.

There's a flash of light, and the drone feed goes dead. Another drone is tapped from a neighboring system, and it reveals a terrible sphere that's growing, growing. It's an explosion that's engulfing everything within millions – *billions* of miles. It's stretching outward, consuming everything in its path. Planets, stars, and entire solar systems are vaporized in the cosmic inferno of a dying titan.

When the light finally fades, it reveals ... nothing. Multiple star systems reduced to less than ash, all wiped from existence. Even the Runaway is no more.

It seems too good to be true. The Heretic wants to believe, but he can't. He knows just what his creation is capable of, having already seen it recover from being splintered into pieces and scattered across space. He may be atomized, but ...

And there.

Cold dread grips the Heretic's hearts. Slowly, pieces of matter begin to grow in the void. They grow and they grow, reforming until the Runaway's screaming mouth emerges from a body now wholly unrecognizable as human. It's a skeletal figure, long and decrepit, with dozens of limbs and a thousand teeth. Its eyes have become one, and within it, there is emptiness.

But the Vytarians aren't finished. At the epicenter of the fading supernova, a new horror takes shape. Matter and light are drawn inexorably inward, spiraling towards a singularity of unimaginable power. The hypergiant's death throes have given birth to a supermassive black hole, its gravitational pull so immense that even distant galaxies feel its hunger.

The Runaway writhes helplessly. He's weakened – still reeling from the largest explosion since the birth of the cosmos. The event horizon calls to him. It beckons, dragging him toward the most powerful trash compact in all the universe, and for the first time in millenia, he feels what it means to be powerless.

Across the Collective Recall, the High Council's triumphant declaration reverberates:

"Now we will crush him!"

A thunderous cheer erupts from Vytarian throats.

"Now we will break his bones!"

The cheer swells, a tidal wave of hope and vengeance.

"Now we will unmake the unmaker!"

Their voices rise to a fever pitch, a symphony of victory.

"We do this for all Chosen! To bring glory to The Distant One!"

The euphoria spreads like wildfire. Through the Recall, the Heretic witnesses Vytarians flooding the streets, their jubilation manifesting in song, dance, and fervent prayer. Arms raised skyward, they chant ancient scriptures, certain that their judgment day has arrived. This, they believe, is their final test – their gateway to ascension, to joining The Distant One in the Edge.

But the Heretic sees what they cannot.

As the High Council exchanges congratulations, the Heretic's gaze remains fixed on the unfolding tug-of-war. He notices a subtle shift – the black hole's pull on the Runaway begins to wane. The abomination's velocity drops from millions of miles per second to thousands, then mere hundreds. And as he approaches the event horizon, where the very fabric of spacetime warps and tears, the Runaway does something he hasn't done in a millennium.

He opens his mouth. Takes a breath.

And this black hole – this unfathomable behemoth capable of devouring entire solar systems – is drawn into him like wisps of smoke. His grotesque jaws snap shut, swallowing the unswallowable.

"I had almost forgotten ..." The Runaway rasps, his guttural voice echoing in the minds of all of creation, "... what pain felt like ..."

He blinks out of existence.

Terror etches itself across the faces of the High Council. The Heretic collapses, wracked by sobs, for he alone knows that what comes next will be a horror none can imagine.

"End this," he pleads, voice cracking with despair. "End us all."

And in his mind, he hears screaming. In all of their minds, they hear screaming. Chaos erupts across the Collective Recall. They watch as Vytarians flee in blind panic, pursued by a mangled creature with an eye like a melting star.

He is here. The Runaway has come.

"You!" the High Council roars, rounding on the Heretic. "We showed you leniency, but it's clear that The Distant One demands your blood!"

A foot presses down on the Heretic's head. An executioner's blade glints in the harsh light.

"Please," the Heretic gasps, "if you have any sense, you'll grant this entire planet the mercy of death."

"This began with you," they snarl, "and so it shall end with you."

And the blade comes down. The Heretic's head is cleaved from his body, and as his consciousness begins to slip, his final wish is for everything they said to be true.

Frantic, the High Council scours the Recall, their desperation mounting with each passing moment. Surely, they think, The Distant One will intervene at any second. He will smite this abomination, this evil made flesh, and they will ascend to join him. They've proven their loyalty. The Heretic is dead, isn't he? What more is there left for them to do?

But the screaming doesn't stop. The Recall is flooded with endless suffering, a torrent of pleas for aid and mercy. Helpless, the High Council bears witness as Vytarians are pulled apart, piece by piece. They watch as the Runaway infiltrates their very consciousness, cutting up their thoughts and marrying the agony of their bodies with the agony of their minds.

"Please!" the High Council begs, prostrating themselves on the floor. "Help us, Distant One!"

A deafening crack splits the air.

The Runaway materializes before them, levitating above their table. His torso is a writhing mass of limbs, his large eye blazing with the heat of a billion dead stars. His form is draped in a grotesque patchwork of blood and skin – none of it his to wear.

"Deliver us from this evil!" the High Council cries.

"Restore that which is holy!" they plead.

"Unmake the pretender!" they beg.

"Destroy the false god!" they shriek.

And the Runaway spreads a dozen crooked arms, tilts his grotesque head and for the second time in a thousand years, he takes a breath. An uneven smile slips across his lips.

He tells them, *I already have.*

12, October, 1991

I'm drowning in vomit. Strong hands wrench me to the side. What's left of my dinner splatters across the deck, and I hack. Sputter. My eyes are bulging, my heart is racing and it feels like a hundred tiny explosions are going off across the surface of my brain.

"Human," Kez's voice cuts through the haze. He turns my face towards him. "Human! Respond!"

A weak noise escapes me. Words tangle on my tongue as I struggle onto all fours. "I'm ... alive," I rasp, each syllable a battle.

"An hour," Wor says, fingers combing through my sweat-matted hair. "You were gone an hour. We readied the vat for your corpse, hoping to salvage what scraps of data we could."

He gestures to a sunken tank, drained of the azure fluid that fills the others. The world's a smear of color, slowly sharpening into focus. "I'm okay ..." I manage. "Just a little ... woozy."

"Did you witness it?" Wor asks. "Vytar's end?"

"Yeah," I croak. "But that was forever ago. Where's the Runaway now?"

Wor and Kez are quiet. It's as though they're not certain how to go about answering the question, like they're worried it'll unearth memories better left buried.

"He remains on Vytar," Kez finally says, eyes downcast. "He is savoring our people's torment. He dissects them—body and mind, and when death claims them, he puts them back together once more. Begins anew. None can escape."

Wor nods, a slight tremor in his voice. "We were off-world when he struck. Monitoring the Edge. When the Recall showed us those images... we fled."

"He'll find you," I say.

"Oh yes," Wor's voice is a whisper. "He will find us, the Earth, everything. Once he tires of our kind, he will deliver his pain upon humanity. Your predisposition toward companionship birthed his turmoil, drove him to confront our god and I do not believe he is capable of forgiving you for this."

I shake my head, mind reeling. It's almost too much to imagine— some omnipotent sadist, torturing millions for thousands of years, remaking them every time they die. "How?" I choke out. "How do you stop that? I mean, they hurled freaking solar systems at him! Supernovas! Black holes! What can a couple Vytarians possibly do?"

"We will destroy him as we were destroyed," Kez explains, resting a hand on a nearby vat. Inside floats a man, half-dissolved, face melting away. "And we will destroy him as he was created. We are designing a virus of hyper-evolution, mirroring The Runaway's own capabilities, but this virus will outpace even his adaptations. It will consume him from within."

My gaze sweeps the room—vats of liquefied humans, tubes snaking out of them into a central console. Atop it sits a capsule, its contents roiling, seething.

"That's it?" I ask, nodding towards the capsule. "The virus?"

"Yes." Wor's pupils contract. "It is unfinished, but we pray it will be ready before he turns his sights to your world."

"How long?" My voice is barely audible.

"Two hundred and fourteen years," Kez intones.

Tears well in my eyes. "Two centuries? That's ... that's an eternity. What if-"

"Correction," Wor interrupts, studying the readout on his arm. "That was our previous estimate. Your Recall data has accelerated our timetable considerably, and assuming your deconstruction goes smoothly ..." His long fingers tap the display. "... It may be ready in as little as thirty-three years."

Thirty three. It might as well have been a *million* knowing what we were up against. "And what do you call it?" I ask. "The virus, I mean."

Kez tilts his head. "Query unclear. A name serves no purpose. The virus has a function and it will either succeed or fail in it, and that is all that we are concerned with."

"No purpose?" I say, incredulous. "C'mon, Kez! This thing is the universe's last hope! It's humanity's! That's a big deal, isn't it? Something like that deserves a name – it deserves to be remembered."

Wor's readout flashes. "Your cortisol is spiking, human. Your clone will have no memory of this, so such an emotional response is illogical. Additionally, we must begin deconstruction immediately if you wish to visit your sister before she expires. The clone will require a day's preparation."

I open my mouth to speak, but I don't know what to say. Tears leak from my eyes. I sniffle, wiping at them as I feel my heart crushed beneath the weight of my grief.

My sister.

Hope.

She's dying in the hospital, and I won't even get to say goodbye. The best she'll get is some lab-grown copycat. And on top of that, there's a mad god rampaging across the universe that could show up on our doorstep at any second.

My legs give out.

I crumple to the floor, and for the first time since I was little, I cry my eyes out. I lean my head against the vat of a dead person, and I start to bawl. For Hope. For myself. For every Vytarian who's dying over and over just to satisfy the twisted whims of a cosmic sadist.

A hand grips my shoulder.

I look up through a veil of tears. "It is time," Kez says softly. "Are you prepared?"

"Sure," I mutter. "Why not? We all die someday, right?"

Kez helps me to my feet, guides me toward an empty vat. "Human– *Isaiah Mitchell*. It distresses you that we have not named this virus. Why?"

I draw a shuddering breath, drowning in my own emotions. "I don't know," I fumble for words. "It's ... it's the most important thing ever created and it's just ... nameless. It feels wrong. Can't you see that?"

"No," he says simply, helping me into the vat.

I step into the transparent tank, wishing I could be as emotionally hollow as the Vytarians. It might make this whole self-sacrifice thing easier. Liquid begins to flow, pooling around my feet. It tingles, like anesthetic.

"What would you name this virus?" Kez asks from above.

"What would I ..." I try to think, but I can't bring myself to focus on the virus, the fallen god or even the end of the damn universe.

All I can think about is her.

My sister. I'm thinking about how much I'm going to miss her, how much I wish I could have said goodbye. I'm remembering the way she'd pull out a board game, close my bedroom door and crank Bon Jovi to drown out mom and dad arguing. I'm remembering the dinner she'd cook us while our parents were passed out on the couch. I'm remembering all this and more.

"Isaiah," Kez says, his voice growing distant. "The name?"

The liquid is around my chest now. I squint up at Kez, my mind already beginning to feel slow and hazy. This is it, I realize. The final frontier.

I give Kez a smile, and I say the last word I'll ever speak.

Present Day

Lisa leads me to the far reaches of the spacecraft, deep enough that crews haven't gotten around to rigging it with lighting yet – so we're doing things the old-fashioned way.

Lisa's making shadow puppets with her flashlight.

"You have to admit this one looks like a giraffe," she says, twisting her fingers in a way that looks nothing like a giraffe.

"We almost there?" I grumble.

She drops her hands with a dramatic sigh. "Yeah. It's just ahead. What's crawled up your ass tonight, Mitchell?"

I bristle. "What's that supposed to mean?"

"I mean, it's usually *me* that's all business. You're the dick everything slips off like cellophane, but now you're all brooding and serious. So what gives?" She swings the flashlight into my eyes.

"Quit it! You trying to blind me?"

"Just needed to see your face," she laughs. "Had to make sure the aliens hadn't possessed you or something."

I roll my eyes so hard I'm surprised they don't fall out of my head. "Give me a break."

"A break? You only just got to work," she quips, snorting at her own wit. Her light catches a scrap of paper tacked above a doorway – D34. "This is our stop, Captain Workaholic. After you."

Scowling, I duck through the entrance. In the far corner, a cluster of portable lamps illuminates a team bustling around what looks like ... Oh God. A field of vats, each one housing a human corpse.

"It's real," I mutter, my stomach doing somersaults. "Christ almighty, it's all real."

Lisa shoulders past me, all business now. "Major Luca!" she hollers. "Major Luca, you in here?"

A woman in a lab coat and dust mask strides over, a camo-green patch on her chest identifying her as our target. "Agents," she greets us, tugging down her mask. "Glad you made it. The bodies are this way."

Luca guides us through the labyrinth of tanks. Lab techs hover over the vats, dipping collection rods to harvest DNA samples. Others drain viscous fluid with handheld pumps. My heart's doing the cha-cha against my ribcage. This is it – the place that's been haunting my dreams, brought to life in all the worst ways.

"Here we are," Luca announces, stopping in front of a gray tarp. I crouch down, steeling myself as I lift the edge of it. Two massive corpses lie beneath, their skin scaled, teeth like serrated knives, claws that could disembowel a grizzly, and tails that look strong enough to crush concrete. Once, I'd have called them monsters. Now they look like old friends.

Their names are Kez and Wor.

Lisa lets out a low whistle, circling the bodies. "Nasty customers, huh? Good thing they weren't up and kicking when we busted in. Bet they'd have gone all Xenomorph on our asses." She mimes a face-hugger attack, complete with ridiculous expressions. Luca chuckles.

Meanwhile, I'm lost in my thoughts. I can't tear my eyes away from the dead Vytarians. How? How could they let this happen? They were the most advanced species in the history of the cosmos, so how the hell did they get shot down by something as archaic as an F35?

"Did the pilot file a report?" I ask, my voice distant.

Lisa's eyebrows shoot up. "You're looking at the first real, flesh and blood aliens that anybody's ever seen, and you're asking about paperwork?" She shakes her head. "Mitchell, I'm telling you – you're losing it."

"The report," I insist, fighting to keep my voice level. "What did the pilot see? Why'd they fire on the UAP?"

Luca glances at Lisa, who heaves a suffering sigh. "Fine, let's get this over with," Lisa says. "The pilot picked up a weird signature on radar. Went to check it out. Says he saw this massive craft flickering in and out of existence – there one second, gone the next. Real Twilight Zone shit. Figured it might be some next-gen Chinese tech, so he called it in. Before he could finish his report, though, the UAP fired off ... something."

"Something?" I echo, my brain working overtime. "Like a weapon, or ...?"

Lisa shrugs. "Your guess is as good as mine. That's what the pilot assumed. Thought it might be a pre-emptive strike, so he gave it hell. Emptied everything he had into it."

"And what was it really? What did the UAP actually launch?"

"Like I said, no clue. Whatever it was, NASA tracked it hauling ass out of our atmosphere. Last ping they got was it screaming past Neptune about an hour ago."

I shake my head, pieces of the puzzle starting to click. Maybe whatever the Vytarians fired took so much juice that they had to divert power from everything else – cloaking, shields, the works.

It's the only explanation that makes a lick of sense. No way in hell an F35 should've been able to touch them otherwise.

"There's more, ma'am," Major Luca chimes in, her voice hushed and anxious. "After I radioed about the bodies, my team found something else. We think it might have been the payload. Or at least, where it was housed before launch."

"Show me," I demand, shouldering past Lisa. "Now."

"Yes, sir." The Major hustles through the maze of vats, and I'm right on her heels, chewing my thumbnail down to the quick. There's a knot of dread in my gut, a creeping certainty that my nightmares weren't just fever dreams – they were more real than I ever was. All around us are tanks of dissolving humans, and I can't help but wonder how many of their clones are walking around topside right now. Did the real Isaiah Mitchell feel anything as he melted away?

I wonder if he'd hate me now.

"It's here," Luca announces, stopping in front of a steel-gray console– another relic of my memories. She points to an empty pedestal on top, a circular hole punched through its center. "We think the payload was right here," she explains, her eyes darting over the rows of vats, disgust twisting her features. "Best we can figure, the aliens were using human DNA to cook up some kind of bioweapon. That's probably what they launched tonight."

"A bioweapon?" Lisa says, breathless as she catches up. "Christ, did I hear that right? Were they trying to wipe us out and just ... missed?"

Luca swallows hard, the color draining from her face. "Maybe. Or perhaps it operates on principles similar to an ICBM, but scaled up. Instead of breaching our atmosphere and circling back, it's punching through our entire solar system. For all we know, whatever they launched is still accelerating out there. It could be coming back."

Lisa fires off a response. Luca counters. They volley back and forth, their voices fading to white noise. At some point, I think Lisa might be trying to drag me into the conversation, but my mind is light-years away. No, it's decades away.

I take a step toward the console, drawn to that empty pedestal. This is where it sat – the virus Wor and Kez had been building to destroy the Runaway.

And there, beneath it ...

A label. It might be the only label in this otherwise unmarked ship, obscured by dust and made faint by years of wear.

Lisa grabs my arm. "Earth to Mitchell. You in there?"

I mumble something in response, but I couldn't tell you what. Words. Just words.

Just like the word beneath that pedestal. It's a word that brings back memories, but not memories of drifting corpses or imploding stars or eldritch horrors and the end of creation. No, this is a word that brings back memories of a hospital room.

White.

Sterile.

Inside of it, a girl is lying in a bed, and her skin is pallid and thin. She's having trouble breathing. Tubes are pouring into her throat doing their best to keep her alive, but she doesn't have long. This girl is dying. And she's the most important thing to me in the entire world.

"Chin up," she's telling me, and her frail hand rests against my own. She's smiling. She's seventeen years old, dying before she's had a chance to live, and she's smiling because she knows that's what I need to see. "Everything will be okay," she whispers. "You'll see."

But I think about our Mom and Dad. I think about how right now, they're passed out on the couch, and how maybe if I'm lucky they'll drink themselves to death before I get home. I think about the bruises up and down my arms. I think about the moment my guardian angel intervened, pulling my dad off of me, just in time for him to shove her backward down the stairs.

I think about the sound her body made as it hit the floor. How still she was.

And now, I'm here, and she's smiling at me, and she's telling me that everything is going to be okay even though I know that it isn't. I know that nothing will ever be okay ever again. "I don't want you to go," I tell her, and I squeeze her hand as gently as I can, tears pouring from my eyes. "Please don't …"

And I know that it's selfish. I know that it's pointless. I know that my older sister is dying whether I like it or not, and that putting this on her at the very end is cruel. But I'm just a kid. I know if I don't try I'll always wonder if it might have worked.

If maybe I had just asked, then she might have stayed.

The machine that's beeping in tune with her heart starts to slow. She leans forward. Presses her forehead to mine. "I have to go," she murmurs. "But don't think for a second I won't be watching over you, Dizzy Izzy."

Beep …

I blink back tears. "Promise?"

Beep …

"Sure," she rasps, pulling me into a frail hug. "That's what big sisters are for, right?"

And we hold each other like that until the beeping stops.

"I'm talking to you!" Lisa's voice cuts through my reverie like a knife.

"Huh?"

"Oh, now he speaks!" Lisa's eyes are wild with panic, her hair a disheveled mess. She fumbles with her flask, taking another long pull.

"What's wrong?" I ask.

She wipes her mouth with the back of her hand, her voice clipped and urgent. "Look," she says. "If this thing really *is* a bioweapon, we need intel. Now. Like yesterday. Just 'cause we've lost visual doesn't mean it isn't coming back to bite us in the ass."

She yanks out a crudely printed map, jabbing at it with a trembling finger. "Here's the plan: I'll coordinate a sweep of Alpha through Delta corridors. You take Echo through Hotel. We're looking for anything – records, data, a Post-it note with 'How to Build a Fuckin' Doomsday Weapon' scrawled on it. Got it?"

"Uh, right," I mumble, still half-lost in my memories. "I'm … I'm on it, Lis."

"Great." She's already moving, practically jogging away, her fists clenched so tight I can see her knuckles turning white. "I'm fucked," she's muttering, over and over. "There's a goddamn bioweapon out there and I don't know jack shit about it … I'm so fucking *fucked* …"

I look back to the console, to the empty pedestal where the virus once sat, and I think to myself that what Lisa's saying isn't quite true. We do know something about this. My fingers brush the dust from beneath the pedestal, revealing the worn label. On it is a single word, scratched by a Vytarian claw thirty years ago.

It's a name.

A virus like this shouldn't need a name; Kez told me as much. But if it had one? Well, I think I would have named it after my guardian angel.

I think I would have called it Hope.

ACKNOWLEDGEMENTS

I love writing, but I hesitate to say writing loves me. A lot of my time is spent second guessing my work. Reconsidering. Analysis paralysis, you might call it. Is this story good enough? Does it even make sense? Am I filling in the blanks with words I forgot to put down on the page?

To put it simply, I'm a cognitive disaster. A messy room, but in the shape of a brain and whatever it is thoughts look like. But thankfully I'm surrounded by wonderful people who help me clean that room, organize those thoughts, and drag me out of whatever pit I so often find myself in.

So, here's to them.

To my mom, who's read my stories since I was a twerp and never stopped encouraging me – thank you.

To the wonderful readers who took time out of their days to leave their thoughts or write reviews – thank you.

To those friends who read my drafts and helped shape them into something approaching sensible – thank you.

And finally, to everybody that's blessed me with frequent smiles, thoughtful discussions, and memories that will last many lifetimes to come – thank you.

As far as I'm concerned, these stories don't belong to me, but to all of you. Without you, this book could never exist. So in that sense, Crooked Gospels is dedicated to you.

And for that matter, so am I.

MORE CHILLS FROM VELOX BOOKS

MORE CHILLS FROM VELOX BOOKS

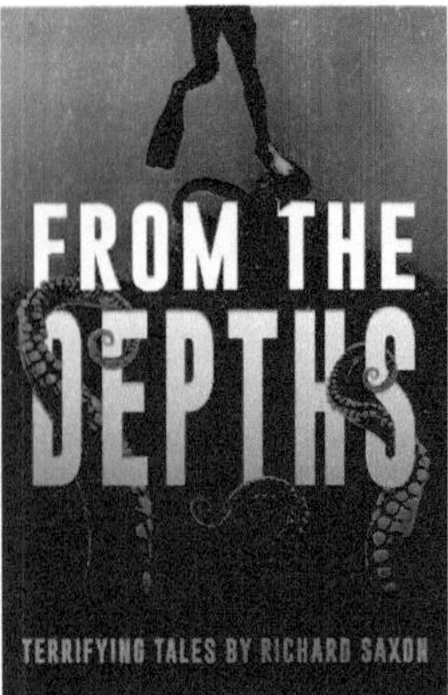

MORE CHILLS FROM VELOX BOOKS

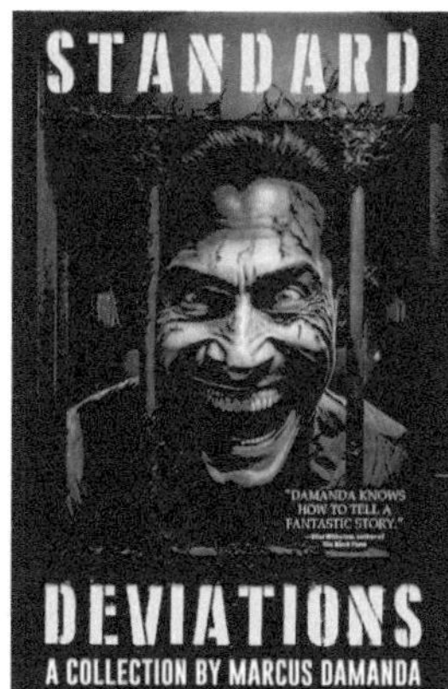

MORE CHILLS FROM VELOX BOOKS